Home of Fire and Tempest

Book Three of the Sorrowborn Trilogy

April Davis

Kevin A Davis

Inkd Publishing

Home of Fire and Tempest

For those who have continued on the journey with us.
For love.

Contents

Introduction

Caitlyn, Dean, and the Wolf Squad have made a fragile home in Columbia with the Alliance.

Tyrell has not forgotten them.

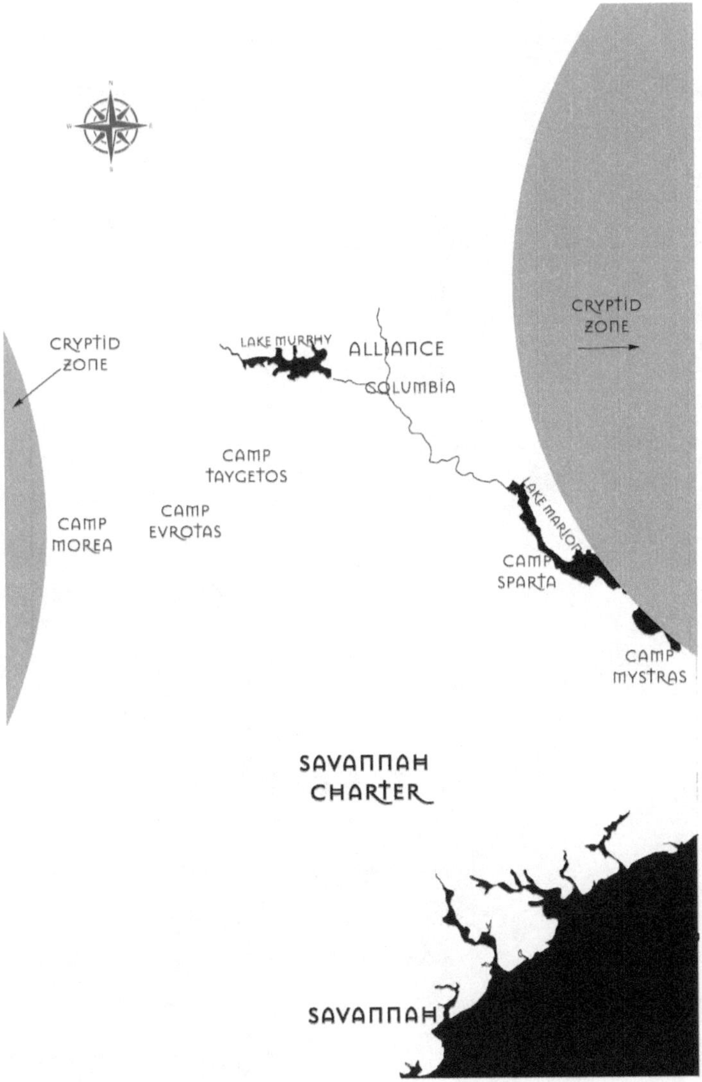

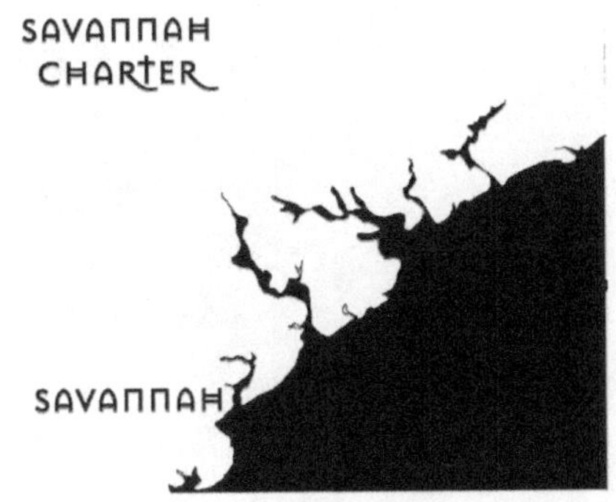

CRYPTID ZONE
CRYPTID ZONE
LAKE MURPHY
ALLIANCE
COLUMBIA
CAMP TAYGETOS
CAMP EVROTAS
CAMP MOREA
LAKE MARIOR
CAMP SPARTA
CAMP MYSTRAS
SAVANNAH CHARTER
SAVANNAH

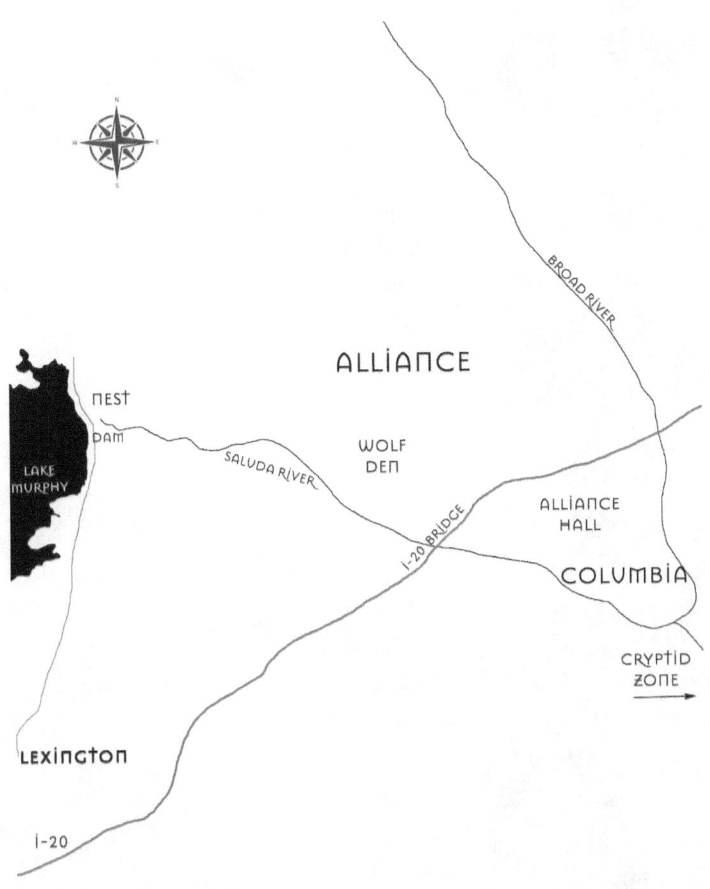

N
W
E
S
BROAD RIVER
ALLIANCE
NEST
DAM
LAKE MURPHY
SALUDA RIVER
WOLF DEN
I-20 BRIDGE
ALLIANCE HALL
COLUMBIA
CRYPTID ZONE
LEXINGTON
I-20

Chapter One

In the shade of the woods, I peered across the rippling water to a sight I'd hoped to never see again. The buildings of Camp Sparta rose from the opposite shore, and the setting spring sun lit the roofs with gold.

I sighed, and on the inhale, sucked in a gnat. My coughing spat brought a shush from Roxie and a roll of Dean's eyes. Shirtless, he lay beside me on the rise above the bank with his black wavy hair hanging against his cheek.

Fog drifted up from the river in front of us, driven by Roxie's magic. My othersense flared from her creation.

"Sorry." I plucked at my lips, picturing little insect wings. Perhaps it was my imagination that I swallowed.

From behind us, Ben asked. "Any hint of Weston?" Pale in the fading light, his peach-fuzz mustache stood out.

None of the Wolf Squad could sense the otherness as I could yet, though I had hope for Fawn. "No."

Dean's strong features screwed into a fake curious stare at my mouth, as if bug parts spread across them. I frowned at him. The little gnats and mosquitoes swarmed our group in the warm evening. The month of April had surprised us with a couple of hot days.

"He's late." Ben had commandeered a wristwatch out of the Alliance's stash in Columbia, and he loved to use it.

I probed Camp Sparta with my othersense. There was no unusual movement there, except for those we hoped to rescue; those rebellious Youth Guard were slowly collecting in the mess hall according to Ben's plan.

Dean studied me. "He'll be fine. It's a long trek to the little bridge." His dark eyes flicked in the direction of Santee, where his family might still live. He never mentioned reaching out to his sister Bettina, not once since we started this mission.

In the dwindling light, Roxie's darker complexion shone as she lay in the brush on my other side. "You told me he passed through the gate just a few minutes ago. It'll take a while."

"It's been eighteen minutes," Ben said.

I rolled to my side, raising my eyebrow at him. Ben's mustache made him appear older, but he and Dean were nearly the same age. "He'll be here. There might have been patrols." I tried to sound reassuring.

Deeper in the woods past Ben, crouched three more members of the Wolf Squad; tall, red-headed Andy, Fawn, and Yatika. Fawn shaved her head while Tika let her black hair grow long. I sensed Penny to the north, where she and Odie watched the military complex in case they moved troops toward Camp Sparta.

Ben had been thorough in planning the rescue, but Dean and Penny had refined the details once the Wolf Squad had convinced me to join. I only came to keep them from getting caught or dying; my othersense could help us sniff out a trap.

Roxie and Fawn were to stay on this bank along with Penny, while the rest of us crossed the river to retrieve and escort the small band of Youth Guard to safety. Some of

Ben and Andy's friends at Camp Sparta shared their beliefs. *More members for the Wolf Squad. How did I feel about that?*

In my othersense, Ben's rhythms hummed with anticipation as he spoke. "It'll be dark soon. Someone will notice a group hanging out in the mess."

Timing *had* been important. The rebel Youth Guard, those not shipped to different camps, bunked with others who displayed loyalty to Tyrell and his military. New "rebels" had blossomed from teens transferred from those other camps.

We believed that the best time to gather them in one place would be during the couple of hours between a busy mess hall and curfew. I hoped we were right.

Roxie rose, backing out of the brush. "Selina?"

My othersense focused on an upper room closest to us. I knew her rhythms from the battle outside Sumter. "Still in her quarters. Alone." Perhaps her new position earned her privileges. I still hated her, but no longer wanted to kill her. Too many had died in Tyrell's war against the Alliance.

Ben pulled out his binoculars to study the windows of Camp Sparta's buildings. "It's pretty quiet over there."

No lamps lit the barracks yet. *Too early to burn fuel.*

Roxie slipped past Ben, heading for the rest of the Wolf Squad. I could sense Andy's anticipation at releasing his friends. Both Fawn and Tika showed light nervous rhythms in the othersense. Their arrival at Camp Sparta came late, coinciding with Tyrell's preparations for the failed attack on the Alliance enclaves. Their friends lived in different camps.

I'd seen the scars on the two women from Selina's wild assault on the other Youth Guard during the enclave battle. When Andy had split the Youth Guard with his call to the Wolf Squad, neither Tika nor Fawn had been aggressive or openly rebellious during the first attacks, which earned them Selina's wrath. After they responded to her attack by joining the side of the Wolf Squad, they held me and my supposed rebellion in the same puffed-up reverence as Andy and Ben. Selina's lightning had stirred them to make a choice.

Ben shifted along the ridge of the bank, scanning the administration building. I couldn't pick out Tyrell with my othersense, but we believed he was there. Weston might have information regarding the camp leader's location.

I searched south for Weston, still not picking him up. Did they have a contingency plan for him not returning? Like Fawn and Tika, Weston came from one of the other camps. Since fewer would recognize him over Ben or Andy, he'd infiltrated Camp Sparta to spread the news about our rescue to those considered rebels.

"Still no Weston," I said, turning back to stare across the water. My hand reached for Dean's fingers. I smiled when he readily clasped them.

I knew it hurt him to come this close to home and family. "Someday—" My mouth dropped open when I tilted toward him.

Moonjir lay on the ground on the other side of my love, his goofy fox face grinning at me with a wet tongue drooping out.

Seeing my expression, Dean spun and nearly jumped up. "Shit," he hissed.

"Hey, lovers. This looks fun." A tiny light sparkled in Moonjir's eyes. His blue fur glowed in the deep shadows, with the pink tips of his one upright ear spiking up like flames. "I see you brought the whole mob with you. Think you can trust them?"

"What are you doing here?" Dean murmured in an annoyed tone.

"Didn't have much of a choice, and I'm not going to let Caitlyn shove me back home when the fun has just started."

I took a deep breath. "What do you want, Moonjir?" *What do you have to tell me?*

"Just enjoying the warm evening with friends. Like you. All friends. A bit impulsive, isn't it?" Moonjir squinted across the water at Camp Sparta. "Coming home like this, I mean. The rescue. Wolf Squad, right?"

"They don't belong here," I said.

"Who does?" He focused on me. "Not really your choice, though. Just along for the ride. The mascot. The icon of rebellion. Not really the leader type, are you?" Moonjir cocked his head, floppy ear swinging. "Or are you?"

My lips tightened. "I'm not." He touched a sore point. I didn't want to be their hero or symbol, the reason I'd resisted this whole mission.

"Just someone useful to rally around." Moonjir reached up and cupped his chin with three nails, eyes flicking between Dean and me. "You two are still an item, I see. Worked out the whole wolfing thing — or still disappointing?"

"Shut up." Dean's face tightened.

Moonjir's tail curled up by his head, a bright blue and pink plumage that I hoped wasn't noticed from the camp. He spoke with mock affront. "Touchy. Or not. I can only imagine."

If someone at the camp spotted us, we'd have to abandon the raid. "We're trying not to be seen over here," I said in a sharp voice. "Now is not the time to play with us."

His lips circled to mouth an "Oh." Moonjir vanished.

Chapter Two

I blinked, staring at the ground on the other side of Dean. My mind raced trying to parse out Moonjir's words. *Was there a message?*

Dean swore, glanced about, then focused on me. "Are you? Disappointed?"

My thoughts raced around the comments being a stupid symbol of rebellion. I didn't want to be a leader. "No. I love you." Of course, I wanted to be closer and even have sex with Dean, but it wasn't his fault. I hadn't cured him.

"I love you too. Will that be enough for you? I mean, if I can never learn to control it?"

We'd tried many times, and he had refrained from running about in wolf form afterward.

"Of course. I love you, and that's enough for me. You?" My heart ached. I couldn't lose him.

He smiled, a bit tightly. "No regrets. Sex is not love." Tenderly, he leaned in and kissed me. "You need to stop trying to save me. I'm learning to accept who I am. You can, too."

"I do." There had to be a cure. Vanya had believed the infection had a magical root.

"I mean it." Dean peered at Ben, then the other members of the Wolf Squad. "Moonjir's right about them, too."

I frowned. "About being along for the ride? Yeah, I don't want to be a leader." *Or a symbol.* "I can help, though."

"They manipulate you. I bet they wouldn't have come if you hadn't agreed."

They would have, and possibly died. Perhaps Fawn and Tika would have remained in Columbia, and Penny. "I don't agree. Ben and Andy were pretty dedicated to this from the beginning. Roxie too." I couldn't abandon Roxie. "What if Selina captured them?"

He nodded, his eyes turning toward the town again. "No regrets, eh?" His words could have applied to his family and sister or our rescue.

Remembering my role, I scanned the camp, then looked south in the direction of Santee. In my othersense, I found Weston at the far edge, running. "Ben."

He strolled to our position, deep enough behind the brush that he barely crouched. "Yeah?"

"Weston is coming." I shuffled backward from the shore, Dean following.

"Finally. Sun's almost set."

The sky above the spring green canopy was streaked with orange clouds, reddened at the western tips over the camp. A lone window in the mess of the middle students' building lit with yellow from a lamp. More would light up soon in the last two dedicated to the Youth Guard.

While Ben strolled south, Dean and I joined the Wolf Squad.

When I caught Roxie's eye, I nodded for her to send the signal to Penny: a splash of water near her location.

The others caught our exchange.

In his Youth Guard coveralls, Andy nearly bounced like

a puppy to us. His freckles dotted his pale face, and the sunset turned his buzz cut orange. "We're doing it. Wolf Squad."

"Easy there, Tigger." Dean grinned at some private joke. "We need to be focused and careful."

"I'm super focused."

"I see that." Dean clapped Andy's shoulder, as if pinning him down.

Tika stood expectantly. She'd braided and bound her long black hair, then tucked it inside her colorfully embellished coveralls, much like I had. All the new Wolf Squad had her embroidered patches. Everyone's clothes sprouted her flowers stitched over tears or holes. "Weston?" she asked me.

"Yes, I can sense him. Are you ready?"

In the shadows, her eyes were dark against golden skin. "Yes."

Her strongest magic was lightning, and I tried not to think of Selina when Tika used it. "Let's hope we don't have to cause a scene. If all goes well, no magic." Even if others couldn't yet othersense like I could, most could "hear" the magic when used. Roxie would cause some noise, holding back the water.

"Yes, let's hope." Tika rarely said much, unless she spoke about cooking, spices, or sewing. That got her excited.

Fawn slid up beside the taller Tika. "Please be careful."

Dean chuckled. "We'll try not to bring you any work."

"I didn't mean that. Just please don't get hurt." The timid teenager peered at the ground to hide her eyes, and the movement highlighted her shaved head. She wouldn't let her brown hair grow out, and she hadn't explained why when questioned by Andy or Penny. Equal to my skill, she could heal the worst wounds and would be waiting with Roxie, safely on this bank, for our return.

"We'll be careful, Fawn." I rubbed her shoulder, and her head lifted. As I spoke, I sensed a full circle around us at the limits of my ability, finding only Weston and Penny outside of those at Camp Sparta.

A bug tried for my eyeball, and I flinched before waving it away. The mosquitoes had gotten a fair share of my blood throughout the evening. I'd be happy to be on the move.

Dean turned, his sharp ears catching Weston tramping through the brush and leaves. Roxie studied me with Fawn and Tika, offering a worried smile. She still worked through her scattered emotions left by Selina's tortures.

When Dean and I headed for Ben, the Wolf Squad followed. Weston's pale skin and sandy hair made him easy to spot in the trees. Taller than Dean and only a few months younger, he had Roxie's skill with water. His history with the Youth Guard differed, as his family had him out on a farm, knowing he could use magic. All of us had our moments of jealousy with his past. He'd gone straight to a camp and never known the labs most of us had.

A scar from a fireball climbed up his neck. Andy's work, according to what we'd determined afterward. Selina and the other Youth Guard had left him on the battlefield to be captured by the Duathua. Instead of opting to be released to return to the camps, he'd begged to stay with the Alliance. The Duathua brought Weston to the Wolf Squad during the trip to Columbia. Dean didn't trust him, but I couldn't see a better place for him.

"Eight in all," Weston said with a ragged breath.

"Gina?" asked Andy in a more passionate tone than I expected. I remembered another fire user with curly dark hair.

"Yes," Weston huffed, stopping to put his hands on his knees, still standing taller than most of us. "And Len." He peered at Ben after that name. Len took to air and performed passably in fire as well. With effort, he spoke the list between breaths. "Vicky, Quinn, Isabel, Elizabeth, Kira, and Nadia."

Yaz hadn't been listed. "Tyrell?" I asked.

"He's here. Obviously didn't see him." Weston straightened, meeting my eye.

"What took so long?" Dean asked.

"Soldier patrol on Pinckney Road. Not actually patrolling, just shooting shit and making me climb through the woods in a wide circle around them. Assholes." Weston glanced at the sun setting like fire in the trees to the west.

"I know we'll be cutting it close."

The sharp scent of pine mixed with dried leaves and earth. Drawing in a long breath, I asked the question. "Selina?"

Weston shrugged; she'd left him wounded on the battlefield outside the enclave. "Bitch is there. She didn't see me."

I sensed Penny and Odie, her peach and brown pit bull, coming from the east at a quick jog. "Bitch is mine, if I see her." She still had scars from our torture; we all did. Carrying her rifle on one shoulder, she joined us wearing her long dark coat that swallowed her small frame. Her pale face and green eyes visible in the shadows, framed in a short crop of brown hair.

My stiff nod to Weston let him lead. "Roxie, let's dig out your new trick." My smile was tense, and I knew it. We took a big risk, but I understood how it felt leaving people behind.

Penny stepped beside Roxie. "Are we doing this?" Odie loped with his eyes on Dean, tail wagging.

I nodded toward the south. "You ready?"

"Been effing ready. Effing bugs."

Silently, we headed as a group to a point upstream

where the two shores pinched the lazy river close enough for Roxie's water magic.

Only two of the people we would rescue tonight originated from Camp Sparta; Gina and Len. The others had been brought in to replace those who I'd tainted, who saw me as a symbol, like the Wolf Squad did. The newcomers came from other camps: Taygetos, Evrotas, Morea, and Mystras. Weston's task included contacting those Youth Guard who'd expressed enough interest in me that Ben and Andy could believe they'd want to leave. Evidently, they'd been right.

My pulse rose, but everyone's rhythms were rising.

Dean took my hand and squeezed. "Belly of the beast," he whispered.

Chapter Three

I'd fought alongside Penny, Dean, Roxie, and Andy in the battle outside the Alliance's Sumter enclave. The rest of the Wolf Squad I'd trained with at Columbia along with a few teens with magic who had tutored under the Seyir. On Denya, the Seyir, those who could use the otherness, had little of the battle knowledge that we'd learned at the camps.

Today we risked Fawn and especially Tika in potential combat. "Let's hope this goes smooth." I glanced back at Ben, then to Tika who had such a mild demeanor. She was most content with a needle in her hand, but she had strong lightning. Harming someone with power didn't require strength, but willingness. A hard lesson for me to learn.

I hadn't wanted to bring a possible battle to Camp Sparta, but Ben and Weston had recruited most of the Wolf Squad.

"We'll be in and out before they know it." Ben offered a cocky smile.

Dean grunted. His natural pessimism had honed the plan once I had agreed to go. Dry leaves and needles crunched underfoot, but his boots barely made a sound.

"If I can do my part," Roxie added.

I flashed her a confident smile. "You'll be fine. We've practiced." Her part in the plan caused me little worry. My eyes flicked up to the canopy of mostly pine.

"The moon," Dean said. "No clouds."

Without cover overhead, the twilight left the sky gray. A bright waxing moon hung nearly directly above. Our biggest arguments had been the timing. Dean had wanted to siphon the Youth Guard off before breakfast, having them come to us one at a time. Then, there would have been too much activity, a rising sun to follow our escape, and more opportunity for them to be missed, raising an alarm.

I focused the othersense. "Except for the windows, no one in direct sight."

Dean scoffed, repeating my words. "Except for the windows."

"No one is standing at them."

He shrugged. I caught his hand touching his holstered pistol.

Weston stopped at the shore of our intended crossing over the lazy river. Roxie had selected the spot with a short sixty-yard distance to the opposite bank. The spread widened to nearly triple that where the blasted out practice grounds of the camp jutted into the water.

"It's 7:28," Ben said.

Roxie dropped to sit a couple yards back from the bank, and Fawn passed us with Odie. A dull roar of otherness welled over the river, and I hoped none of the Youth Guard would hear it this far away.

As I stepped forward, Penny brushed past. She would take the first position once Roxie did her thing. Odie let out a light whine, and she gave a warning shake of her head. "Odie. Shh."

I followed, exposing myself to the camp. The shore

dropped steeply, and Penny scrambled down with her rifle slung across her back and black coat flapping.

Roxie created a bridge of solidified water that ceased flowing with the current. Penny stepped onto it with confident strides, and her boots sunk the bridge, but not below the surface. We called it hardened water, though it was more like rubber than ice. Occasional murky ripples splashed over the top and slid off as quickly.

The scent of marsh grass and fish wafted in the breeze. After almost toppling and planting myself face first, I slid on my ass down the bank.

"Crap." Dean scrambled close behind me, his hand grabbing the back of my coveralls.

"I'm okay." I straightened, scanned the otherness, and stepped onto the three-foot wide bridge. Like Penny, I sunk a quarter of an inch into the surface.

It didn't ripple with Penny's continued crossing, so I took another step, conscious of those watching me from the shore. *I could swim, if I needed to.*

Penny reached the far shore and climbed a tree before I sloshed off the end. The shallow bank lay only a couple paces from a trail I'd patrolled hundreds of times. The far end of it exited at the road, Bass Drive, right where the guards watched the gate.

Dean and I passed under her where she'd cover with her rifle. Our meeting place was a dozen paces down and behind the brush but with a clear view of the side of the southernmost building in the camp — where the Youth Guard waited for us to rescue them. My chest tightened.

Andy passed to take a position ten yards to the east while Tika crouched between us and Penny.

Ben and Weston were last.

"Good luck," I whispered as they reached our position.

"Thanks." Ben winked with a broad grin.

The shallow inlet stretching from the main river dug almost to the road. I'd snuck out of the camp many times to traipse through the reeking muck where the fence ended. Weston waded in, dark water to his hips. His sandy hair and pale skin seemed bright in the moonlight. He exited dripping mud and lilies, crouching as he climbed to the far bank where fire and air practice had cleared all but the shortest grass.

Ben followed, wasting time to grin back at me and Dean before scuttling toward the building where the Wolf Squad once ate and slept.

I ran a wide scan, but no one had moved or even shifted very much. I had gotten near enough to sense the closest Youth Guard. The bundle of them in the mess buzzed with nervousness.

"There's only seven," I said to Dean.

"What?"

"Weston did say eight, didn't he?" I couldn't remember all the names.

"Yeah. Maybe cold feet." His gun rested on his right knee where we squatted.

I focused on the Youth Guard on the second and third floors. Two on each level, one in each bedroom. They buzzed nearly as much as those we intended to rescue.

I straightened and almost stood as I readied myself. Ben had just reached the shadows of the building where the upper walkway covered the sidewalk. Weston stepped inside the mess hall.

"Dean." I swallowed. "I'm not sure about this."

He squinted at the building. "What?"

Wells of otherness formed over my head. Along the whole trail from Andy back to Penny there were four wells of activity. Two more grew on the opposite shore where Roxie and Fawn waited.

"Oh, Dean." I drew as much as I could reach. Spreading the stolen otherness overhead from Andy toward the water, I drew in air, rustling the trees. It condensed as I formed a thick, dense shield with the power; I tried to spread it out to protect our entire line of people, but I couldn't reach Penny, and certainly not Roxie.

Fire blossomed to my left, brighter than the moon. Orange reflected off the water, and the stench of burning trees wafted under a hot breeze.

"Windows?" Dean asked, but he didn't wait, firing a deafening shot beside me.

In my othersense I felt Roxie and Fawn's rhythms spike in pain. Odie as well. Penny dropped from where she'd been thrown to the bank, unconscious from what I could tell from her rhythms.

Camp Sparta had turned into a wasps' nest of activity. All along the top two floors, Youth Guard opened doors, and wells of magic formed overhead again. I drew them in with a snarl, strengthening the shields and still trying to stretch to Penny.

The sky over the building roared with otherness, louder than anything the Youth Guard had created.

Even as Dean fired two more shots, I heard Tika's scream. Not from pain, as I momentarily feared, but of rage.

Half a dozen searing white bolts of lightning split the roof apart; debris flew outward as they struck. The fat, impossible torrents temporarily blinded me, forcing me to turn away. In that flash, I saw the roof destroyed — possibly the building behind. I feared for Ben, Weston, and their charges inside. *Yaz.*

After that, the only otherness that I sensed blossoming was Andy's as he pelted the railings and stairwells with fire. The Savannah flag roared into flames along with smaller banners and once-inspirational slogans.

Youth Guard were dying or dead inside the rooms and on the walkways.

Blinking, I sensed for Ben's familiar rhythms and the small group he led inside the bottom floor.

Tika's vengeful lightning struck the next building where Youth Guard poured out of their rooms along with what might be a couple guards. Far fewer rhythms vibrated in the inferno that Tika and Andy created.

"They're dying." I held the shields about us, though I wanted it all to end.

Dean's muffled voice seemed as far away as Roxie. We might have to swim across to retreat.

I sensed a new group of rhythms, soldiers moving quickly toward us. Too fast. "Dean, troops. Some sort of vehicles."

My sight still slashed with thick lines, I peered across the compound. Bright headlights barreled through the north gate while another set raced down Bass Drive. They'd try to encircle us.

Dean tugged at my sleeve, pulling me to a crouch.

I searched for Tika next to us. Her lightning had stopped. Andy bombarded the two buildings with fire, but none of the Youth Guard attacked us anymore. They had all died or fled. What had we unleashed on them?

Weston, Ben, and six others had exited the mess hall at the back, near the river. They ran for the inlet closer to Tika. Fire engulfed the front of two buildings.

I almost laughed insanely when Ben stopped to lob fire-balls at the back of the building. By morning, there would be nothing but ash.

"Andy," I yelled. He glanced over, and I pointed at the north gate and Bass Drive, then beckoned him toward me with a gesture. "Soldiers."

Penny still lived, I could sense that. Roxie had grown stronger, perhaps with Fawn's healing.

I rose to a crouch and nodded for Dean to follow me toward Tika. Her dark eyes locked onto mine. Firelight reflected from the growing inferno. I could almost believe it came from within her as well. She might have had no expression, if it weren't for the hardness around her eyes.

"Tika, are you okay?" I asked.

She nodded, then turned as the headlight of an approaching vehicle flicked on her face. Her teeth bared, and I felt the storm she set over the soldiers.

Lightning lit her face, then flashes of orange and red.

Weston led the way into the water of the tiny offshoot from the main river. It rose to his chest. Dark shapes began to spill in behind him. I drew what otherness I could and propped a shield behind Ben as he escorted the last of them down the bank.

"C'mon," I said to Tika, but passed her to check on Penny. The rhythms of the soldiers were gone, vibrating in pain or running away. The last threat pulled through the southern gate, and I hoped they had sense not to follow. "I need to get to Penny. She's been hurt."

Flames ate at the treetops ahead. The attackers had either known exactly where she'd been or missed their target. Across the river, fire danced in random spots near where Roxie had been stationed. This trap had been planned well.

Dean spoke, but I couldn't understand him over the ringing. Andy and Tika waited with Weston and helped those we'd rescued. Two were missing of the eight. *Had Yaz still been in Camp Sparta?* I could ask those we'd rescued later.

Not bothering to crouch, I jogged toward Penny. The

fire in two trees grew, dropping flaming sticks that would soon light the dry leaves and needles.

Otherness welling up behind me forced me to stop and spin. Andy's fire blossomed in the woods by the road. The soldiers there spiked in panic, not pain – at least not much. Shivering, I resumed the last few paces to the river's edge.

I reached Penny, strewn on the shore with the muzzle of her rifle dipped in the water, but she hadn't let go. The inferno of Camp Sparta lit her like daylight. The reek of burning hair clung to her, but when I laid my hands on her, I knew she'd barely been burned. Her brain had swelled from the fall. Healing surged through me, and I pushed away a rising well of sadness. I'd mourn later. Some of the Youth Guard dying I might have accepted, considering what they had thrown at us, but this massacre, and perhaps Yaz, I couldn't simply accept.

I sensed Roxie's magic well up over the river. We wouldn't have to swim.

Dean's muffled voice broke through. "Caitlyn, we need to leave." He stepped into the water, handed me Penny's rifle, and picked her up.

Weston reached the bridge, leading a line of six unsure rebels onto the water. They followed with Ben smiling at the back. Andy and Tika watched the compound and flames for anyone foolish enough to brave the radiating heat.

A simple rescue had become a fiery massacre. How many old friends of ours had died?

Bullets flashed across the river from the north. I'd let my senses drift. Two boats with half a dozen soldiers raced toward our escape. "Soldiers!" I pointed at the dark vessels, painted with firelight and crackling with gunfire.

Dean grumbled ahead of me. "Crap."

Tika's magic welled over the water, and I slammed into her, dropping us to the shore. "Lightning and water."

Ben spun on the midway point of the bridge, and I thought he'd been hit. Then his and Andy's magic engulfed both boats in fire.

Andy whooped. The explosions rocked the river, sending low waves upstream. One of the rescued Youth Guard slipped, a young girl from the shape, but one of the others grabbed as her foot splashed, and they both fell onto the bridge.

Tika's eyes were moist with an otherwise unreadable expression when she helped me up. How would she handle this?

At Tika and Andy's insistence, Dean and I stepped onto the bridge before them. He strode as if on land, and I tried to keep pace and not end up swimming.

Penny grumbled in his arms without moving. "Put me down, you effing freak."

I smiled, weakly, at what little good I could hope for out of this mess. Ahead, Roxie's rhythms felt weak, and that wouldn't bode well for the next leg of our escape.

Chapter Four

As Camp Sparta burned across the river, it shone red and orange light into the forest ahead of us. Soaked, Roxie and Fawn sat in waterlogged leaves amid smoking brush and trees. Their burned coveralls bore the marks of the betrayal more visibly than Penny.

Ben led the six rescued Youth Guard down our escape path while Weston waited for me. The air stunk of burning wood and the sharper, more chemical odors from the sinking boats. Odie whined as he ran back to check on Penny and Dean.

"What happened?" I asked. "You said eight."

"Elizabeth never showed." Weston's rhythms vibrated with frustration. "Vicky went down from gunfire when we exited the back. Dead or wounded, I don't know."

I never heard gunshots, other than Dean's. "Do you think Elizabeth betrayed us? We knew it was a risk."

Tika, pale-faced, passed us to follow the rescued Youth Guard. She stared at the ground, her rhythms distraught in my othersense. Her power had been intense, so perhaps she recoiled against it now. I understood that feeling.

Weston noted Roxie and Fawn rising. "We'll ask them

when it's safer. They might guess where we're headed." He nodded past the burning buildings, and I presumed he meant the military. Their camp wasn't in flames, yet. The woods were dry.

I motioned him forward, along with Dean carrying Penny. "Roxie? Fawn? You okay?"

"A bit worn. You? Penny?" Roxie brushed at her singed hair, grimacing.

"Penny took a spill." Smoke thickened around us, swirling in the breeze. I gestured for her to follow Dean as I swept behind with my othersense. The few people I found were headed away and in pain. "I'm fine."

"Me too." Andy scoffed lightheartedly from behind as we marched. "Thanks for asking."

Fawn stuck by Roxie, silent. Her tan scalp had a couple red splotches.

We traipsed into the section of burned woods that led to the metal shed where I'd first kissed Dean and he'd turned. On the north shore of the lake where I'd paddled him away in werewolf form had waited a much larger boat. The memories seemed so long ago, but it had been just weeks.

Roxie's drawn face made her appear tired. "You going to be okay for this next bit?" I asked.

A weak smile flashed on her face. "Not much choice. I'll be fine." She swallowed, dropping her voice. "Tika?"

"Yeah. I hadn't expected it. She's usually so quiet and reserved."

Andy heard, and his cheerful tone made me cringe. "You see how she split the roof wide open? Lit the place up. Fried them good. Teach them to mess with the Wolf Squad."

"Andy, they were people just like us. Some might not have even been attacking us. I mean, considering the situation, she acted to save some of us, but we don't need to be happy about anyone dying."

He sniffed and didn't respond. Andy had set the front of the building and some people to flame, forcing others trapped inside to climb out the back windows where there were no stairs. My stomach churned at the memory.

The inferno glimmered through the woods when I glanced back, but moonlight lit the forest floor. The blackened trees seemed more ominous with the scent of burning wood carried on the breeze. I focused on those we'd rescued, who were marching in a line ahead of Dean.

In my range of othersense, I found no one following or waiting ahead. If they knew about us and beat us to our boat, we'd be in trouble. Our pace quickened. Dean didn't hold us back, despite Penny. Odie padded attentively beside them.

"We're getting close to the shore." Fawn pointed to our right through the trees, where moonlight glittered on water.

I sighed in relief.

"Were you afraid they'd get to the boat?" Roxie asked.

"Yeah. I can only hope they used their faster motors in the river and they don't know about our escape plan. They had more than two craft last time I checked." I snatched glances of the shore through the trees.

Each glimpse of the lightly rippling lake gave me hope. Ben chatted up the new group, and I watched them as much as they snuck glances at me. Len strode sharply at the lead alongside a pale-haired, short man, who I guessed would be Quinn. Gina had curly black hair and walked closely beside a slight woman with long brown hair. One of the others appeared to speak constantly as she gestured. None had any belongings except what they carried in their pockets, much like me when I'd escaped Camp Sparta.

Whiffs of pungent plants in the breeze reminded me of living in the northern marsh as we neared the shore.

Penny struggled slightly in Dean's arms, and he hushed her calmly. "I'll let you down when we get to the boat. Nothing is easy."

Weston, Len, and Quinn reached the boat first and were pushing it out as the rest of us bunched along a soggy shore. Unlike Dean's little boat, there were three pontoons affixed to the bottom and a little canopy stretched over the top. It had a steering wheel like a car, but Roxie wouldn't need it.

The teen with animated gestures slid past Dean and Odie to face me. "Thank you, Caitlyn. I thought we were done for, but you had the place on fire. My name's Nadia, short for Nadeschda. Russian on my mother's side. We're Wolf Squad all the way." She made her last gesture to the others behind her.

I forced a smile. "Tika and Andy did most of the heavy work. Well, they all did their parts. You can thank them — and Ben, for refusing to leave you behind."

At the mention of her name, Tika peered at me with haunted eyes, then turned down again. I'd have to talk with her.

"I'm Andy, Nadia." Pushing past me, he loomed above the teen and offered a hand.

Dean had worked his way to the boat as it bobbed, stepping into the water while Ben jumped in to lead Penny to a long, padded seat. "We should get going." Dean's voice hit that commanding note he often used with the Wolf Squad members.

Gina splashed into the water with the teen I assumed to be Isabel, and they climbed up easily. Weston helped while the stout Quinn marched back toward me.

His face dotted with short whiskers spaced too far apart,

he wore a grimace as he reached me and extended his hand. "What's the plan?"

"We'll go over it when we get going." I swallowed, my lips twisting. They didn't know anything about the Alliance. "Everyone should hear."

He snorted. "Which camp will we hit next? Surely we can be better prepared than this shit show."

I blinked. "No other camps. I'll explain when we're all in the boat and underway."

"No other camps? I thought you were the Wolf Squad — rebels against these friggin' camps."

My assumption had been that the rescued Youth Guard would be like Andy, somewhat fanatical, but not rude and confrontational. Quinn expressed zero gratitude.

"We will talk about our plans when we get going." I strode past him toward Dean, who waited for me knee-deep in water with the boat almost loaded.

"Our plans, or yours? Sounds like you're just running away."

I certainly am. Silently, I waded into the cold water and climbed up the front of the boat. Roxie knelt at the back, where there had once been an engine. Everyone had spread into seats or sat cross-legged on the deck. With Odie at her feet, Fawn sat beside Penny, who curled up on a length of padded cushions on the right side. As Dean shifted the craft to point north, I walked toward Roxie while I scanned the lake with my othersense.

"Shit. We've got company, Roxie." I turned south, but no moonlight reflected off the lake.

Dean scampered up the side. "All in."

Quinn's swearing rose above the murmurs.

Roxie called the otherness, and most of them dropped to the deck when she churned water under the hull with a lurch. I grabbed the bars on the back and held on in a crouch. We turned slower than we had on the trip south, but that could have been the extra weight or her fatigue.

A single bullet whistled past, but there were three muzzle flashes. Two dark shapes cut wakes in the lake, where I sensed six soldiers, three in each boat. Had they known we'd be here, or was it just Tyrell's assumption?

As a fourth muzzle flash lit the night, Andy cried out. The spike in his rhythms confirmed he'd been hit.

I drew in the otherness.

Focusing three feet behind Roxie's churning water, I drew in air and formed a shield in the shape of a quarter dome rising from the froth up over our heads. A second volley of bullets wedged into it and hung suspended before I'd even finished.

The nose of one bullet pointed at me, with the bulbous shape trailing along behind as Roxie picked up speed.

One of the foolish soldiers lit a floodlight on us, and immediately I felt one of the people behind me draw in the otherness. I hoped it wasn't Tika.

A second draw and a third pull on the otherness coated the military boats in fire. One man glowed orange as he dove into the water. Twin explosions sent a flock of birds from a tree on the shore, then the night was silent except for the roiling water under Roxie's power.

"How did you friggin' do that?" Quinn asked from behind me.

I dropped the shield, and the bullets plunked into the lake. Turning, I found he'd stabilized his footing and stood close behind me. Ignoring Quinn, I spoke in a tight snarl. "Andy."

Dean and Isabel, the slight woman with long brown hair, were already crouched over the lanky teen. I had to push past Quinn to reach them. Andy's left arm bled as he stared up at the little canopy over the center section with his jaw tight in pain.

"We got you, Andy. Is the bullet still in him?" I asked.

Isabel's eyes were wide as she nodded at me. She'd already probed with healing, so she could act even in a crisis. *Good.*

"I'll get it out." I drew in otherness, focusing on the odd power that let me manipulate metal. Gravity shifted lightly, and Len gasped. The bullet reacted to my call, liquefying and oozing out of the bloody hole in Andy's arm. It had reached bone before stopping.

Gravity reasserted as I released my otherness and tossed the blob aside. Fawn and Isabel were both holding Andy, and I sensed them each trying, then pulling back as the other attempted healing.

Fatigue tugged at me, but healing came the easiest, and I remembered what we had done at the barn with the uncaring Kisharn and his acolytes. "We can work together. Drop in, as if just probing."

Fawn nodded, following me into Andy with the otherness. Her head cocked as she sensed me there. A familiar rush flowed up my neck and cheeks at the odd melding of our powers. Isabel rested a hand on Andy's neck, and she inhaled as she found us.

"Deep wound first." As one, and yet separate, we nudged his body to knit muscle and flesh.

A grin spread across Fawn's face. "Amazing."

"Was that air?" Quinn asked, nearly at my shoulder. "I can friggin' do air."

"Yes. I'll try to show you, later." If he had a proclivity to air, I might be able to teach him, but not in the middle of trying to heal someone.

"Good. We can use that when we free the other camps."

My jaw tightened. "First, we get back to the Alliance."

First, I heal Andy. "I don't plan on starting a war with Tyrell. They'll be coming to Columbia soon enough."

"Alliance? What's that?" Quinn's voice tinged with anger. "Wait, Columbia is crawling with friggin' Duathua."

I had hoped to ease everyone into the conversation, as it would be a long trip back down the Congaree River. "The Alliance is a community of humans and Duathua working together toward—"

"Nope. Not happening. I ain't going there."

Andy had nearly healed between the three of us, so I withdrew and patted his chest. He watched me, and the tightness in his jaw eased. "It's where we live. All of us. You've been lied to about—"

"Not Friggin' going there!" Quinn pushed his ugly face closer to mine.

Dean slid between us, his chest brushing Quinn back. "You heard the kid, Roxie. Pull to shore. We've got one less. No regrets."

I stood, rocking with the motion of the boat. "We can't leave him behind."

Quinn, however, had gotten Dean's implications. All the Youth Guard knew Dean had been infected. He checked with pale-haired Len, who offered no support, then he swore and turned his back on Dean and me.

I didn't like the man, but maybe he'd calm down on the ride. I searched the other faces, but they were just stunned. "The military has killed any of the Duathua ambassadors they've sent and told us lies about them. If anything, they're a lot like us. No one needs to stay with the Alliance, but it is where we are headed back to."

Weston and Fawn nodded. Ben smiled. "They are really strange, but nice. You get used to it."

I bowed my head to him. "Thanks. We'll go about an hour before giving Roxie a rest." Weston had tried to replicate what she did, but couldn't steer the boat while propelling it.

We had two wounded from the rescue and had gained a jerk. I just wanted to get back safely. As Nadia started pounding out questions for Ben, I checked on Penny. We weren't safe yet.

Chapter Five

I sat beside an unconscious Penny during our first rest with the moon still lighting the half-submerged trees Dean had tied us to. With my othersense, I scanned the south for humans. We were close to the top of Lake Marion as the Congaree River wound west of where Dean and I had set up in the marsh. It seemed a lifetime ago, but the marshy scents brought back the memories.

Quinn had stayed away from me and Dean, speaking angrily with Len, Weston, and Ben about his disappointments. Ben, at least, tried to assuage any concerns about the Duathua.

Nadia chattered from the front of the boat. "I should be sleeping, but I can't, not after all this. We're Wolf Squad now. Duathua! What will they be like?"

Tanned Isabel and Kira with rich brown skin sat with the excited Nadia, nodding. The boat seemed so much smaller with all the new people.

Roxie lay at my feet on the deck beside Andy, who slept with a stolen seat cushion under his head. His expression appeared pleased, or at least content.

"Okay?" I asked Roxie. Her rhythms vibrated irregularly. She looked worn but not asleep, despite her eyes being shut.

"I'll make it. Do you think he knows where we're going?"

"Tyrell's pretty smart. I'm watching for anyone coming from that direction."

"Let's hope he doesn't have another of those helicopters."

I cringed at the thought.

Dean climbed into the boat, scoffing at her concern. "Yeah, that'd make for a fitting end. Who do we think ratted on us? This Elizabeth?"

Weston and Len both glanced over at Dean's question. Len spoke, interrupting Quinn's tirade. "She made like she thought you walked on water. A good act if she did turn us in." His expression became frustrated, as if Quinn's dour mood infected him.

"Did you know her?" I asked.

"We're both out of Camp Mystras, so I guess I knew her better than others at Camp Sparta." Len had a long face, making the sparse whiskers on his chin more prominent — like a goat.

If Elizabeth had been our traitor, then she'd killed Camp Sparta. Would she mourn the night's events as much as I or Tika?

Len cleared his throat. "Um, speaking of Camp Mystras, are we going to free them next? There's a lot of Youth Guard there who want to join the Wolf Squad."

Exhausted, I closed my eyes. "We ended up with a lot of people dead or injured. Do you really want a repeat of tonight?"

Quinn spoke, of course. "These two don't look dead. We only lost Vicky, and she was weak anyway."

My face tightened, but I kept my eyes shut. "I meant the Youth Guard at Camp Sparta as well."

"They deserved it."

I opened my eyes to search out Tika sitting with Fawn at the back, staring into the lazy river. "No one deserves it. Just because it couldn't be helped, doesn't make it right." The last I said for her benefit.

"We should go to Camp Mystras next. This time we'll plan better. Len knows who to speak to there."

Tired of the recurring argument, I focused on Roxie. Selina had tortured her because of me, but still she resisted heading to Camp Sparta until I'd given in to Weston and Ben. If she'd asked me, I would have agreed earlier. I told Quinn the same thing I'd told Weston and Ben, "I'm not in charge. We can all do what we need to."

Dean gave me a sharp glance as he sat beside me, taking my hand into his. He smelled like swamp water, but he still looked cute.

As Quinn grumbled and spun away, Dean whispered in my ear. "They want you to lead. You could tell them not to go. Most would listen to you."

I shook my head. It would be time for Roxie to start churning water with her magic to propel us again. We'd continue this way into the morning, taking short breaks. We'd brought enough supplies to get us back to Columbia. I had never realized a single river ran from the city to Camp Sparta until members of the Alliance had mentioned it. They'd considered this boat useless since they had no interest in wasting fuel on it.

By the time we reached the edge of Columbia, Penny and Andy were awake and as annoyed with Quinn as I felt. The morning smelled fresh, though the burned-out city on each bank seemed like it should have stunk of ash. The shores held new green growth sprouting among the black skeletal remains of trees, and any buildings within sight were scorched and crumbling.

Odie spotted the Pahawan warriors flying low over the ruins or perched on the branches and rooftops. Our new crew didn't see any of them. We passed under a bridge that the Alliance had blockaded from one end to the other with abandoned vehicles.

"Lovely friggin' place," grumbled Quinn.

Most of us had already decided to ignore him, but he'd grown cozy with Ben, Weston, and Len. Roxie looked exhausted, and her rhythms were low and erratic. I sat on the back seat where she knelt.

"Almost there." My comment brought no response from her. "Maybe Nur has a batch of that goat cheese." The friendly Duathua scientist had remained close with us, even after Vanya had died and I'd sent Wati away.

Roxie kept her voice low. "It was pretty horrible to see, once I doused us and got a clear view of the camp buildings. Jordan? Yaz? So many I wouldn't want to get hurt." She hadn't talked about the disastrous rescue until now.

"Tika's pretty shook up about it. I've talked to her a couple times, but I'm not sure I'm getting through."

"It didn't feel this way when we fought outside of Sumter." Roxie shrugged with one shoulder. "Those were soldiers trying to kill us with guns, until the end." Her eyes were dark underneath when she turned to me. "Are you going to do this again at Camp Mystras?"

I shook my head. "Honestly, part of me is like 'Yeah!', but I can't risk that kind of slaughter again. I hate that there are people trapped in camps like we were."

"I think Quinn is getting a group together to go."

"I know. I'm not in charge. He can do what he wants."

"They look up to you, Caitlyn."

"Fine." *It's not.* I hated being their symbol. "If I don't go, more will be safe."

"He might end up dead. He's not very strong. Weston and Ben are, but there's a reason Tyrell didn't take Quinn to Sumter." Roxie almost sounded angry.

At me?

I glanced forward where the little wooded islands sprouted up in the middle of the river. The stronger current this far upriver rippled around the land. To the north, the Alliance's main community lived on the hilly peninsula between the Saluda and Broad Rivers. Smoke from cooking fires rose above green woods, and a couple taller buildings were faded but not burned. Duathua flitted over treetops. Quietly, Gina watched from the front of our boat, apparently the only one to have caught sight of the cryptids.

We had been concerned how they might react, but had decided to bring the newcomers straight here. I left Roxie's side and held onto one of the bars of the canopy. "We're here," I said in what I hoped was a calming tone. "We've got a place in the northwest that's about a two-hour walk from where we'll dock."

"The Wolf Den," added Andy from his spot on the deck.

I forced a smile. "As named by Andy. There are several available homes near ours, and he picked the one next door to house you. A couple of you will have to double up in rooms unless we work on a third house."

Gina hadn't turned from her view. "Do they live with us?"

"The Duathua? Not really. We're in an area that hasn't been heavily populated. We've got a hand pump in the back." That had impressed me the most when we'd moved in; it pulled water out of the ground. "There are a lot of humans living in apartment buildings nearby, but that's about it."

Nadia perked up at that comment. "Why don't we live there?"

Dean raised his fingers up as claws in a mock threat and growled. His pantomime quieted Nadia, though I knew it and the "Wolf Den" comments bothered him.

We were nearing the island where rowboats were tied to trees or posts. Another of the blockaded bridges was visible past the rocky waters of Block River. "We're going to have to take turns carrying Andy."

Penny shot me a warning glare. Even though she'd slept most of the trip and her vibrations were off, she wouldn't be carried since she could stand. I wouldn't even suggest it.

"I can walk." Andy rose on his good side.

Fawn spoke before I could. "No. You won't."

A hint of cooking fire wafted with the scent of pines on the breeze. Dean moved to the front of the boat and grabbed a rope as Roxie eased us into the calm inlet. Still, she caused the rowboats to bob.

Once Dean had us tied beside the other boats, I sent the newer members to shore. We had supplies to pack up, but I handed the blanket we'd brought to Fawn. "Ben, Weston, can you get us some branches for a stretcher?" Clouds drifted in front of the sun angling to the west. We had plenty of time to get to the Wolf Den and get the new people settled before dark.

"Are we Wolf Squad now?" Nadia asked as she splashed into water and mud.

I turned to find her addressing me. "If you want. You're free to be whatever you desire."

"Wolf Squad," Andy called out.

Giving him a flat look, I zipped up a duffel bag and

placed it in the front of the boat. Some of them might not wish to stay with the Alliance, but it was safer than the options. The werewolves and Oni steered clear of even the Columbia ruins due to the flying Pahawan. Tyrell remained a concern, and we couldn't avoid him forever.

Penny, Roxie, and Odie led our procession while I stayed with Dean and Ben carrying Andy at the rear. "Let's see how this goes," chuckled Dean.

"It only took a day for me." Ben's mustache still seemed sparse, like it needed to be washed off.

I'd been out cold and quarantined during the Wolf Squad's first day with the Duathua. "Should we worry about Quinn?" I asked Ben.

He shrugged, almost undetectable with his burden. "Don't know. He seems angry over everything."

"What's his best power?"

"Air. He's not strong at all."

Penny started the group over the small bridge to the mainland. The new people peered around, but little could be seen through the trees.

When we climbed up to the pitted interstate, they got a clear view of one of the Pahawan flying in their glass-like Kudaru armor with a three-tined Rizulat in their hand. Beside a rusting bus, the group stopped to gawk.

Weston nodded. "Duathua warriors. Pahawan. They are the military of the cryptids."

Quinn swore, but he didn't draw in the othersense.

Gina grabbed Isabel's hand. Nadia just smiled, then spoke. "Will we see one up close? Three pairs of wings, right? I mean, obviously they don't attack, or you couldn't stay here. But just flying all about you all the time, that's insane."

Nur had said she'd drop by in the evening to check on

us. I fought for a comforting smile. "You'll meet one close up tonight. She's a nice lady; you'll like her."

I ignored Quinn's scoff.

By the time we'd walked a couple hours, the novelty of seeing the Duathua faded. The interstate had no one else on it. For as many people as there were in the Alliance, they weren't moving about much with spring crops to plant.

When we crossed the fields to Bush River Road we came close to members of the Alliance grouped outside an old hotel, much like the people of Santee had. I wondered about the fire from Camp Sparta and how much of the surrounding woods would go up. Dean had to be concerned for his family.

We were all weary by the time we passed a complex of two-story apartments with cook fires trailing smoke above their roofs.

"Do humans live there?" Nadia asked. "Duathua?"

I shook my head as Penny turned the front of our procession down a cracked street to the right toward the Wolf Den. "Just humans. Most of the Duathua are settled to the north near the Broad River. We're fairly close compared to the areas we walked through."

"Then why were they flying all over?" Quinn asked.

"Be glad they do." I relaxed tight lips. "The Pahawan spend their days patrolling the outer edges. Werewolves and Oni might not like crossing water, but Tyrell's soldiers will." In reality, the more distant patrols would warn us of troop movements well before they reached the city.

We passed through the Wolf Den's neighborhood of abandoned, neglected buildings that members of the Alliance had never considered worth fixing enough to live in. One had a fallen pine lying in the middle of a broken roof.

As Penny brought the group to a stop at the corner of St.

Andrews Road, I stepped around them to the grass out front of the house and motioned to it. "This is the place we've prepped for you. Rather, Dean and Ben have been prepping for you. They're handy with all that."

The building had an open, empty porch called a carport that led to a single room with a fireplace. The rest of the brick house rose two stories, with all but one window still intact. I continued, "There are five bedrooms, so like I said, two of you will have to double up. We scavenged good mattresses, bedding, and some other furniture. Want to take a look in the daylight before we head over to the Wolf Den for dinner?"

Nadia strode to the crumbling drive of the carport. "I'm starving, but I need to see."

I followed her, waving Dean and the others to our nearly identical house next door. "They dug a latrine back there. Over it, they rigged a plastic outhouse called a Porta Potty. They're common in the city."

The funky-smelling kitchen had decent equipment compared to the bare slots at Camp Sparta, and we'd found the drains worked, mostly. From a second-floor bedroom, I pointed to the hand pump where they'd get water. While everyone else poked about with growing excitement, Quinn remained gloomy. He made it difficult for me to like him.

When we arrived as a group at the Wolf Den, Ben had a pot of beans and chicken cooking. The Duathua kept us supplied. As I settled everyone in the large living area and lit an oil lantern, Odie made his rounds.

I watched everyone as we ate. Would they choose to settle in and make a life in Columbia, or leave, possibly to die in rescue attempts? Fawn, Roxie, and Tika had seemed content and had only joined the trip to Camp Sparta when I agreed. Andy remained unquestioningly loyal, though he'd argued for me to go with Ben and Weston. How would the new people shake out?

A knock came from the front door, and I jumped up. "That would be Nur. She's a Duathua scientist." I eyed Quinn as he rose, causing the others to follow.

Nur smiled, her long fingers folded around a canvas bag. Taller than me, she wore her usual beige skirt with a colored hem and a woven satchel belted about her hips. "I am grateful to see you. I hope all went well on your excursion." Her large eyes, set into stiff gray skin, peered past me. The scales on her head shifted in what I recognized as curiosity.

Stepping aside and waving her in, I introduced her. "Everyone, this is Nur. You'll likely see her often." Going around the room, I named the newcomers, then explained why Andy was convalescing in his room along with Penny's fall, both of which she waved off.

"I am hopeful you will find some peace here." She lifted her sack toward Ben. "Dried peas, as promised. We'll have extra chickens brought over tomorrow to feed everyone. Are any of you healers?"

Isabel smiled awkwardly and raised her hand.

"Excellent. One of the requests from the Alliance is to have healers, such as Fawn and Caitlyn, learn to help plant growth from the Seyirs."

I explained, "Seyirs are the humans who work with the otherness, such as we do, but they're from the same world as the Duathua. You'll have the opportunity to learn new skills, if you want. Food is important with so many people."

Nodding, Isabel paled. "Okay."

I'd been remiss in helping. "We'll work as a group." I nodded at Fawn who'd learned more than I had.

We talked briefly, and when Nur left with Penny and Odie, the tension in the room eased.

Nadia bombarded me with questions. "She? I mean, no shirt, and you could tell — nothing. Do we rely on them for food? What do the other humans do, avoid them? Why do they have humans on their world?"

Dean must have seen something in my expression, because he spoke. "It's been a really long two days. Ben, can you settle them in next door? We'll clean up here. Plenty of time tomorrow for answers."

Ben checked his watch and nodded.

As Dean cleared the room, I had a brief moment with Tika. I couldn't imagine anything I said would take away her pain, so I drew her into a hug. She stifled sobs against my shoulder, but held on. When he noticed, Dean raised his eyebrows silently and headed outside with buckets to fetch more water.

An hour later, Dean and I lay together in our bedroom, larger than the others, and cuddled. Emotions tumbled inside me between Tika and Quinn.

"Hey, no regrets." Dean placed his hands on my cheeks and kissed me.

At first, my feelings warred, then gave in to his embrace and let it soar me away from worries into passion. My hands worked across his bare chest, muscled with almost no hair. Working down to his sides, my body flushed warmly, and I pulled his hips closer. I knew what I risked, but I wanted more.

Dean coughed and pushed away, suddenly growling in the darkness.

I'd caused him to shift. "I'm sorry." My selfish desires had ruined the night.

Nails scraped on the floor, heading for the door. Dean's silver furry form took shape with movement.

"Stay." We'd avoided too many incidents, and only the Pahawan had spotted him inside Columbia. They knew his silver fur. One bad situation, and we'd be asked to move. The Alliance had been clear when they accepted us. "Please stay." I'd rather he rode out the shifting safely, in our room.

Dean scratched on the door, and I rose with reluctance. I couldn't hold him. He'd explained the limitation of his mind in this form where passion dominated.

Tears ran down my cheek as I walked across our room.

Chapter Six

From the back door of the Wolf Den, I watched Dean run between the fragrant pines, glowing when the moonlight caught his silver fur. Exhausted, I cried silently before turning to head back to my empty bedroom.

Sleep came fitfully, and each time I awoke, I would check the back door for Dean.

The moonlight had retreated when Dean returned, climbing naked into our bed. As I stirred, he spoke huskily. "Sorry."

I shook my head in the darkness. "It was my fault."

"Nothing is easy," he whispered.

"We'll find a cure."

He sighed, a weary sound. "We've tried. As much as I want — *us*, know that love will be enough — at least for me."

Wincing, I fought tears. "We'll find a cure." I no longer believed it.

Against him, I fell into a deep sleep, waking only when someone slammed a door downstairs. Sunlight slanted in from one of our bedroom windows against the faded white walls.

Dean rose from atop the blankets beside me and faced

the door. "It's late." He retrieved his clothes from the floor. "I'll get us some water."

The temperature still cool from the night, I pulled my coveralls to me as I yawned. "I need to check on Andy."

He left without discussing the failed evening, and I understood. If I brought it up, there would be a reminder of something he felt a certain shame over. He foolishly believed that shifting could be controlled.

Carrying my coveralls, I went to the small bathroom where we kept a slightly damp towel and a pail to rinse with. I had never forgotten the shower, hot and luxurious, at Vinnie's house. He kept his werewolf son imprisoned on the property. Had they survived the soldiers when Tyrell moved through to attack Sumter?

After a quick wash, I dressed lethargically, fighting a waning mood after yesterday's events. Digging fingers through my hair, I settled it enough to braid. When I stepped into the hall outside my door and reached the steps, nothing sounded from downstairs. I crossed through the empty house to head out to the latrine.

Afterward, I grabbed one of Dean's pails while he filled another and left the bucket on a counter in the kitchen before heading up to check on the others. Fawn's voice came from Andy's room, but I entered anyway. "Any better?" I asked.

Andy grinned from his mattress on the floor, and sitting beside his bed, Fawn nodded her shaved head as she spoke. "He's well enough for a trip to the latrine. Maybe Dean could help?"

I rested my hand on Fawn's shoulder. "I'm sure. Where's everyone else?"

"Ben and Weston are next door. Tika and Roxie are still in bed."

"I'll check on Tika," I said. "Glad you're feeling better, Andy."

He waited until I reached the doorway. "Are we going back out — to free more Wolf Squad?" His tone sounded hopeful.

"I think I've had enough adventure for a day or two. I'll consider it, but I believe Quinn intends to, no matter the risks." If I agreed, most, if not all, the Wolf Squad would likely join. Someone might not come back next time.

His expression dropped. "Okay. I just remember what it was like."

I turned to exit. "So do I." Heading for the closed door to Tika and Fawn's room, I drew in a deep breath.

A sharp knock came from the front door, and as I turned to the stairs, it opened.

"I brought some company," called Penny from below. She lived farther north, but visited nearly every day.

My chest tightened. Had someone spotted Dean last night? I paused at the top of the steps. An extremely tall Duathua leaned down to follow Penny through our door, their head scales tinged with red. They wore the skirt of the Duathua, not the armor of their warriors, so this didn't concern Dean. "Hello." I took the steps briskly. The scent of cooked eggs set my stomach rumbling.

Despite the promise of a warm day, Penny wore her long black coat. "Caitlyn, this is Jural. She just made it to the Alliance." Odie panted in the doorway, then padded inside.

"Greetings, Seyir." Jural straightened cautiously, her eyes watching the ceiling that she came close to reaching. Then her piercing gaze followed me as I descended the stairs. She had used the title they gave the Denya magic users; only the Pahawan did that with me.

"You just arrived?" Did that mean the Duathua came

out of the cryptid zone, or someplace else? I gestured for Jural to follow me into our communal sitting area.

Through an open window, I could see Bella grazing from where she'd been hitched on a tree in the front yard. We had chairs, pillows, and boxes to sit on, but we'd need more with the new additions.

The back door opened deep behind us in the house, and I assumed Dean had retrieved water.

Jural waited to speak until she'd navigated the arch. "I Displaced at forty days ago. Survived many Oni there. Iandil's scouts aid me." Her accent and wording came awkwardly.

Forty days on Earth. Iandil, the Duathua who had instigated the Alliance and continued to search the depths of the cryptid zone for survivors, had lived through Sumter. "So, when did you arrive in Columbia?" I waited until Jural picked a tall stool before I flopped into a thick pillow.

"The morning before."

Yesterday? Why was she here to see me? A chill rose up my neck. "And you wanted to visit me?"

Jural smiled; I easily recognized the expression on the Duathua's stiff skin. "Iandil spoke of you. They sent I to Nur. She much to say. You are an unusual Seyir. You returned one Duathua from the Displacement."

I drooped. Other Duathua had come to me, wishing for me to try. I'd reluctantly refused, and the Alliance, through Nur, had squelched the idea until we'd studied it more. Besides Moonjir's questionable word, I had no idea if my friend Wati had been sent home or somewhere else. Despite myself, I peered at Jural in the othersense, building the vision of her connections. As expected, they clustered, with only a few newer ties to those here on Earth. Those newly brought through the Displacement might be easier, according to Nur's theories.

"You've come to ask me to send you back?"

Her expression remained affable. "Not. I would study this world, not leave it. I came to hear your experience of Wati."

Dean came from the kitchen with a pail and mugs. He studied the new Duathua without a word.

"Jural, this is Dean, my partner."

She cocked her head. "The half werewolf. It is pleasure to meet you, Dean."

Ignoring the werewolf comment, he raised his handful of mugs. "Water?"

"Thank you."

I took the moment to absorb what I could of her odd speech. I probably should be impressed she spoke so well, considering the time she'd been around people speaking English. *Days maybe?* Jural was obviously old, considering her height. The Duathua never stopped growing. She just wanted to know about my experience with Wati, but I hated dredging up those memories.

When we all had water, Dean promised me some food and headed across the house to the kitchen.

"You will tell of me?" Jural asked.

"About my experience with Wati? What I did?"

"Yes, those."

I obliged, talking first of the training I'd learned under Vanya to describe the connections I could see. So far, none of the other Wolf Squad could. Though some of them meditated with me each day, others had given up. I spoke of pushing Wati and the resistance I sensed before it finally yielded. As quickly, I let Jural know my concerns of not knowing for sure that the young, joyful Duathua had been sent to Denya.

The latter statement caused Penny to close her eyes. She'd had strong feelings for Wati.

Dean brought flatbread and jam for breakfast and lounged on the floor beside me. I bit into mine hungrily as I finished talking, savoring some of the last sweet blueberry jam we'd stored.

Jural studied me, then dug into the bag at her side, retrieving a glass sculpture of an unusual fish. "You see connections this?"

I focused my othersense and found the connections of everyone in the room, but nothing on the object. Swallowing a bite, I shook my head. "No, should I?"

"I thought." Jural drew in the otherness, surprising me. Few of the Duathua I'd met could.

She focused it in the room, expanding until it enveloped us all. I resisted snatching at it reflexively in defense. Her eyes glanced at the glass sculpture as if expecting something to happen.

"I see your otherness in the room and the connections on everyone here, but nothing to objects like the fish."

"Fish." Jural repeated. "This speech." She dissipated the otherness. "We train you. Any." Her gaze turned to Penny, who just raised her eyebrows in response.

"What training?" I asked.

"We listen." Vanya had called her meditations the same, but I imagined Jural meant something different. She put down her mug. "Eyes on."

"Open?" I asked.

She nodded. "Breath." We followed her inhale. "Breath." She exhaled slowly. Extending her own foot, she said, "Hear toe."

Dean chuckled. "Mine or yours?"

Jural answered lightheartedly. "Yours. Listen. Breath."

I sat in silence for a minute, breathing and feeling ridiculous.

"Toe speaks you. Blood. Energy. Rhythm."

The stairs creaked, and we all turned as Tika peered around the corner. Jural smiled. "Come us."

A hint of a grin flashed on Tika's face before she perched on a crate near the archway. It pleased me for her to join us, even if we listened to toes.

Jural walked through her beginning statements for Tika's sake, adding, "We own body. We tell body. Body tells us. We control all."

Dean snorted.

"All." Jural emphasized the word for him.

Chapter Seven

After we spent over an hour with Jural meditating on our toes, she bid us goodbye, asking to return the next day to continue the meditations. I reluctantly agreed. Whatever she expected to show us didn't appear to come quickly. Penny smirked as our visitors stepped outside.

"What do you think?" Dean asked me as I headed upstairs to check on Roxie.

"About my toe?"

"You know."

"I learned a lot from Vanya, but we could speak better. It came quickly. I won't insult Jural and tell her to leave."

"Good."

I gave him a quick glance before tapping on Roxie's door.

"I hope you're bringing breakfast," she said from inside.

Dean rolled his eyes and headed for the stairs. "We'll get you something," I said, opening the door.

Her eyes were dark, but she sat on her mattress with her face shining wet from a quick wash. Roxie had dressed and likely would have been downstairs in a minute if I hadn't come up.

"Fawn checked me over already. I'm tired, but fine. Who was that I heard downstairs?"

"A Duathua Seyir named Jural. We were, um, meditating."

Roxie's eyebrows lifted. "*Okaay*. What are you going to do about Quinn?"

Since we were waiting for Dean to bring breakfast and she hadn't made any move to rise, I dropped next to her onto the mattress. "What do I need to do? He's got issues. They aren't mine."

"He's trying to take over the Wolf Squad." Her tone growled slightly, as if it angered her.

I shrugged. "Some might choose to follow him. That's fine. I don't want to be some symbol of freedom — or a leader."

"He might get them killed."

My face grimaced before I could calm it. "I know. It's the same situation that Ben put me in. Do I keep risking you, Penny, and Andy to save them?" With the door open to the hall, my voice softened. "Tika? Fawn?"

Her lips pinched in frustration, then relaxed with Dean's footsteps sounding on the stairs. "Maybe you just need to make your position known. You *say* you're not the leader, but most of them look to you as one."

"Not you." I smiled so she wouldn't take it seriously.

"Of course not. I'm no fool."

Dean brought Roxie a tall mug of water along with flatbread and jam. "Roxie's right. Shit or get off the pot."

My eyebrows knitted. "What?"

He placed Roxie's breakfast next to her feet. "Nothing is easy. You can say whatever you want, but they still follow you."

I couldn't tell Quinn or Ben not to do what they wanted. They'd just sneak away. I did feel responsible for their welfare, and that wouldn't go away just because I made them understand I wasn't their leader. My stomach hardened as I remembered the devastation we had unleashed on Camp Sparta, then finding Penny knocked out of the tree and Roxie in a burned section of the woods.

She smirked as she took a bite of her breakfast. "Mmmm."

I rose, wanting to run from all of this. "Dean, feel like a walk, maybe to the dam?" The walk would take a couple of hours each way. I needed to think, and escaping for the day would help me relax.

He studied my eyes, then nodded. "Sure. Not much of a dam, with the most of the water drained out of the lake."

"We'll pack a lunch."

A small smile crept on my face as I headed downstairs. As I hit the landing, the front door opened, letting in my least favorite person.

Quinn's grimace hardened when he found me so close. "We need maps. Camp Mystras is southeast of Camp Sparta in a place called Moncks Corner, m-o-n-c-k-s."

Len followed Quinn, pushing alongside him. "I know the area well. Patrolled it for years. I've got some ideas."

It appeared that everyone stood outside the front door of the Wolf Den. I shifted toward our seating area. "I can check with the Alliance to see if they have maps."

"They friggin' better. I'm not sure what their game is, but if they're at war with Tyrell, they should know the terrain."

I kept my voice smooth. "They don't want to be at war with Tyrell or the Savannah Charter. They've sent ambassadors."

Quinn rolled his eyes. "I don't friggin' care. We're going to start with Len's people. Free them. Where do we go for the maps?"

They'd made a decision. *All of them?* I was almost tempted to send Quinn blustering against the Alliance. They rarely called an assembly except for a major concern. Most neighborhoods coordinated the sharing of supplies. Finding someone in the Alliance to request something like maps from might take the day. "I'll get them for you."

"We'll need supplies. Weapons." Quinn pressed closer, forcing me to back into the room.

Dean chuckled, peering down at the irate teen. "They aren't giving you their weapons, kid."

Quinn's face rippled into a snarl, but he held back, as if fearing Dean. "Whatever. Maps and supplies."

As the rest of the newcomers filed into the house, I weighed their expressions. Of the women, Nadia appeared excited, while the other three seemed resigned. "I'll go for the maps today. Supplies will be more difficult. Winter just ended, and stores are —"

"We're not waiting for the friggin' crops to harvest." Quinn glanced back at the hall with the front door and stairs. "We'll need the boat and Roxie."

My eyes tightened. "You don't get to choose who goes with you." I doubted she'd agree if I wasn't going.

"You don't get to friggin' stop us."

Even Ben and Weston wore sheepish expressions, as if embarrassed by Quinn's aggressive behavior. I offered them a smile I hoped comforted them. "No. I certainly don't. You are asking for help. I'm trying to accommodate."

My demeanor seemed to aggravate him, and Quinn stepped closer — too close. Dean simply slid in front of me, pressing the shorter teen away. "Back it up, kid."

Quinn retreated, pulling in the otherness. As quickly, I drew it from him. His eyes widened, and he froze, his face turning ashen.

"FYI, bullyboy, I ain't motorboating your little crusade."
Roxie stood in the doorway, her face hard. "Not unless
Caitlyn is going. If you all would like to survive, I'd suggest
you consider the same plan. Ben and Weston might be
strong enough to live through an actual fight; bullyboy ain't."

Dean chuckled, and I poked his side to make him quit,
before I spoke. "Let's start with your maps. I'll work on
those today. Moncks Corner? Southeast of Santee?"
Through the window, I watched Penny galloping up on
Bella, with Odie loping alongside. As she launched off, I
worked through the small crowd toward the front door.

Quinn sputtered behind, but I ignored him. They'd left
the door open, so I closed it.

Penny relaxed when she saw me. "The Pahawan are
meeting and asked that you attend."

The last time I'd met with the warrior Duathua, they
discussed their defense plans and potential Wolf Squad
positions. Then again, Dean had been roving in werewolf
form last night. "Is something wrong?"

Shrugging, Penny pulled out a water bottle from a
saddlebag. "Not an effing clue. 'Get Caitlyn.' They aren't
talkative around me."

Dean stepped out, closing the door behind him. The
others watched from the window. "What's up?"

"Pahawan want a meeting."

He grimaced. "Go. I'll try to get Ben's help fixing that
roof." Clicking his tongue, he knelt to pet Odie.

Penny smiled, tucking her water away. "Having fun
with the kiddies?" she asked.

"You're not much older."

"Neither are you, but you've had to grow up." She
hopped atop Bella and patted the saddle behind her."

It would take an hour and a half to get to the Alliance

meeting place on foot. Half that on a horse. "You'll go slow?"

"Of course. Do you think I want to listen to your effing screaming?"

She pulled me up while I used the stirrup. The Alliance humans raised horses. Still a rarity, more and more younger colts grazed in fenced-in fields.

Penny whistled for Odie, who dawdled, enjoying Dean's attention. His nails scratched on asphalt as he chased after us down St. Andrews Road; we rode toward the cross street that would bring us to Bush River Road. That path would lead all the way to the large buildings where the Alliance met. The saddle was already bruising my butt.

Thicker than they'd been since the last rains, clouds gathered in the northeast ahead of us. Fires had taken some houses in this part of Columbia, but not like they had in the main city to the southeast. On a side street past a burned-out shell lay a community of tall mansions where the people farmed what had once been lawns. Water dictated prime locations for the Alliance to inhabit, and though the road rose in an incline, something had made the houses there appealing.

"Do you think he's coming?" asked Penny. "Because of Camp Sparta?"

"Tyrell? I doubt he would over Camp Sparta, but the Savannah Charter plans to liberate Columbia. Maybe."

She snorted. "Effing *liberate*. Kill off the Duathua."

"Yep." I hoped this meeting didn't involve Tyrell and almost wished it had to do with Dean roaming about as a werewolf. Maybe we'd end up exiled to the outer fringes of Columbia. After dealing with all the new Youth Guard, I might welcome it.

The path took us over the main highways that cut

through the area. Unlike Santee, many of the vehicles had either been scavenged for the bridge blockades or moved neatly into the brush at the sides. People had taken over some of the larger buildings and congregated in small clusters near those. Near them, rows of tiny green shoots rose amid fields. We needed rain, according to Nur, or the crops wouldn't produce much.

At the top of a low hill, every building showed some activity.

Penny pointed to a Pahawan in shining Kudaru armor flying away. "They've spotted us. They'll report that we're coming."

The Pahawan had a tight organization, much like Tyrell's military. I'd interacted with them more than the Duathua scientists or crafters, other than Nur. "No doubt we'll get an earful for being late."

"I made effing good time getting to you; they can't expect us to run the whole way back."

In a massive plaza, the Alliance used dozens of grand and small buildings for their meeting hall and other "official" buildings. Our destination waited where Pahawan silhouettes stood or sat on the largest of the buildings.

The sign outside read "Office Depot," and we'd all guessed at the meaning of the words. An office had been where people worked before the Sorrow, or so Dean said. Depots had been where trains let off people or where they stored ammunition. There'd been no sign of guns.

"A lot of Pahawan," murmured Penny.

"Guess so." I rarely came this far, but it seemed as many as other meetings.

The crumbling parking lot showed signs of cars long removed and stunk of oil like a gas station. Birds nested in the spires sprouting from the pavement. Supposedly the poles had held huge bulbs that lit the area for miles.

"Are you coming in?" I asked her.

Penny shrugged. "I'll find some grass for Bella and hang in the back."

She pointed to a green swath by the road and left me to enter on my own under the watchful eyes of the Pahawan perched on the roof above.

Layers of Kudaru, hardened air created by the Seyir from Denya, covered broken windows making the massive interior visible. The door creaked as I opened it. The Alliance had polished the floor and walls inside, but debris still hung from concrete ceilings. It had been a sight to see the Duathua fluttering about the place during Alliance meetings.

My footsteps clattered on cracked plastic tile as I walked toward the back. A Kudaru amphitheater rose in a grand half bowl against the corner. It reflected sounds into the main room when a thousand or two met for Alliance meetings. The crafters had created the structure with green and blue glass-like Kudaru that was a marvel to admire. It made the rest of the cinder block building appear dull. Even Dean had thought it cool.

Today, only five Pahawan waited at a table that flowed up from a dais in the middle of the amphitheater. I swallowed at their silence with only my footsteps to echo in the hall.

"Caitlyn," said Henweyay. The Duathua called her Haarseer, which meant military leader of the Pahawan, or something like that. Roxie would likely remember.

"Henweyay. I hope everything is okay." Still two dozen paces away, I hurried my step to join them.

"It is not. We would not bother a Seyir otherwise." Her high-pitched tone gave no hint of the seriousness of her statement. Though she was seated, I knew from previous meetings she stood taller than Dean.

"I'm sorry to hear." Sometimes I wished the Duathua did not need as much back and forth in a conversation. They could take tips from Dean. "What has happened?"

"The humans are gathering forces to the southeast. Trucks and weaponry."

The door at the front opened behind me as Penny and Odie slipped inside. I nearly stopped, ready to run back and prepare the Wolf Squad. "How soon will they be here?" My pulse rose.

"Not soon. They are not moving." Henweyay had dark scales on her scalp. Her expression remained fixed, though one of the others lifted their chin. "Our scouts just found the stockpile. It is an area where they have not congregated before. They attempt to camouflage it."

Taking a breath, I moved onto the Kudaru step before the dais. "Any estimate when they'll get to Columbia, or even leave?"

Henweyay made an unfamiliar gesture with her long fingers. "None. I have heard you retrieved six new Wolf Squad. Two injuries, but all returned."

"Yes." *Why had they called me here?* They could have sent Penny with word of all this.

"Will they fight with us?"

Considering Quinn's bloodlust, likely. "I don't know. We're just getting them settled in."

"They are strong?"

"I doubt they are as strong as the first group. They were left behind when Tyrell attacked Sumter."

One of the other Pahawan tittered in their strange language. Not all the Duathua deigned to learn English. Henweyay gestured, her eyes studying me. "Are there more you could recruit to the Alliance?"

I almost laughed. Gratefully, Quinn and the others weren't here. If they went off on their mission, the Pahawan might supply them with everything they requested, if it meant more Wolf Squad. "Maybe. Is that what you asked me here for today?"

"Yes, and to question their willingness and strength. After Sumter, we fear we would have to—" She stopped when the door to the front opened again.

I turned to find Nur — and Jural — stepping into the hall. The newer Duathua appeared to tower over Nur. Their wings blurred, and they both skimmed the floor toward us. The Pahawan buzzed with low, quick conversation in their own tongue.

Nur and Jural both studied me as they approached. "Apologies," said Jural loudly as she flitted down. "Haarseer. We have word your scouts find warriors to the east."

Placing a hand on my shoulder, Nur chirped low comments in the Duathua language to Jural. I let her adjust my focus toward the dais.

"This is true, Seyir. Do you have suggestions for us, or is this a concern for the Alliance assembly? We have sent word to our elders and humans to prepare to convene." Henweyay's tone didn't appear to alter, but I had difficulty noting inflection.

"A suggestion." Jural stepped forward, climbing up to the dais. "I would accompany Caitlyn." She pronounced my name better than she had earlier this morning. "I — believe we teach each other."

I frowned. *What could I teach her?* The meditation this morning had hardly been fruitful, and she had never asked about any of my skills.

"She has not discussed any plans with us yet. I could assign a Pahawan for your safety were the two of you to leave Columbia." Henweyay's "yet" did not escape my notice.

"No Pahawan needed," Jural said. "Thank you." Turning, the Duathua Seyir smiled as she descended to stand beside me, facing the five Pahawan.

Henweyay spoke with her group quietly before refocusing on me. "I will return to my previous question; do you have any intention of gathering more Wolf Squad? I ask because we have over thirty thousand humans here in Columbia, a tenth of that in Duathua. Fewer than four thousand are skilled and able to fight the human military, and our weapons are less than adequate against theirs. Without your Seyir abilities in warfare, we should propose evacuation to the Alliance assembly when it convenes."

I'd known that many Pahawan had died in the fight at Sumter, but some weapons had been retrieved as well. My heart fluttered as I imagined leaving Columbia. They placed a lot of hope and pressure on people like Tika and myself who could kill Tyrell's soldiers and Youth Guard.

Quinn would gather a group on his own, but they'd be safer if I accompanied them.

"I believe many of the Wolf Squad intend to rescue more Youth Guard. I would hope they'd help defend Columbia." A sigh escaped my lips, knowing Roxie, Tika, and Andy; all of them would want to come with me on whatever harebrained plan Quinn, Ben, and Weston had cooked up. "I will join them."

Chapter Eight

I fought shivering from a chill that rose up my shoulders as I faced the five Pahawan. *They can't be expecting the Wolf Squad to save the Alliance.* At my side, both Jural and Nur focused ahead to the dais.

Henweyay tilted her head forward in a motion that made me believe she appreciated my answer. "What will you need for this mission?"

I cackled, then stopped myself, trying to shake away an unbalanced feeling. "Well, weapons. A dozen, maybe? The boat we just used because the next camp seems to be in that direction. Food. A stretcher, evidently. First aid supplies." Dean wouldn't believe this when I returned. "Oh, a map. Someplace southeast of Santee. Conch — no, Moncks Corner."

The Pahawan listened carefully, one nodding at my mention of the town.

My thoughts raced, searching for what else we might need. I glanced at Jural. "Crap. A bigger boat. We barely fit on the way back."

Finally, I appeared to hit on something that stumped

the Pahawan as Henweyay glanced about the table. "One that will fit on the Congaree River?"

To the east of the Alliance lay a large lake, still massive, even after the dam had been partially drained a decade ago. Some boats rested on their sides on the shore. Those might be too deep for a river.

"Yes." Roxie had navigated some tight spots on the Congaree River. Larger might not work.

"What about a second boat of similar size?" Henweyay asked.

I shook my head. "Only one of us can propel it through the water without fuel."

The Pahawan leader didn't pause. "A second boat with fuel would work. Correct?"

My eyebrows climbed. The Alliance only allowed fuel for military use. *Which is what the Wolf Squad is.* Dean knew boats. "Yes."

Henweyay stood. "Thank you, Caitlyn of the Wolf Squad. It might take two days to have a boat prepared and supplies stored upon it. The map we will attempt to get you tonight so you can begin planning your strategy. Thank you for your cooperation."

In a group, the Pahawan flew from the dais toward a side door, speaking in their native language.

Stunned, I took a moment before glancing at Nur. "What have I gotten myself into?"

Nur cocked her head. "Protecting the Alliance. I would not see war, if we could help it. Leaving this place, where we have begun to prosper, could cause many to starve. I believe your Savannah military would follow — wherever we went."

Jural said nothing, but patted my shoulder, as if in encouragement.

The empty amphitheater appeared to glow green and

blue with the distant light of the front windows. I studied the intricate curves that made up the structure of ascending rows of benches and a curved half dome, all built with no apparent seams.

"Caitlyn?" Nur asked.

I sucked in a deep breath and turned toward the front door. The two Duathua did not fly as we walked, instead keeping pace beside me.

Penny smirked, waiting until I drew closer to speak. "Effing idiot."

I chuckled, but Jural spoke slowly. "This *is not* proper action?"

"Yeah, sure." Penny shrugged. "Schmuck."

The word sounded odd. I frowned. "What?"

"It means effing idiot." She started for the front doors, holding them open for Odie and us.

The day had warmed, and the scent of cook fires wafted on the breeze. My stomach growled. Clouds scattered across the sky straight above, but blue sky stretched ahead.

I answered Jural's earlier question before asking one of my own. "It is good that we help the Alliance survive. Tyrell is mistaken to attack instead of accepting the Duathua."

She nodded.

"Also, we rescued six Youth Guard. We can help more." I'd need to talk with the new members. Learn their skills. "I have a question for you, Jural."

"What you teach me?" she asked.

I offered a half smile, tugging up one corner of my mouth. "Exactly."

"This soft Kudaru you create. Kudaru I create well. Your skill intrigues."

Seyir had asked about the ability, yet to replicate it fully. I'd tried to teach all the Wolf Squad, but with no results. "Sure, of course." Did she really intend to travel with us to do so? Quinn likely wouldn't stop with one camp; there were two others mentioned.

Penny raised her eyebrows. "We should go make Quinn's day," she said.

Jural smiled. "I return this evening. To train. Each of us."

I ignored Penny's chuckle. "Sounds great," I said.

As we split off to retrieve Bella, I smacked Penny's arm. "You're enjoying this."

"Ef yeah."

<hr>

By the time I arrived home for a late lunch of cold chili, it only took another hour before the entire Wolf Squad, except for Andy, chatted in the main room. Penny hung with us, enjoying the show. As expected, my news elicited excitement and concerns.

I leaned against the wall, scraping less than tasty beans out of a bowl. Dean studied me intently.

Quinn strutted in the middle of the room like a stunted rooster. "Wait, you mean to tell us that all of a sudden you're friggin' waking up to the idea that those kids at Camp Mystras need your help? Did you bump your head?"

Only Dean had known where Penny had taken us. Roxie had likely dragged the information out of him, based on the inquisitive expression on her face. "Yep. Convinced me, you did." I stuck a spoonful of chili in my mouth to keep from saying more.

"Map?" Quinn asked.

"On its way," I mumbled through chewing.

"Who's going?" Quinn motioned for Ben to raise his hand.

Ben and Weston were quick about it, with Nadia and

Len following close afterward. I flicked my hand up before returning to my meal. If Quinn wanted to be in charge, I'd be happy to follow.

Dean and Roxie waved obliging hands in the air along with Penny, who chuckled. After the rest joined, Tika raised her hand last. I almost wished she'd refused. If Andy didn't heal enough to go, I guessed Fawn would stay despite her offer.

"Good. We're going to need sketches of the compound from Len and Nadia. Paper? Pens?"

I scoffed. "I rustled up some weapons and a second boat, but paper's asking too much. Weston?"

Weston rose from his perch on the windowsill and headed for the door at the end of the building. His room sat on the ground floor while the rest of us slept upstairs. "I'll get the chalkboard."

"Friggin' chalkboard?" Quinn demanded.

Roxie leaned in over Dean. "Second boat? How's that going to work?"

As I swallowed, others in the room peered at me questioningly. "Fuel." It wasn't quite as rare as paper, but close.

"Fuel," she repeated. Her eyebrows shot up. The fireball at Camp Sparta had singed one, and I just noticed.

"If they have friggin' fuel, you won't need to do your thing. That's good."

Roxie pursed her lips and crossed her arms.

I moved the empty bowl to my lap. "Fuel is scarce." Telling Quinn that the Pahawan agreed with him would just involve a longer "friggin" conversation. The Alliance wouldn't give any more than absolutely necessary. "Roxie will have to move the first one like before. Dean, will you steer the second ship?"

He smirked. "Pilot. Boat. Sure. Same type?"

I shrugged lightly. "Didn't ask. Something that fits in

the river. They'll have it ready in a couple of days and waiting for us with the other one, along with supplies."

Weston returned with a blackboard three feet across and set in a wooden frame. It still showed our plans from Camp Sparta. I winced at a crack that ran in a line across the map; it lay where Roxie and Fawn had waited on the opposite shore through the spot where Penny had been knocked from the tree. *Coincidence.*

As Weston laid the board on the floor and pulled pieces of chalk out, Quinn and Ben knelt expectantly beside it.

"Len. Nadia." Quinn waved them over. "What's the layout of Camp Mystras?"

Dean craned his neck, interested, and I nudged him in the side. "Try to make sure they don't end up killing us or the camp," I whispered.

Roxie heard me and joined Dean as he stood. Penny followed behind them.

Alone after Nadia and Len joined the planning, Tika sat near the arch near the front door with her knees drawn up and her arms wrapped around them. Her long black hair swept over one dark brown eye and draped down her sides.

Bowl and spoon still in hand, I stood and walked over to sit beside her. "How are you doing?"

Tika tilted her head to peer into my eyes. "I couldn't sleep. Are you going to do meditation this evening? I thought it might help."

After everything that had gone on so far, I'd forgotten about our sessions. I'd tried to reproduce what Vanya had taught, but our time together had been short before the Seyir had been killed at Sumter. "Sure. We could all use it." *Better than toes.*

"Yeah." She turned her head, watching the jabbering cluster in the middle of the room.

"You don't have to go."

Tears had formed in Tika's eyes, which she wiped on the sleeve of her Youth Guard coveralls. "I want to help. I just—"

I waited for her to finish for half a minute before I spoke. "Wasn't your fault. Actually, fighting with our powers is scary. You'll do better now that you know what you're capable of."

She nodded silently, and we sat together listening to the plans.

Gina, green-eyed with pitch black hair more like Roxie's than Tika's, walked toward us awkwardly, so I gestured to the pillow on my other side. "Sit."

She appeared about my age and height, but her stiff position had her looking down at me. "Are we Wolf Squad now?"

I chuckled. "Of course, if you want. Should I have some sort of ceremony?"

Tika leaned forward to speak. "I'll make patches for everyone." She tugged on the patch she'd made of the wolf emblem for her own coveralls to show Gina.

As Gina smiled, I patted her arm. "I never made up this whole Wolf Squad rebellion thing, but I've stopped resisting it."

She frowned as if unbelieving. "But you fought your way out of the camp to get free. Tried to bring your patrol with you, until Selina stopped you. Nearly took out the whole administration building doing it because you were so powerful."

I blushed. "I was just trying to free Dean and run off with him." For a moment, I almost mentioned that Roxie and Eric had just tried to help, but I didn't want to mention Eric. "I had no idea what kind of rumors followed me."

"Yaz told us some of it, then we learned more when they sent us to Camp Sparta."

My eye twitched. "Yaz. You know Yaz? What camp?" *Does she hate me?*

"Camp Taygetos."

"Why'd they send her there?"

Gina shrugged, black hair rolling across her shoulders. "A couple of Youth Guard ran away after you left, and Tyrell swapped people around. He sent some of us to Camp Sparta to be tested for the advance on Sumter. I didn't make the cut. No bother at the time, then we heard about Ben and Roxie joining the Wolf Squad, and I wished I'd tried harder. Thank you."

"For what?"

"Coming to rescue us."

Ben made that happen. I smiled and fought a shiver, not telling her that I'd argued against the plan.

A Pahawan delivered the map to Penny at the front door, but I remained with Tika and Nadia while Quinn gathered a crowd around it in the center of the floor. Dean and Penny would keep the plan safe; I trusted them.

The Duathua warriors' visit reminded me of the army building forces southeast of Columbia.

"What's Tyrell's plans?" I asked Gina.

"He knows you're here — that the Wolf Squad is here. They still plan on liberating Columbia." She swallowed. "Will we be safe here?"

"How soon? When will he attack?" My voice rose.

Gina pulled back, as if intimidated. "I don't know. He doesn't tell us anything."

"I'm sorry." Calming my voice, I patted her arm, hoping to reassure her. "We'll be safe, one way or another." *Just perhaps not here.*

The three of us sat in silence for a while. Quinn and the others ranged between arguing and agreeing on the plan, but they had days to deal with it. The sun had dropped, leaving long shadows outside. Ben had already mentioned prepping dinner amid their discussions.

Penny rose when a knock came at the door, and I considered standing as well but just leaned forward to peer past Tika.

Overly tall Jural with her red-tinged head scales, Udal wearing her yellow shawl and metal pin, and Nur, shortest of the three, stepped inside.

I'd forgotten Jural had wanted to come by this evening. The conversation dropped in the room as Quinn and the newer members stared, slack jawed, at the three Duathua.

I jumped up, wondering what Jural would expect from me and why all three had come.

Chapter Nine

As I moved around Tika to greet the Duathua, the otherness blossomed behind me. I snuffed it and spun on the group. "Behave yourself, or you'll end up in the woods with the Oni."

All eyes focused on me, but Quinn's scowl and clenched fists made me believe that he'd been the culprit.

Nadia, bless her soul, rose from a crate by the window and approached to extend her hand to Jural. "Hi, I'm Nadia, short for Nadeschda. I've never properly met a Duathua."

Jural tilted her head and enveloped Nadia's pale hand in long gray fingers. "I am pleased to greet you. Are we both new to this place?"

"Columbia? Definitely. First night, and I could barely sleep; I'm so excited. I haven't seen much here, but at least we're safe. How can you be new too?"

"I arrived from the lands at the east. There much trouble there." Jural turned to me and smiled, though I doubted the others would recognize the expression through the thick Duathua skin. "Caitlyn, I have come on training. Have you quiet place?"

The room had been noisy when the front door opened, but I heard only breathing now. "Yeah, we can use the back patio where we usually meditate."

Tika rose at the mention of our evening activity, her expression questioning.

I pointed past the Duathua toward the entryway. "It's out the back door. Would you mind if we take half an hour and do our usual group first?" My eyes flicked toward Tika and caught her hopeful expression.

"If we not intrude." Jural waited for my reply while Nur and Udal stepped back.

"Not at all. Vanya taught me, so you'll likely recognize it. She was a Seyir from Denya."

"I will enjoy. Thank you." The tall Duathua gestured for me to lead the way.

As I passed Udal, she spoke. "I'm going to check on Andy, though I am sure you have done well in your healing of him. I will be only a moment and then join you."

I pointed upstairs. "Fawn's worked on him as well."

Ben called behind me. "I'll get dinner cooking for everyone."

"Thank you." I walked us through the kitchen, leaving my bowl and spoon on the cluttered counter. We used the appliances for storage, though locals had explained their previous usages before the Sorrow.

Refreshing, cooler air of the patio washed over me as I stepped into the outside room, reminiscent of the outdoor kitchen at Camp Sparta in structure at least. In this porch, a low brick wall rose from the floor and supported aluminum frames. Ben and Dean had patched the screen sides with mesh taken from buildings in the neighborhood, but the tin roof still leaked during heavy rains. Ben's camping chair sat against the wall of the house near a wire and cloth construction that he'd repaired.

"We just sit on the floor. It's dry after the past week." As if a threat, thunder rumbled from somewhere distant. The day's clouds had promised rain soon, but I hoped they'd wait a bit.

Tika and Dean had followed behind Nur and Jural. More hesitant figures milled behind them in the darkness of the kitchen.

"Everyone's welcome," I called to the open door.

Fawn and Weston, usual attendees, brought a wide-eyed Gina and Isabel with them.

Wind rustled through the new and old pines growing outside as I settled onto the cool floor, and Dean dropped beside me. He'd rarely attended the evening meditations after the first couple of them. I didn't ask why he joined us now.

Nervous in front of the Duathua, I drew in a deep breath. "Close your eyes. We are going to listen for the otherness. Some of you can hear it when it is used, but we are going to listen for it when it rests."

I gave everyone a minute to settle and sit listening. In our previous meditations, Fawn seemed the closest to hearing the otherness. Everyone except Dean heard some version of the otherness when we used it.

Udal joined us, so I repeated my initial statement. She had to know all this already, growing up on Denya.

"I hear a hum from the otherness at rest. There are changes in the vibration when it is in someone. In the beginning, you are searching only for the light hum around you. Life force. Otherness."

I gave them a few minutes before I spoke again. "It pervades everything. When you recognize the initial hum, you can move your 'listening' to others and note the change.

"I first listened by imagining to reach out to the otherness. That moment before I pulled it in. Practice that now, reaching out but not grasping, as you listen."

We meditated for a little over what I guessed to be half an hour, giving anyone a chance to announce they'd heard the otherness before I ended the session. Awkwardly self-conscious, I studied Udal for a reaction. What was her experience with the otherness? *The same or different?*

Before I could voice any question, Jural spoke. "Soft Kudaru would example you."

Nur spoke quietly in their language, and Jural restated her question. "Would you show an example of soft Kudaru?"

I nodded, pulling in the otherness and air around us. The wind outside in the pines had grown stronger, as if heralding a storm. My shield formed near the metal ceiling above us, and Jural tilted her head, watching as if she could see it. I knew where it was, but beyond a slight wavering of the air, like heat off a road, nothing showed to my eyes.

Others followed her gaze, and Fawn spoke. "I can hear that." She rubbed a hand over her shaved scalp.

Gina, Tika, and Weston nodded, leaving Dean to roll his eyes, while Isabel cocked her head like she searched for the sound.

Udal rose onto her gray knees and stretched a hand toward my shield, pressing her fingers into it. "Interesting. Explain?"

My lips tightened; I'd tried many times. "I gather the air — and pull it together like a clenched fist. I thought it would make Kudaru armor at first."

"That stack air," said Jural absently. I heard her call the otherness and draw more air, but didn't know where. She dropped her hand to a point a foot from her face and poked a finger through the empty space. She seemed disappointed at the lack of resistance, waving her hand in the area. "Explain more?"

I scratched the back of my neck where my braid started, then released the shield. Air rustled people's hair. As I manifested another, I explained once again.

"I pull in air and don't stop while I compact the first of it. My body seems to clench, like—" Wincing, I searched for a better example than taking a crap or having an orgasm. Dean would have never let me live that down. "— like I'm in pain and trying to hold it back. I push harder, imagining the shape and thickness of it. Where I want it to be. All this only takes a second, and I know where it is. When something tears at it, I can feel it weakening. If I draw in more otherness, I can rebuild it."

Jural drew in otherness and tried without success once more. She nodded to herself and resumed sitting on the floor. "Thank you, Seyir. I would again try tomorrow."

"Of course."

She brought out the tiny Kudaru figurine and called the otherness. "We listen. Eyes on. Breath." Her inhale sounded exaggerated. "Breath." Jural exhaled slowly. Extending her own foot, she said, "Hear your toe."

The group extended feet as Dean chuckled.

"Listen. Breath."

I focused. Just because I had failed earlier in the day didn't mean I couldn't learn what she tried to teach me. Vanya had gotten through to me. My own attempts at teaching how to build a shield to someone older and likely more experienced in the otherness proved how difficult it could be, just not impossible.

"Toe speaks to you. It's blood. It's energy. It's rhythm."

Inside the house, they were chattering to each other as pans rattled. Smoke from the cooking fire wafted in the stiffening breeze along with the scent of promised of rain.

"We own body. We tell body. Body tells us. We control all."

My toe remained silent, and the meditation brought me no new revelations. I dipped into the familiar othersense, and the connective bonds between people and the world around us formed white lines that crisscrossed. Jural's trails bundled in one direction, except for a cord now attached from me to her. The connection between Gina and me glowed stronger as well. Many of ours led upstairs, where Andy slept.

This intertwined group, Wolf Squad and Jural, would soon head south to Camp Mystras and danger. We could have lost Andy, if the bullet had hit lower. I couldn't imagine losing one of them, as I had Eric.

I focused on my toe, leaving our upcoming mission to the future.

Chapter Ten

Two days after meeting with the Pahawan, I sat straight on a padded seat at the side of the boat while Roxie churned the water to propel us south across Lake Marion. In the twilight sky, the water had sunk into creepy blackness crested by moonlit ripples. The low drone of Dean's engine ebbed in and out against the splashes.

My othersense hadn't detected any people at all since we exited the Congaree River into Lake Marion. Penny lay on the deck ahead of me, with Odie curled against her legs.

Andy, more restive since his gunshot wound, sat beside me. "That rain is going to follow us."

The weather had made the past two days difficult, including the launch from Columbia. The wind pushed the clouds south. I worried about soldiers, not getting wet. "It'll hide the moon." Nearly full, it fought wispy clouds, bathing us in unwelcome light more often than not. "I don't know how we'll get past the Santee bridge. They always have soldiers on patrol." Quinn, of course, had suggested we kill them, as if that wouldn't bring down the entire military for our pass on the way back.

"They might not even be there."

Our first rain in a while behind us, Dean thought much of the area around Camp Sparta might have burned through the dry trees. "I'm not counting on it."

I could sense the group in Dean's boat, Quinn, Weston, Ben, and Nadia, as they slowed. Standing, I held onto the bars of the canopy and peered over Len, who lay on his stomach at the bow. Dean headed for a tiny island of trees clustered in the lake. The branches and tops cut dark silhouettes against the stars to the southwest. "Roxie."

She turned to me, then nodded as she noted we drew closer to Dean ahead. Her pull on the otherness eased, and we slowed.

"This is where we switch," Andy said.

"Rest, then we'll tow them."

"I missed all the planning fun, and um, toe watching."

"Not that bad. The toe watching." I could make out the red-tinged scales of Jural's head where she sat on the deck near Roxie's bench at the back. Tika and Kira kneeled on the cushions there. All of them were trying to learn Roxie's technique.

Gina, Fawn, and Isabel sat in the middle seat facing me. Over the past days, long-haired Isabel had connected with Fawn over healing skills, and the two were rarely separated.

Len sat up and hung his legs over the bow as Roxie eased us toward the trees that perched on spits of sand so small you couldn't stand on them. It wasn't much of a resting place.

Quinn held the strap of the rifle he wore proudly on his back and yelled to us far louder than he needed for us to hear him, "Alright, we'll rest here one hour."

He silenced when Dean shushed him and admonished the surly teen in a quiet tone. "Sound travels over water."

Len jumped off my boat with a splash and tied us to a

tree as Weston did the same for Dean's ten feet away. The current slowly shifted us.

Quinn stepped to the side of his boat, speaking in a hushed tone but with his usual arrogance as he explained what we'd all discussed a dozen times. "We'll rest for one hour. Roxie will take the lead and tow us so we're quiet while we pass under the bridge. Caitlyn, you'll keep a lookout for any activity."

I gave him a polite thumbs up while Penny chose a different digit. "Effing blowhard."

Roxie took the bench to lie down and close her eyes for an hour while we bobbed in silence under cloudy moon-light. A cool sprinkle started as she rose, and we tied Dean's boat to ours with a long rope. All of our rhythms vibrated quicker as Roxie nosed our vessel into the current and we churned southward on Lake Marion.

Birds startled and flew from one of the clusters of trees as we passed. The dark horizon fuzzed into stars ahead. Somewhere up there lay the two-mile bridge that spanned Lake Marion at Santee, where Camp Sparta and the military had protected the residents from werewolves.

Standing beside Roxie with my back to the water she churned, I sensed the first soldier and pointed. "One, to the left." We'd discussed this carefully together, outside the boys' club that Quinn had formed.

She eased back, barely propelling more than enough to guide us in the current.

I couldn't see any of the three bridges; the closest would be the oldest. Land supported about half of the highway toward the northeast side. We needed to keep clear of that. Penny, Len, and Tika watched from the bow according to plan, as they had the best night vision.

Floating forward, I kept shaking my head when she

glanced at me. I only had one soldier that I could sense, and his rhythms vibrated calmly. Calmer than mine.

Those in the front murmured, and Andy relayed in a whisper. "Starboard, 90."

I swayed to keep balance as water splashed when Roxie turned us sharply to the right. A thin, ghostly line of gray formed to my left, causing my heart to leap into my throat. We were close. If I could see the first bridge, a soldier could likely see us.

"Two and three." I pointed at two more soldiers vibrating almost straight ahead where the closer bridge faded into the darkness. Wide-eyed, I searched under the gray line to make out dark posts that cut the dim reflection of moonlight on the water south of the bridges.

Far behind me, Quinn hissed something, his words drowned under the splashing water. Through my connection with Dean, I could sense where they were, but kept my eyes on the bridges

"Port 45. Ease to 90," whispered Andy from the center of the boat. "Pillars."

We were still a good distance from the first bridge, but I could make out where dim moonlight reflected and where the land blocked it. My pulse began to relax.

Quinn barked in anger behind us, and I focused my othersense to Dean's boat, where vibrations spiked in irritation. What was going on? "Crap," I whispered.

Murmurs sounded from our own boat, as they'd probably heard Quinn. The vibrations of the two soldiers ahead hadn't changed. Their focus should be on the bridge, watching for werewolf packs. The scent of burned woods wafted to me for a brief second before the breeze from the north blew it away. My eyes wandered to the right; toward the direction of Camp Sparta. At least Yaz hadn't been there. We'd never been close, but she was sweet.

I blinked as a gunshot rang out over the water. It took me only a second to call the otherness to form hasty shields on each side of our boat. My face tightened, and I chanced a glance behind; I couldn't reach Dean's boat to protect him. I still tried. It withered at the distance.

"Get effing down." Complained Penny from the front.

The soldiers' vibrations had spiked. They had to have seen us, but their rhythms seemed more in reaction to the gunfire. They'd been quiet up to that point.

The supports under the bridges were clear now, as was the land to the left. From our weekly patrols over the bridges, I knew we were at the halfway point.

Water churned angrily as Roxie launched us forward; only to have Dean's tethered boat behind cause us to lurch when the line drew tight.

"Caitlyn?" Roxie asked.

There'd been only one shot, but the soldiers on the southeast shore were moving. At the edge of my othersense, I couldn't determine more than activity. "I'm not sure."

We were almost to the first older bridge, with supports of the newer bridges visible. She aimed us easily between the wide span of the poles.

A distant gunshot echoed, and chagrined, I knew in that instant that the first had come from Dean's boat. Too loud. No wonder Dean had grown so angry. I'd bet a piece of cheese that it had been Quinn. Idiot. "Get down, Dean. And don't shift."

Roxie flew us under the bridge, and I moved our shields between us and the soldiers on each side. When I'd pointed out on the long bridge where I believed the soldiers' posts were located, both Penny and Dean had believed it too distant for a lucky shot. I wasn't taking a chance.

The next problem would come when Tyrell learned of

the incident. Would he make a connection with the southern camp and send a warning?

Another distant crack sounded from the right as we veered for the space between the post of the newer bridge, then a barrage of shots sounded from an automatic weapon. Bullets pinged off metal and concrete, but nowhere near us. I sensed the soldier on my left running toward us along the bridge, but we were in the middle and a mile from each end.

Some idiot in Dean's boat fired back, just as rain sprinkled onto my face. The blessed clouds buried the moon. I sensed Dean's angry vibrations and hoped he didn't start throwing them overboard.

We burst from under the last of the bridges, and I shifted the two shields and reinforced them to join in a quarter dome at our back. Dean and his crew would be exposed, and I couldn't do anything about it. My legs wobbled as I turned to peer at the boat Roxie tugged behind us. I buttoned Dean's jacket tight around me against the weather.

Dean's team was crouched on the deck at least. Rain marked ripples on the water's surface, random dots crashing into each other.

I flinched when a distant gunshot echoed, and again when another followed it. The ghostly gray bridge dwindled behind us, with rain helping to mask our escape. The automatic weapon fired in bursts, but no one in Dean's boat spiked with pain.

The soldiers stopped firing after a moment, and the rushing water blended with the pattering rain.

"Will Tyrell send word?" I asked Roxie.

"If he thinks it's us, yes."

I closed my eyes, released the shields, and called out to Andy. "Course?"

He had the map and compass. We needed to aim right for the next leg.

"How tired are you?" I asked Roxie as we waited for him to light a flashlight.

"I'm fine."

"Liar." I leaned my head on her shoulder, watching the rain.

Dean fired up his engine behind us, and I reached down to bring in the rope that someone had untied from their boat. Andy changed Roxie's course by a couple degrees. A dot on the map far from patrolled areas. Our next stop wouldn't be for a while.

Our rhythms calmed, even Dean's, and I dropped the othersense. The light rain slowly soaked us until the night felt chilly.

At a shallow shoreline of trees, we stopped on time, 9:13 p.m. according to Ben, and the argument between Dean and Quinn flared. The jerk had fired his rifle at a random shape on the bridge, not even near the ends where the soldiers guarded.

Roxie shook as she climbed overboard into knee-deep water in the rain. "Are you going to stop that?"

I joined her, shaking my head. "Gotta pee."

They were still glaring when we returned with Penny from the woods. Roxie climbed into our boat to sleep as Quinn tried to stomp through the water toward me.

"Dean's out of control. He threatened me."

Penny snorted, patting a damp Odie at her side. "Did he call you an effing shit-brained nincompoop that would have more use as an anchor?"

Quinn frowned. "What's a nincompoop?"

"I'd find you a dictionary, but that's like offering a hat to rock." Penny climbed onto the bow, slapping it for Odie to jump.

Glaring, Quinn jerked his head to follow me. "He can't treat me like that."

Obviously, Dean could. I shrugged. "I'm not in charge."

Quinn sputtered as I sloshed past him toward Dean. Nadia was off using the woods, but I bet the boys had just peed off the side. The sharp scent of gas hung from the boat.

Dean slid onto the bow as I approached. "What kind of shit do you think we're in for *now* with the military?"

"You think Tyrell will know it's us?" I grabbed his hand and rested my head on his wet jeans.

"I'd make that assumption. It smelled pretty torched up. Maybe he left someone else in charge who isn't that smart."

"They won't call it off."

Dean pulled my head up and slid down into knee-deep water. "No regrets."

I kissed him. "Quinn's crying that you yelled at him."

"I heard. Dick. If I hadn't been using the engine as a damned tiller, I might have been able to stop him. We might have slipped right under their noses."

"That was the plan."

"Dick," Dean growled.

Kissing him again, I whispered, "I thought you might shift. You were so angry."

"I almost did shift."

"I love you."

"I love you, Caitlyn. Let's try and survive this."

I gave him a hug, squeezing out some water; even my coveralls under his jacket were wet. "The rain might help."

"Tying Quinn and leaving him in the boat would help."

I seriously considered Dean's suggestion. We planned to hide vessels in the wooded shore near Pinopolis before midnight and hike the two hours into Moncks Corner. Our plan might work, if Quinn didn't decide to shoot something.

Chapter Eleven

The night rain had drenched me through to my underwear when our group reached the sign for the burned-out bowling alley that served as our first checkpoint. I'd been using my othersense to make sure no one wandered about in the storm around any of our three groups, but now I expanded it, searching for a cluster ahead that would be Camp Mystras. Are they waiting for us?

Unlike Camp Sparta, this camp lay on the east edge of the town, far from the bridge. We'd spent the past hour winding down backstreets where the town folk slept. With so few people this close to the river, I easily found the dense cluster ahead.

"Got the camp," I said.

Dean and Andy nodded, dripping water from hair and faces. Tika and Fawn gestured toward the sign and headed to take their positions there.

We'd be sending the nine here to rally before we trekked the two hours back to the boat where Roxie slept. Gina and Jural guarded her. The area had been abandoned except for one cluster of people, but we weren't taking chances.

"What are we walking into?" asked Dean as we started sloshing forward on the road.

"I don't find any clusters waiting to ambush us. About as many people as Camp Sparta in one building. Too dense and too far for me to tell if anyone's awake. Another structure with maybe six people next to the main one." That partially fit our expectations.

"That seems light." Dean shook his head, spraying water. "Len said over a dozen in the admin building. Nadia agreed."

"They've been gone a few weeks; maybe Tyrell's moving people around," Andy suggested. "Any guards?"

I blinked water out of my eyes and focused on my splashing boots. "According to Len, they'd be just inside the doors. I'll be able to pick that up when we get closer."

Checking on the second group in my othersense, I found Quinn, Len, Nadia, and an annoyed Penny vibrating behind us, already close to Fawn and Tika. Much farther down the road where we'd passed, I sensed Weston's group. We hoped that four or five teens walking at night wouldn't be of interest to anyone who spotted us.

Pointing to my left, I spoke without lifting my head. Another cluster, probably the school. Like Santee, close enough to the camp that the younger ones could learn, but housed separately.

A bent pole reached down out of the gray ahead with a dead traffic light barely showing until we got closer. Somehow the ruined pole seemed sinister. Tall woods rose on each side of the road, sheltering us from some wind but not the downpour.

"We're close." I pointed slightly to the left of where we headed. "I think I can sense the military building far ahead."

"Len said about a mile up the road, toward the bridge."

Andy sounded more excited than he had been this morning. He really should have rested another couple days.

"That seems about right. Too far for details. No one massing on the road or moving toward us." I released a breath. Quinn's mistake didn't appear to be biting us in the ass.

Dean cleared his throat. "Good, and the camp?"

Through the rain, I couldn't see the two-story building that housed the Youth Guard at Camp Mystras, but I could make out the individual rhythms. No fence surrounded it, and no gates barred entry.

"Most everyone is sleeping upstairs. A few pairs downstairs. Three guards at the edges, so those are the entries. There are two more people awake in a room, maybe sitting."

I gestured as I spoke. "Nobody outside, on the roof, or waiting in the woods. The admin building has six sleeping people, well-spaced, so I think in their own rooms."

"We good to set up as planned?" Dean asked.

"Yeah, nothing out there but raccoons," I answered.

Len and Nadia believed there were nine Youth Guard who would join the Wolf Squad, and nearly a dozen maybes. We weren't going to risk contacting any but the nine. Quinn and his team would be along soon to handle that phase. I hoped he didn't screw this up.

We reached the intersection with the building just coming into view, but instead of turning down the street, we stepped into soggy grass. The water rose to our ankles. A couple signs were there along with an old wooden electric pole and a few metal boxes buried in the ground. Dean pressed against one of those and then sat on it.

"We should have been the group to go into the admin building," Andy grumbled.

"Could have joined Quinn's team," I said. Penny had

accompanied Quinn, planning to keep the grumpy little tyrant in line.

Len and Nadia were from Camp Mystras, so they would know the area best. I could sense them behind us, closing fast. Nadia's voice broke through rain and wind first, and in a minute they cautiously approached our location.

"All clear." I hoped Quinn wouldn't spook and shoot me. "Six sleeping on the second floor of admin. Three guards at the doors in the main building. Two people awake there in a room on the ground floor."

"Friggin' rain. I'm soaked." As he approached, Quinn slid in the grass, nearly falling. His pack flopped side to side. "Friggin' grass."

I frowned. He wasted time. "I'll monitor, and we'll move in if there's any trouble."

Nadia sloshed to me while Len and Penny wisely waited on the road. "Only six in admin? Should be more. Maybe in a nearby building?" She adjusted her soaked pack. All of Quinn's group had brought equipment for their break-in.

"We're clear all around here." I kept my tone pleasant, but they needed to get moving. We'd riled up the bridge guard at Santee and had to go back under the damned thing to escape to Columbia. I didn't relish doing that in daylight.

"Having an effing picnic, or what?" Penny started around the corner toward the side street. Conflicted, Len faltered, then followed her.

Quinn, appearing to not want to be left behind, swore then followed too quickly. His right foot slipped forward, causing him to split and splash face first into the muck. Penny chuckled, but didn't slow down.

Dean rocked as he laughed in silence.

Nadia and I both tried to help Quinn up, but he just slapped away our hands and dragged himself to his feet.

I smacked Dean's shoulder when he kept chuckling after Quinn's team had left. "This is serious."

Weston's group walked down the last stretch to us. His and Ben's rhythms were relaxed, but Kira and Isabel vibrated nervously. I'd tried to talk them into staying behind in Columbia.

Supposedly, Isabel could heal remarkably, though her other skills lacked. Tyrell hadn't brought anyone who could only heal for the attack on Sumter.

"We're clear," I said to Weston when he approached.

Ben wore a glum expression; he'd wanted to be in Quinn's party.

Weston's sandy-colored hair appeared as dark as Ben's when wet. He stepped with care into the flooded grass. "All good?"

"So far. Quinn's group is still on the side road. No activity in the building." I gave him the rundown on the positioning in Camp Mystras and the lack of activity around the military base to the northeast.

"And now we wait," he said.

Ben checked his watch. "We're running late. 1:13 a.m."

We'd run the times repeatedly, concerned about our return crossing under the Santee bridge. If it came too close to dawn, we'd have to pull the boats on shore and wait for nightfall. "The rain and clouds might give us cover. Let's hope Quinn and his group get the room assignments and keys quickly."

Camp Mystras kept the Youth Guard quarters unlocked, but Len believed there were keys for the outer doors in the major's office. For our plan to work, we needed one door. The guards didn't monitor an unused maintenance access. They kept it locked, and it needed a key on both sides.

One of my many concerns revolved around Quinn's

reaction if they didn't find keys. He'd been ready to kill the soldiers guarding the doors. I monitored them as they crossed the street, heading to the second building in the back that I couldn't see through the rain. Penny's vibrations I knew from our time together, and Quinn's had become easier to separate. He vibrated higher and erratically.

"They're at the admin building now." If all went well, we'd remain on this corner with Weston's group, focused on getting the new people down to Fawn and Tika. If something went wrong, we'd know soon enough.

"Clustered, perhaps at the major's door." As I spoke, even Kira and Isabel stepped into the flooded grass to listen. Nervous, my stomach roiled.

Eventually, the little party split up. "I think Quinn and Len are inside."

Ben mentioned the time, and Dean shut him up. All our rhythms had risen. None of us wanted to see another disaster like what happened at Camp Sparta, except perhaps Ben, who'd supported Quinn's "Burn it all down" plan.

It took only a minute before one of them returned outside. Quinn, however, remained in the office. I spoke, unsure. "I think Len is back outside. Quinn's in the office." That hadn't been the plan. I sensed everyone else in the building sleeping.

Penny vibrated with irritation. After a moment, she moved inside to Quinn's location, and both of them grew annoyed. "I don't know what Quinn and Penny are doing, but Len and Nadia are heading for the quarters according to plan."

Dean swore. "If he messes this up —"

I checked on Weston and Ben. "Do you know what's going on?"

Weston wiped the rain out of his eyes, avoiding mine.

"Maybe he's looking around to see if there's anything useful."

"Like?" I asked.

"Extra uniforms, weapons, equipment, information on the other camps. Who knows?"

The three of them had likely planned this. "Wonderful." I turned back toward the camp.

Len and Nadia grew visible as dark movement in the gray before they disappeared,, heading for the barracks. The original plan had Penny and Quinn on their way back to a point across the side street as a first rally for the escaping Youth Guard. I would have only needed to monitor the guards in the main quarters that way; now I flicked back and forth between the buildings.

"Len and Nadia are inside with no reactions. Moving for a stairwell. No, one is heading to a lower room." At this close distance, my othersense gave me a fair indication of height, relative to my position.

"Here goes," said Andy.

Other than the keys, the major's office held the bed assignments. Hopefully, each of the nine had roommates who slept soundly. Supposedly, Len and Nadia would know the people on the roster.

"Quinn?" asked Dean.

"Office. Penny's moving out." I tracked her for a moment. "Coming here, I bet."

From the lower room, two people emerged. One headed for the stairwell, the other for the maintenance door. "Andy, can you take up Quinn and Penny's position? We've got someone coming out. Let Penny return to report on whatever Quinn is up to." I gave Weston and Ben a flat glare.

He splashed away, running for the street.

Penny passed him on the road marching toward us; meanwhile, another of the nine stepped out of a room and moved for the stairwell. "That's two. No movement from the guards." This far from the bridge and any cryptids, maybe the soldiers took this position lightly.

Quinn remained in the office. I ground my teeth, but checked on the activity in the quarters. "We've got three."

Breaking into a run, Penny flew by Andy, who had just gotten into position. I cringed at her angry vibrations.

I called off number four when she came splashing up.

"Effing dipshit. He's stuffing duffel bags in there." For emphasis, she tossed a new bag into the grass. "Coveralls."

Ben checked his watch. "It wasn't supposed to take this long."

Sloshing through the water, Penny marched to him, forcing him to step back. "You effing knew?"

I pointed toward Weston without taking my eyes off the figure heading to Andy. "They both did."

"Ef both of you. Anything else we should effing be aware of?"

Voice low, Ben mumbled. "Nothing. I swear."

"Five," I counted. "Penny, thanks for letting us know. Better get with Andy in case this turns sideways."

Grumbling, she splashed away from Ben, kicking the duffel as she passed.

"Ben. How about grabbing your duffel?" I froze as either Len or Nadia entered a room, and both occupants awoke. "Crap."

Dean rose off his perch. "What?"

"Number six's roommate woke up." I started for the street, with most of them following me. My othersense gave me a lot of information, but not enough in a situation like this. The three hadn't moved, but I knew they were all awake with rhythms rising. None had called the otherness; that had to be good.

Number seven moved out of a room, but I barely

focused on their movement toward the stairs. I didn't have time to check on Quinn.

Slowly, number six moved out of the room with either Nadia or Len, leaving the other occupant alone; awake. Flashing through the rest of the house, I didn't find anyone else roused from sleep or alarmed guards.

"I'm not sure what happened," I said haltingly, "but I think we're okay."

The first rescue trotted toward us. A hulking teen larger than Dean, he wore a broad smile despite being drenched.

Weston and Kira teamed up and intercepted him. "Follow us," said Weston. They'd lead him part of the way down the road and send him on to Fawn and Tika to rally and wait for us.

"Eight," I counted to the group. "Wait. Nadia and Len are coming with them."

"What happened to the ninth?" asked Ben.

"I don't know."

Dean studied me. "Quinn?"

I shook my head, watching the second rescue run toward us.

Ben moved forward. "I'll get him."

"Stick to the plan," I said.

He twitched, but nodded his head, water dripping off. Isabel stepped up beside him, and they escorted the second escapee around the corner. From there, we'd forward each of the new people down the road, and they'd have Weston's group to direct them to the rally point by the burned-out bowling alley. In small groups, we'd lead them back to the boats.

Weston's group would also act as our rear guard if we had to retreat in a hurry.

"Shit, Dean. I'd almost like to leave him." I wouldn't, though.

"Nothing is easy."

"We might not make the bridge on time."

"Might not."

Len and Nadia exited the building with the last rescue. I fumed as Quinn continued to dither in the office. "I'm going."

Dean smiled. "*We're* going. Those kids can turn this corner on their own. Most of them probably know where the bowling alley is better than you."

"Fine, let's go get friggin' Quinn."

Chapter Twelve

I waved number three toward the corner. "Take a right. We've got people to point you down to the bowling alley where we're gathering."

The soaked, lanky boy just grinned. "Wolf Squad."

"Yeah, take a right."

Penny jogged toward Dean and me as we approached. "Getting the effing dick?"

"Yeah." I motioned toward the corner. "Take our station and get everyone going once Nadia and Len show up." I gave the latter instructions to Andy, so everyone wouldn't be waiting for Quinn.

Reaching almost the point where we'd cut across the road to the building, I nearly fell trying to stop. I'd focused my othersense too tightly on Quinn. "Dean, we've got someone moving on the grounds."

"Where?"

I searched the admin building and came up with five slumbering forms. "Back parking lot, according to their map."

"Latrines."

"In this weather?" I fought the urge to pee at the

mention of it and started forward again. "Let's hope it's a long crap." The person seemed stationary.

A drive curved in from the road, pouring a river of rainwater to the street. We sloshed up to the curb and grass, slowing with glances toward the main building. A guard stood just inside the glass doors there.

We made it to the south entrance and found it jimmied by Quinn's team. As we slipped inside, I could hear my breathing. The muffled rain and wind beat against the windows and roof. My boots squelched as I crept down the dark hall.

Dim light came from the middle and opposite end, but I counted the left-hand doors. The major's office lay near the main entry on this end. As we neared, I winced as I heard a dull thud from inside. Quinn didn't even try to be quiet. We didn't have time; the person outside moved toward the admin building.

When I opened the door, Quinn jerked up from a file cabinet, then searched the room as if for his weapon. His rifle lay beside me on a desk. The window behind him let in a little gray light, but he didn't recognize me. Charts covered the walls while shelves, tables, and chairs crowded the space.

"What the hell, Quinn?"

"Caitlyn?"

"We've got to go." The moving person outside ran for the building, likely not enjoying the weather.

Dean closed the door behind him most of the way, but didn't latch it.

"Great, I need help with these." Quinn pointed at two stuffed duffel bags.

"Keep your voice down. We've got someone awake."

"You said they were sleeping."

"They *were*. Grab whatever and go. Now."

"You're not friggin' in charge."

The outer door with the jimmied lock clattered as wind pushed against the one to the office. Dean cocked his head, watching me.

From the faltering movement of our unwelcome visitor, they too had heard the sound of metal rapping in the wind. They paused in what I guessed was an entry. I knew where people vibrated, but could only imagine their relation to the walls. My chest tightened with every second the person paused.

"Hello?" a man's voice called.

Dean glanced at the partially open door. He didn't risk closing it.

Quinn moved toward his rifle, and I grabbed it before him. Dean had his gun ready and stepped between me and the opening.

"Too loud," I whispered in his ear. If it came to defending ourselves, I could kill silently with a touch. I cringed at the thought.

The man drew closer, cautiously moving into the corridor outside the office. I hoped he might pass us, but he must have seen the partially open door.

Motioning Dean to stay put two paces from the entry, I pressed against the wall beside the frame. Was I really going to kill him?

Dean nodded, weapon pointed.

The hinges creaked hesitantly, and a balding head leaned inside our room.

He gasped at the sight of us before I spoke. "Don't move." Pressing the rifle muzzle against his chest, I grabbed his shoulder. He wore a soaked, brown coat.

"I—" The man let me tug him into the room. In my othersense, none of the other five people in the building had awakened.

"Kill him," said Quinn. He reached one of the duffel bags and searched for the zipper. Perhaps he had found weapons in the major's office.

Dean took the panicking man from me and pulled him inside.

I latched it with a light click, then stepped to Quinn and pushed him away from his bags. "Stop it."

Quinn's eyes darkened. "We have to kill him." He drew in the otherness, and I snuffed it away.

The bald man's face slackened, even as Dean nudged him into a nearby chair.

As Quinn moved forward, as if to continue searching the bag, I rested a hand against his chest. If he turned this ugly, we all might pay the price. "Have you ever killed anyone?" I asked.

"Not friggin' yet."

"I have; with a touch." My voice a mere whisper, I hoped it conveyed the kind of threat that Dean or Penny managed. I met Quinn's eyes and held them.

His face twitched as he eased back.

I let him pull away from my fingers, but held my hand there. "Take your bags. Sneak out the way we came in. We'll follow after we deal with this." Why would someone *want* to kill?

Our captive watched the exchange silently. His vibrations were easing. He'd certainly heard Quinn's intentions, considered my interference, and accepted Dean's threatening gun with quiet reservation.

Quinn snorted and snarled with the same breath, then shrugged, pointing toward the bags. "I'm friggin' outta here."

We all waited as he grunted and staggered under the weight of his booty, but I did open the door for him.

As soon as the latch closed, our captive spoke. "You're Caitlyn, and you're Dean."

I'd intended to tie him up and follow Quinn, but his comment piqued my interest. "How did you know that?"

He straightened. "I'm Minister Higgins of the Department of Outer Resources. Your descriptions are detailed in all reports, if you can get access to them. After your attack on Camp Sparta there has been little else we've been talking about here. I am surprised that you stopped your soldiers from killing me."

Soldiers.

While Higgins talked, Dean searched about the room, perhaps for something we could use to tie him up. My love studied my face, perhaps guessing at my curiosity. "We need to go."

Minister Higgins appraised Dean silently. He likely knew about the werewolf infection.

I nodded Dean off to find something to tie Higgins with while I held the rifle, though not aimed at the man. "You're not military?"

"Not even close. We're at the opposite spectrum of the government. We find resources, while they use them."

I had never considered much about the Savannah Charter except for their military. It made sense that someone had to supply food and clothing. "Doesn't sound like you appreciate what they're doing."

He cocked his head in a shrug. "We need protection against the cryptids, but this expansion is draining us."

"Expansion? You mean the attack on the Alliance? Columbia." My tone darkened slightly, causing his vibrations to rise. "Sorry. There's no need for the army to attack us."

Higgins relaxed. "It's true then; you work for the Duathua now."

"With. It's an Alliance of humans and Duathua. Mostly humans. They've sent ambassadors to you. They want nothing but peace. The Oni and werewolves harass from one side and Tyrell the other."

"We've never had any ambassadors from the Duathua or the Alliance." He appeared honestly surprised.

The military could have intercepted them. "They've tried. You've done nothing but attack all of us, humans as well as Duathua."

Dean returned with rifle straps, motioning Higgins to stand.

"We rely on the military to protect the outer regions. The werewolves are a plague." He winced, glancing at Dean, then stood offering his hands.

"Turn around," Dean grumbled.

What if the government knew nothing about the true nature of the Alliance or the Duathua? "Would the rest of the government have an interest in letting us be? An ambassador, or whatever, to agree to peace."

Higgins stiffened as Dean tied his hands. "It's complicated. Sergeant Major Tyrell holds a lot of power in the government. He's got — a sway over many of the ministers. I don't think he'd allow there to be peace."

"On the ground. Face down." Dean gestured Higgins toward the back of the room.

Any hope I'd imagined faded at Higgins's last comments. There might as well not be a Savannah Charter, just Tyrell.

Dean tied the man's feet together and lashed them to his arms.

The man studied me, or my reaction to his words. "Tyrell began his rise when he started the labs. Years later, they let him have some for his Youth Guard."

I blinked. "He saved me from the labs." Even as I

protested, I believed the man based on his slow shake of his head.

Dean gagged him. We left him arched on the floor in the room, silent except for the rain that pattered on the window.

Tyrell's involvement in the labs wriggled in my brain, but I couldn't doubt it after all I'd seen.

I never even asked why Higgins was here. There wasn't time. We still had the Santee bridge to get past.

We almost jogged to the exit, then dove back out into the storm. Wind blustered my hair, and rain drenched sodden coveralls. I still held Quinn's rifle while I searched about with my othersense. No alarm had raised Youth Guards or soldiers, and Quinn's angry little soul stood on the roadside with Andy and Penny.

"How's the rebellion going?" asked Moonjir from beside me.

Two strides from the drive out to the street flowing with runoff, my heart skipped a beat or two. Dean nearly stumbled on my other side.

"Scared the crap out of me," I snapped.

Moonjir didn't have a damp bit of hair on him. "Sorry. I was going to pop in earlier, but you were fraternizing with the enemy."

"What?" I sloshed through the drive, heading for the street.

"You were chatting with the gentleman you left tied in the office. General politics. You need to polish your speeches a bit before delivery." His footsteps caused bigger splashes than mine or Dean's, but his furry blue and pink toes were fluffy and dry.

We hit the street and crossed as water poured toward the opposite side or down gullies at the edges. "What do you want, Moonjir?"

"To restate my previous inquiry: how is the Wolf Squad insurrection proceeding? The recruitment here hardly seemed worth the effort. Eight new Wolf Squad? All without the excitement of the last raid. Where's your flair?"

"No one got hurt here."

"One man's pride."

"Could have been worse."

"True. Well, let's hope the weather keeps. Watch your toes, Caitlyn."

I started to comment, but Moonjir had vanished. Had the last bit been related to Jural's meditation, or was I searching for meaning in his banter?

"He's right," Dean said.

"About what?"

"Let's hope the weather holds. It might get us under that bridge."

Penny wore a furious expression when we arrived, and Andy had taken one of the bags from Quinn. None of us spoke until we reached Weston and Kira.

"What's that, Quinn?" Weston poked at the duffel bag.

"Coveralls, three guns, and friggin' papers on the other camps." Quinn sounded pleased with himself.

I explained about Higgins, stunning Weston into nearly a stop. Quinn kept walking ahead of us.

When we reached Ben, he sounded less excited about the haul. "We're thirty-eight minutes behind schedule," he explained.

Quinn snorted and pulled his duffel bag off his shoulder. "Take this. We'll be fine."

I let Weston fill in Ben and the others about Higgins. Tyrell's position in the government had always been an assumption; it chilled me to learn how true it had been.

Puffing up to fit his ego, Quinn split the new members off with the Wolf Squad while I silently considered Higgins and Moonjir. Neither of the conversations helped the present situation. If anything, they depressed me.

Penny, Dean, and I ended up escorting Jimmy, built like a brick and inches taller than any of us, and Lorabelle, who had a heavy southern accent, hair as pale as mine, and a burn scar from her left eyebrow down the entire side of her face to her neck.

Despite a couple of sharp comments from Penny, I kept the conversation off Higgins or the Santee bridge.

Jimmy explained about the missing member of the nine, Maria. "She never let on to any of us what she planned, just up and scooted off one night. Headed northwest. They tracked her down, though. Brought her back just to show us, I believe. Then sent her packing for Camp Taygetos, the new one."

"Where was she headed?" I asked. Northwest would have brought her into safer territory, but possibly populated as well. My time at the labs had burned into me that populated areas weren't safe for our kind.

"She wanted to live on a farm, like where she grew up. We all have fantasies of going home."

I didn't really remember home. Some hadn't been as young as me when they were sent to the labs. Pushing down envy, maybe jealousy, I offered an understanding smile. "You'll like where we're headed, then." My expression wilted. Tyrell had troops building to take our glimpse of happiness and security away.

The rain never let up, and when we gathered at the boats, we had to help bail out the rainwater pooling on the bottoms. Odie sniffed all the new people, even ignoring Dean for the chore. I lost count of their names.

We had one last obstacle ahead before we could reach Columbia: the Santee bridge. Quinn explained the situation to the new rescues. "We're headed to Columbia, but we don't have to deal with the Duathua for much longer. Once we get some new supplies, we'll be on our way to take friggin' Camp Morea and the soldiers there."

"Duathua?" exclaimed one of the new men.

"We outnumber them like thirty to one. Besides, they don't dare mess with Wolf Squad." Quinn's statement caused me to cringe.

From exchanged glances, I thought a couple of the new rescues might turn around and head back to Camp Mystras. I shot a glance toward our boat, where Jural sat on the deck with only her reddish head scales visible. How would that go over?

Ben complained about the time. "We're late on our schedule."

"Wouldn't be if we hadn't friggin' pampered some officer," said Quinn, shooting me a glare.

Dean squeezed my hand. "Love you. Ignore the shithead."

"Love you, too. You're the one riding back with him."

He groaned and headed to prep his boat while Quinn glossed over the threat that awaited us at the bridge. We had enough supplies to easily camp the day, but I'd rather not if we could help it.

Quinn might be bull-headed enough to want to try for it in daylight even if the weather didn't cover us. Luckily, Dean and Roxie were in control of our movement.

I scanned our growing numbers and turned for the boat.

Someone behind me screamed.

Chapter Thirteen

Ahead of me, Jural had stood up in our boat beside Roxie and Fawn. The Duathua's height and translucent wings made her stand out even in the gray rain.

I turned to the crowd, hands held out. "She's a friend. Her name's Jural." There had been no real reason for her to come, as we had not even spoken a word during the trip.

One of the new women, a tan teen who reminded me of Tika, fell back to the ground, still screaming.

"An effing friend," Jural agreed from the boat.

Ignoring her, I explained and pleaded with the new people. "Where we are going, there will be more Duathua. The Alliance is based on cooperation between our two races. Columbia has survived because of the strength this has formed."

Quinn snorted and opened his mouth as if to say something, but Penny just laughed pointedly at him. "Effing wimps." Odie trotted behind as she made for the boat. "We have an actual threat ahead of us with Tyrell's soldiers. Sunrise is coming."

Gina moved forward as quickly, smiling as she passed me to climb into the boat with Jural. Her movement stirred

Andy and Len until the Camp Sparta crew moved as a whole.

Face dark with annoyance, Quinn approached, hand out for his rifle that I carried, but I just waved him away. Scowling, he looked back to Weston, who now carried one of the duffel bags.

Lorabelle and Jimmy stepped forward next, joining our boat, while the other six newcomers followed Weston and Quinn to Dean's. As I climbed in, Odie greeted me, excited for all the company.

"Who's a good boy?" Jimmy sat on the deck, focused on Odie. It earned the oversized teen an appreciative glance from Penny.

Gina and the others looked exhausted, but they chattered lightheartedly, as if relieved we hadn't experienced another disaster like Camp Sparta. I didn't mention Higgins or how close we'd come.

At the back, Jural found a seat on the deck to watch Roxie, who still yawned after an almost five-hour nap.

Tired, wet, and chilled, I wanted to spend the ride with Dean, but it served us well that he had experience with boats and could keep an eye on Quinn. I sat in the rain at the back, helping Gina and Fawn bail the occasional bucketful of water that accumulated. My othersense ebbed and flowed with my concentration, but I found no threats.

Jural took up a wide space with her long legs. "Your rescue was successful," she said in surprisingly correct English.

"It was."

"Yet, you are stressed."

I was, but didn't want to bring everyone down as well. Instead, I remarked on her speech. "I can understand you better."

She smiled and leaned into a nod. "Thank you. It is so very much easier when I can listen."

Jural had been silent for the trip, and quite alert. "Is that why you came with us?"

"That, and to learn from each other."

I wanted to describe the conversation I'd had with Higgins, but it could wait until our first rest before the bridge. Lightning pulsed the dark gray to the east into a lightening of the clouds without distinct form. The thunder took four seconds to reach us, grumbling across the water.

"We'll have time for that when we let Roxie rest, if you'd like." I'd suggested to many to take what naps they could, but monitoring with othersense, I'd wait until we were clear of the Santee bridge and Lake Marion.

"That sounds — delightful." Jural seemed unsure of that usage, and it might have been a little bit of an exaggeration, at least for me.

Roxie pushed past our first planned rest, opting for only one instead of two before we reached the bridge. We needed to beat the sunrise, and it would be close.

The storm had lessened by the time we stopped, and Jural took me on my word to leave the boat for a meditation. "This one will be yours, with an example of your Kudaru shield for me to study. I will take the first break after the bridge."

Gina, Fawn, Tika, Weston, and Dean joined us, though some of the new members considered the offer. Jural's attendance might have dissuaded them.

Long-limbed live oaks dominated the rainy, musky forest on the south bank of Lake Marion where we stopped. For my example, I formed an umbrella, blocking us from the persistent rain.

"I would leave this up while we listen for the otherness, but we need to hear everything at rest." In truth, I couldn't hold shields indefinitely, especially as tired as I'd become with all the walking and no sleep.

After Jural attempted, without success, to emulate my form several times before nodding for me to continue, I dropped the shield, letting the rain pounce on us. Dean groaned; he rarely joined my meditations. Did he think she was leading? I pushed away a moment of exhausted irritation and began.

The storm didn't help as it drenched us and punctuated quiet moments with rumbling thunder. I grew tempted to end the meditation after a few minutes.

Gina, who had only attended a couple of sessions, suddenly spiked in my othersense. She spoke in a whisper. "I hear a hum."

My heart sped. "Good." I'd begun to believe I would fail trying to train others on this. "Okay. Listen to it."

"What am I looking for?"

"Variations. Rhythms. Changes. Just keep listening."

Weston frowned while Fawn and Tika both drew in deep breaths, clenching their eyes in concentration. Gina wore a pleased smile throughout the session, though by the end she hadn't identified more than the first sense of a hum.

From the shore, Ben called out that an hour had passed. When we returned to the boat, Jimmy was sitting on the bow with Andy and two of the other newcomers from Camp Mystras: Jerome with skin as richly brown as Roxie's, and a handsome teen named Keith whose bangs hung wet over his eyes. They rose when we climbed out of the rainy woods with Jural.

Jimmy introduced them to us, and both of the newcomers managed to greet the tall Duathua with respect, though their necks craned to do so.

Dean gave me a quick kiss and turned for his boat.

"How's it going?" I asked.

"Nothing is easy." He rolled his eyes and headed back to his boat.

When I woke Roxie, she stared into my eyes for a long minute. "The rough part next."

"If the storm holds, we'll only have you tow Dean the last mile."

She rose slowly. "I'm so tired."

As Roxie spoke, Jural climbed into place. "Why not help her? You are skilled at healing."

"She's not injured, just tired."

Jural smiled. "You can — restore her."

When I looked at Roxie, she raised her eyebrows and shrugged. "I'm game."

I'd never considered that we could alleviate exhaustion. *This could be useful.* "Lie back down."

"Gladly." Roxie dropped back onto the cushion.

Fawn slid in beside me, then surprisingly, Lorabelle. I had never asked about her predominant skill.

"What are we looking for?" I asked Jural.

"Simply heal."

I touched Roxie's wet forehead and cheek, Fawn her arm, and Lorabelle her leg. "Lorabelle," I said, "we can work together on healing. When you go in, search for us. Once we all are together, we can meld yet work separately. We'll sense what the others are doing and learn from it."

Relieving the exhaustion proved easy as the flesh, or cells, of Roxie's body reacted to the otherness. Some elements of the blood responded. Her body drank our combined ministrations as if we poured otherness into it.

"How do you feel?" I asked.

"Refreshed." She rolled her shoulders as she sat up. "Better, but I could still sleep if you gave me the opportunity."

"Little chance of that."

"Yeah." Roxie stood. "Better. Thank you." As she moved to the rear, she reached up and patted Jural on the shoulder. "Thanks."

Andy had revised directions for us based on his best calculations from the map. "I'm hoping this is right. I didn't have to do much math with the original plotting." He peered against the rain at the gray sky. "But no sun, so there's that. Let's do it."

At a presumed mile from the bridge, we had our best eyes on our bow, with Dean towed behind. I pressed my othersense as far as I could, waiting for guards to show up at either bank.

Minutes passed with Roxie easing us at a slow pace. The rain and thunder continued, offering us plenty of cover. My shoulders tense, I craved one of Dean's back rubs. Have to wait on that.

"Caitlyn? Anything?" Andy asked. "We should be able to see it any minute."

In my othersense, I couldn't tell rock from water, but I found no one within range. "Maybe your calculations?"

I focused on my right, where the bridge should stretch onto land, and found life. Just small animals, but not the fish underwater. I lined it up as best I could to our course. "I think you're right, Andy. We're close."

"But?"

"No guards that I can tell." I searched deep ahead into Lake Marion on the other side of the three bridges. "It's odd."

Penny called from the front to Andy. "I see the bridge. Land to the right. We're good."

"Should I speed up?" Roxie asked.

"No. I'd rather creep underneath slowly."

The boat quieted except for Odie, who thumped his tail

when Jimmy scratched his ear. Thunder rumbled deep to my right, almost behind us.

The first bridge came into sight with no hint of the guards in my othersense. The land rose on the right, where I sensed rodents, maybe rabbits or possums.

We passed underneath with a moment of respite from rain and a gust of marshy scents from the dark concrete posts. The second concrete bridge waited for us, while the last and oldest bridge lay beyond with smaller gaps between squarish supports.

"Ef me," Penny said from the front. "This is wrong."

My skill prickled, agreeing with her. With slow churns of the water, Roxie brought us back into the rain toward the shorter old bridge. There were no cars stacked on top, but it had long been unused, even before the Sorrow, except for fishing. The military had removed the northeast end, perhaps long ago, as I'd never seen it connected.

Had Tyrell given up on Santee?

We were twenty feet from the square gray poles when Jural spoke. "I do not think this is safe."

I frowned at her comment. "Neither do I."

The Duathua made an odd gesture with her fingers. "They have built something. I can feel their workings. Things attached." She pointed to the top of the bridge, overhead, then to one side, then the other. "Many things."

The bow of the boat had already gone under the edge of the bridge by the time I reacted. "Roxie."

Penny pointed to a flat gray box strung overhead, affixed to the concrete. Taut cables stretched from either side of it to the supports.

I threw a shield over us, extending ahead and to the sides.

Metal scraped the bottom of the boat, even as Roxie churned the water in an attempt to stop us.

A cable twanged.

The bridge above exploded in bright light.

As a cloud of dust and metal filled the surrounding air, the storm became an ebbing silence to my ears. A burned stench of chemicals assailed my nose. Concrete the size of heads embedded into my shield or rolled down into the water to splash, though I couldn't hear it.

I fell to one knee as we rocked with water splashing over the sides.

Roxie gestured with a wince to the front, then back. We'd already sprung the trap; if we could, we needed to get to the north side.

"Go!" I yelled. My voice vibrated, but I couldn't hear. I pointed forward, through the dust cloud, and bolstered my shield until it nearly wrapped around our boat. *Dean*. How far had the blast extended?

Roxie lifted us with her churning, concrete scraped the hull, then we shot out into the rain.

I turned, waiting for Dean to follow us through. The line between us tight, his boat emerged through the fading cloud and pulled behind us.

Gina tugged at my arm, motioning to our right.

Two sets of dim lights flickered in the water slightly ahead and to the right of our position. I reached out with my othersense, and it only took a second before first one trio of soldiers, then another, came into my range. They were over a mile off.

Shaking, I rose and stepped to Roxie, tapping her shoulder and pointing toward the lights. Then I gestured us veering away. "They can't see us," I called.

They might hope we remained trapped under the bridge.

Whether she heard me or not, she churned the water, and we angled to the right side of Lake Marion. Holding onto her shoulder, I tracked the soldiers. As we sped into the storm, they raced for the bridge.

A single chunk of concrete remained in my shield, and I rolled it off with a simple shift before releasing the otherness. Andy tried to yell something to me, but then motioned to his own ears. I gestured with my hands that we were moving away from the soldiers, they were out of my range.

We'd survived. Quinn had nearly brought us to disaster, but somehow we'd raided Camp Mystras and were headed to Columbia.

Andy pointed north, then to the maps. He lifted his hands in the air.

I didn't worry about the navigation.

Dean knew these waters. He'd get us home.

Chapter Fourteen

Groggy, I smiled at the barricaded bridges of Columbia as they came into view under a sunny sky. The warmth felt luxurious, though my damp coveralls stuck to my skin. Many of the Wolf Squad slept while I sat in the back with Roxie, Jural, and Gina.

"You okay, Roxie? We're almost home."

She smiled warmly. "I'm good. Those refreshes after a nap really help."

We'd used Jural's healing trick at each stop. When the sun came out, Jural ran one of her sessions, though I still hadn't reached any result or even knew what to expect. Her English rivaled Nur's.

Gina craned her neck, studying the bridge as we passed underneath. "I was scared; during the explosion."

My reactions had been muted, as dull as my hearing. I'd been through too much over the past weeks. "It's a healthy response." I leaned my head back, closed my eyes, and let the sun warm my face.

"How do you stay so calm?" Gina asked.

"I don't, really. I'm tense and worried. Keeping everyone safe is first, though."

"Why then?" When Jimmy spoke, I snapped my eyes open. His gentle tone and expressionless face gave no hint of his meaning.

"Why what?" I asked.

"You let Quinn act like the boss, but people look to you."

I frowned. Jimmy had barely been with us for a few hours. Quinn had been obnoxious most of the return trip, the whole trip, but nothing I couldn't ignore. Even Dean paid the jerk no mind.

Roxie raised her eyebrows, smirking.

"I don't want to lead the Wolf Squad. He does."

"Why don't you want to lead?"

I don't want to be responsible for everyone. "I'm not sure." Leaning forward, I tugged at the wet coveralls stuck to my knees. "I'd like to just have someplace comfortable to rest."

Jimmy shook his head with a slow thoughtfulness before he spoke. "I don't understand, but I don't have to, do I? It's your choice."

"It would be safer if you said you'd lead." Roxie's smirk had vanished. "He's going to get someone hurt."

I studied my sodden boots. They wanted me to be a symbol of something I wasn't. This rebellion had been their idea. Living someplace quiet with Dean mattered not trying to save everyone.

The new people didn't notice the Pahawan flying low on the horizon until we were almost to the docking island. Having Jural with us made the sight less spectacular for them.

On the walk back to the Wolf Den, both houses already seemed to be included in that name. Quinn wanted to be in the lead, so Weston and Ben kept him on the path. I found myself near the middle; Roxie and Penny talked close behind.

Ahead of us, Jimmy carried one of the big duffel bags. Dean wore a pack over one shoulder with the remainder of our supplies.

"There's some useful stuff in the haul, like docs and maps. Can't fault Quinn for that." Dean held my hand lightly, his last two fingers hooked into mine.

I'd kept my comments about Quinn's behavior to a minimum, but based on Dean's quiet chuckle, my expression oozed attitude. "What did you think of that Higgins?" I asked.

He shrugged with more of a twitch to his face and head than shoulders. "Not much. They've got problems, not surprising. Tyrell being a dick is hardly news."

More than anything, the fact that Higgins, a government official of some sort, knew nothing about the Duathua ambassadors bothered me. I'd related the conversation to Jural, but she gave no response. I wanted to mention it to Nur or someone like Henweyay.

Less than half an hour after I'd thought of the Haarseer, a Pahawan flew down to me at one of the overpasses. "Crap." We had reached a point suspiciously close to the buildings where the Alliance met, and I just wanted to crawl into bed.

The newer members of the Wolf Squad froze or even stumbled off the road as the Duathua warrior in Kudaru armor with a large Rizulat trident landed lightly on the asphalt.

"Seyir," they said in a formal voice. "Might the Haarseer request your presence?"

Dean patted my shoulders. "I'll get the kiddies fed and settled in. We'll have to double bunk at this point."

My eyes widened.

He laughed. "Not in our room. The non-leader still gets some privileges."

Jural moved toward us from where she'd been talking with Gina and Fawn. Roxie gave me an apologetic smile. Penny nodded to the Pahawan as she stepped beside me, while Odie begged some pets from Dean.

Climbing over a concrete barricade, I headed for the road that led to the mall and meeting place. Jural and Penny accompanied me as the rest of our troop kept on the highway. The Pahawan took off ahead of us. "They probably want to know how it went," I said to Penny.

"They could just effing count," she replied.

They could have. "Perhaps they want to know if we'll be continuing."

"Quinn and Ben haven't talked about anything else. Effing Camp Morea."

Gina had mentioned it as a question. I sighed. "I'm too tired."

"Isabel, Kira, Andy, and Gina. They've got friends there. The whole camp, according to Andy."

Jural peered down at me. "You do not wish to help your people? This Jimmy and Lorabelle seemed very happy that you released them."

Ugh. "Every time we go, there's a risk people will die or get hurt. Andy could have been killed. If you hadn't noticed the bomb, we might have died at the Santee bridge."

"It is good that you want to protect your people."

I hadn't been alone with Jural during the trip, so I asked her the question I had twisting inside. "How did you know — at the bridge?"

She raised a hand, trailing it in an arc and rubbing a long finger against her thumb. "I could see the connections between the — items — and those who had put them up.

Fresh, new. There were many items. One at each section of the bridge. There were many connections."

I frowned. "I've seen connections between people, but not between objects."

"When people create or invest themselves in something, a similar connection or bond is created." With a smile, she pulled out the small Kudaru figurine. "There are so many that our senses dismiss them. You can recognize more recent or important ones."

I shifted into the othersense, studying the strange clear fish in her hands, but there were no connections bound to it that I could see. Shaking my head, I twitched, feeling like I disappointed her.

"We will keep trying. Your accomplishment with your friend Wati, among other things, gives me hope."

"What does Wati have to do with this?" I gestured toward the figurine. What other things?

Jural clicked her tongue. "We have old — ancient — writings that we call the Epics. They describe the unbinding your people did here on Earth that began the first Displacement."

I'd never mentioned the conversation with Vanya to Penny. "Something about the Sempiternal, here on Earth."

"Yes. Exactly. The Seyirs of that time had great powers, but we do not understand their desired outcome, only the rough understanding of what they did and the aftermath. It involved a structure they called pillars and disrupting the bindings. A side effect of their actions caused gravity to fail."

Penny whistled. "Effing shitheads."

I couldn't connect all the impact Jural attributed to me, some long-dead Seyirs, and the ability to see a connection to her fish; or my toes. Maybe after a night of sleep, something might make sense. Letting the conversation die, I marched to the meeting place of the Alliance in silence. The sun, still warm on my skin and starting to dry my clothes, angled toward the west.

At the entrance, Penny gave me a quick hug. "I'm heading home. You know the way back to the Wolf Den. Thanks."

I frowned. "For what?"

"Not getting us effing killed." She winked and strode away with her rifle strapped on her back and the long coat rustling at her heels. Odie pranced alongside.

Henweyay waited alone for me on the dais, greeting me and Jural equally. "Seyirs. Thank you. Your mission went well. None missing or wounded, and you have brought recruits." The Pahawan's comments were not questions. Her scouts had likely been reporting on our progress.

"Has Tyrell made any movement toward the Alliance?" I asked.

"None. When will you be leaving on your next mission?"

My heart sank. I'd avoided the inevitability of this on the return trip, dismissing questions with deliberate vagueness. "We'll need to rest and plan."

She lifted a satchel off the table and strode down the stairs from the dais. "I have appropriate maps of the southwestern area between Columbia and the city once called Augusta. These should cover most of your planning needs. We have resources available. The safest path for ground travel to avoid the new military buildup near Jones Crossroads would be to head west, then south. We've notated sightings of their scouts, homesteads sympathetic to the Alliance, and those supporting the Savannah military."

Henweyay's words splashed across my dull, sleep-deprived brain, and I numbly took the leather satchel. "Resources?"

"Weapons, which you already have. Ammunition if needed. Vehicles, military and otherwise, that we've got stored. Fuel. Inflatable boats. Our stockpiles are inventoried, so we can quickly determine if we can supply your requests."

Silently, I counted the number of Wolf Squad who had said they'd been taught to drive. It hadn't been considered when I'd been at Camp Sparta, but they'd taught Roxie, somewhat.

"Boats?" I winced, realizing my vocabulary had been reduced to single words. Dean spoke more than that.

"There is no direct watercourse from Columbia, but the Savannah River runs south into the Augusta area. The other camp at Aiken has smaller tributaries nearby. I will send a messenger to your Wolf Den tomorrow morning to see if you have a list by then or require information. I have scouts dedicated to those locations who can give detailed reports."

I imagined an armored Pahawan sitting in the main area at our house among all the newer members. They'd be terrified. Lifting the satchel, I nodded to Henweyay. "Thanks. We'll look at these tonight." Actually, I'll be sleeping. Quinn and the others could come up with a plan.

Jural walked with me to the exit. "I will come by in the morning, if that is acceptable?"

"Of course. We'll train." I forced a weary smile.

By the time I reached the house, my feet and thighs were chafed, hunger gnawed at my stomach, and I could sleep on command. The sitting area smelled like stew with an abundance of garlic. Dean had saved flatbread for me, and the sitting room had new and old Wolf Squad members piled onto every surface.

Quinn followed me and Dean to the kitchen. "We're hitting Camp Morea next."

I handed him the satchel while taking a bite of bread. Plenty of stew filled a still warm pot. "Fabulous," I mumbled.

"What?" Quinn opened the satchel.

I swallowed and repeated my statement. He scowled and headed for the others. Leaning against a counter, I stared at a stain on the ceiling. "I'm tired, Dean."

"I can corral these yahoos. Take a nap. Got them all settled into rooms. Nur came by. There will be extra mattresses here by nightfall."

"No problems?"

"Quinn's room has a leak in it." He grinned. "I gave him a bucket."

Stuffing the last of the bread in my mouth, I turned and searched for a clean bowl and spoon. "Didn't get the roof fixed?"

"Most of it. Nothing is easy."

"Let me get a couple of hours in. Then I'll be back down to hear the details. The Pahawan have military vehicles, fuel, inflatable boats, whatever we need."

"They, too, have seen the light of your cause."

I gave him a dead stare, then took a bite of garlicky potato and pork stew. Ben had cooked; it tasted good. "Camp Morea, eh?"

"Andy's excited."

"Not as much as he is about Gina."

Dean appeared surprised. "Really?"

"Not sure she feels the same, but he moons on her."

"Didn't notice."

"I spent — how many hours with them? She's a nice girl; wants to see your library."

He shrugged. We had almost forty paperbacks and a precious dozen hardcovers in crates in our room.

I paused with a spoonful of stew before my lips. "Let's

see if we can at least get one day of rest. Do we need everyone?"

"Less would be better," he agreed.

I scraped the last bite out of the bowl, and he took it along with the spoon. The kitchen floor seemed more appealing than walking up the stairs. "Carry me upstairs?" I joked.

When he grabbed me up in his arms, I squealed.

Chapter Fifteen

Two days after we returned to Columbia, I sat in the front seat of a Jeep Wrangler, scrunching my nose against the persistent reek of gasoline. An anxious Roxie drove while Penny, Dean, and Odie took up the backseat. I didn't feel as rested as I would have liked.

Somewhere ahead, Jural and two Pahawan scouted over the road to the northwest of Columbia. They wouldn't be needed until we got deeper into what the Alliance called "the wild zone" where human gangs carved out territory. Before planning this trip, I'd never heard of people like that.

"Three hours in this effing stench," complained Penny behind me.

"Less. If Ben were here, we'd know to the minute." Dean's joking tone hid his concerns. None of us four were happy with Quinn's plan.

I'd been able to whittle down his initial numbers based on drivers, but we still had thirteen, including myself. Speeding ahead, Quinn and Weston drove the lead vehicle, another Jeep, while the rest paired up in the four cars behind.

The sun rose behind our caravan, leaving long shadows

from the woods across the broken asphalt. A cluster of abandoned, burned cars forced Roxie to ease half off the road to get around.

"We're going to sit half an effing day, anyway. I could have ridden Bella."

I tilted my head back, speaking to the ceiling rather than turning in my seat. "You wanted to go south of Lake Murray, rather than north."

"Yeah. I'd have kept to the woods mainly. I doubt any effing scouts would have seen me."

Dean snorted.

We were past the first burned-out town, Newberry, when the Pahawan flew low over the trees with Jural. Quinn never slowed, but Roxie pulled to a stop and let me out.

Henweyay had insisted on the scouts, and I hadn't minded. Three steps away from the Jeep let me take in a breath of fresh air. Dean grabbed one of the red jugs of gas, and Jimmy and Lorabelle topped off their tank as well.

Jural fluttered to the ground beside both Pahawan. One of the scouts with bluish-gray head scales pointed down the road. "They aren't close to your path, but there's one of the roving bands hunting. They have horses and rifles about two miles from where the road splits to the right."

"So, stay left."

They nodded seriously.

His map flapping in his hand, Andy jogged toward us, past Jimmy and Lorabelle. "Trouble?" he called out. He'd desperately wanted to ride with us — with me — until I suggested he team up with Gina, who had a lot of practice driving.

I shook my head, waving him back. "Stay on the route."

Tires chirped to my left when Quinn turned around and sped back in our direction. I'd rather we didn't have to explain anything to him. He might decide to get in a gunfight with the band.

"Thanks," I said to the Duathua and raced for the Jeep. Seeing my haste, Dean capped the tank.

Quinn's scowl convinced me we wouldn't move forward without some sort of conversation. With one leg in the Jeep, I sighed.

"Have fun," said Dean from behind me.

"Oh joy." I waited for Quinn to come to a stop, bumper to bumper, and walked forward.

The little prick waved impatiently for me to approach. "What is it?" he asked. The night before, he'd shaved his head, much like Fawn did, but it didn't suit him well; neither did the dozen hairs on his chin. Was he growing a beard?

"Nothing. Stay on the route. They have a sighting of some armed people, but they're just hunting."

"And they made us friggin' stop for that?"

"No. I chose to stop to hear their report."

He growled and put his Jeep in reverse with a thud. "Weston and I think we should move straight on to Camp Evrotas afterward."

From the passenger seat, Weston tightened his face to near a wince. I stepped toward them to argue, but Quinn spit dust and stones from his tires, angling off the road.

"Idiot." I climbed into our Jeep. "You hear that?"

Roxie nodded, waiting for me to close my door. "We talked them out of it once. If we pack the vehicles from Morea like Andy believes we will, they won't have a choice unless he expects everyone to walk."

I slammed my door. "He would."

She sniffled, fighting the cold that had taken down two of the new men from Camp Mystras. "Weston and Ben will agree, but I think the others would rather drive."

"If there's enough effing fuel. I don't think they have a lot left." Penny chuckled. "It would be funny if Quinn ended up walking. Might take him a couple of days with those short legs."

Henweyay had cautioned prudence in using what fuel we had. Most gas and diesel had been scavenged and used early in the Sorrow. The Savannah Charter grabbed any they found for the military; it seemed the Alliance had done similarly.

Somewhere around a town called Saluda, a pack of werewolves had been spotted by locals friendly with the Alliance. The Pahawan let us know so we wouldn't stop for any breaks, but they hadn't been able to confirm.

At midday, we drove through a soggy area still puddled from recent storms to reach our stop. Stretches of mud made it difficult to find places to park all the vehicles. A vine-covered bridge across a small river had crumbled into the far shore, possibly intentionally. The military often destroyed smaller crossings it didn't want to guard.

I slogged along the edge of the woods with Dean. "I hadn't thought it might be a swamp."

"We lived in a swamp; this ain't one."

"True." I smiled. For a bit, it seemed that Dean and I might have lived alone in peace. Tyrell had made that a short dream.

He waved off a bug and pointed. "That looks good. Tree cover."

We checked, then waved Roxie in. Jural and the Pahawan returned from a quick scout of the area. They wouldn't go any farther with us but would wait here.

Jural landed beside me. "It seems we have some time, Caitlyn. We could each benefit."

"Sure," I said.

Dean straightened, more interested than I was. He

joined Weston, Gina, and Isabel in our little circle amid an appreciative crowd of gnats. Penny and Roxie sat closer to the water with Odie, out of earshot, so they could talk.

This time, Jural started with her toe-gazing meditation. As always, she held her little figurine as if on display. "Listen to your body. You are in control. It speaks with the connection of blood. Bindings of energy. Subtle rhythms."

I could sense it in the otherness, those subtle vibrations, but no connections or binding. The white lines of connectivity that I saw came from deep in our center mass and extended to those we knew.

"These ties are songs or a language we have just learned. In learning them, we control them. They pulse up, then down, back and forth."

Focus drifting off my toe, I imagined the flow of blood, and perhaps recognized the rhythms, as twisting lines flickered a pale blue in the otherness. I glanced up to Jural, about to ask her, then stopped.

A thin tendril of green led from her figurine to her chest. I blinked, unsure.

"What we have made, touched, grown, we have connection to. We control our bodies, our blood, our thoughts, our emotions." Even as Jural spoke in that quiet, lilting voice, she brought out a second figurine made of Kudaru, a long-legged bird with a long pincer beak. It, too, linked to her with a green tendril.

My mouth hung open. When I began to form a comment, she shook her head slowly and smiled. "Breathe in your thoughts and emotions, command them with your breath out."

Pointedly, she nodded toward my chest. "See those things we have attachments to. The toe is ours. The body is ours. The emotions are ours."

As she spoke, I peered down at green and orange

tendrils that sprung from my chest and danced along the edge of Dean's jacket that I wore. A multitude of colored tendrils stretched from the leather to Dean himself. I gasped, causing him to look up then grow a concerned expression.

In a single blink, the world exploded into vibrant threads. They ran from people to their clothing, into pockets, and some just trailed out to parts unknown.

"I—"

"Shh. Listen."

My breath quickened to near panting. The connections wove around me, filling all the space, as if to suffocate me. If I focused on a single thread, it became less overwhelming.

Dean watched me, worried. His threads snapped into focus over the others.

"As conscious as you wish to be with the connection, you can dismiss them. You are in control. Breathe." She spoke as if to all, but I took the words as my own.

Similar to how I controlled my othersense, I let go of the threads. They vanished to the edge of my consciousness, and I let out a long breath. Everyone had noticed my irregular breathing, my panic, and kept flicking glances at me. I forced myself not to apologize.

Before she finished, I tested myself once more, and the threads exploded into my awareness. They scared me, and I let them subside.

She had everyone stretch "before Caitlyn begins," and cocked her head in a very human way for me to follow her. Dean's jaw tightened, but he let me go alone.

"You can see now." She made a gesture upward with her fingers. "I did not want to disturb the others to discuss it. Not everyone is searching for the same result."

I frowned, unsure who she meant or what they

expected. "Do you not want me to mention what I saw?" That made me uncomfortable.

"The learned is yours. Express as you will. I did not want you to interrupt."

"I'm seeing the connections between an object and — a person who has a feeling for it." I sucked in a breath. "The bomb on the bridge. You saw the soldiers' connections to their work."

Jural beamed, and it made me proud. "You are quite remarkable, Seyir. At least, you are open enough that you grasp quickly. More so than many who might spend years. I myself, have not learned what you created, this soft Kudaru."

"Let's go try."

The group didn't question me when we returned, and they listened intently when I demonstrated and described creating shields. We spent over an hour in my session on othersense, especially as Gina pushed harder, trying to get further than she had already.

I let Dean separate me from the group after we finished. "What happened?" he asked.

"I can see something like the othersense, except connections between people and things they are attached to. Like your jacket."

We walked along the crumbling road in the sun, away from the bugs in the woods. He frowned and shrugged. "Is that what we're supposed to be searching for?"

"No, not everyone. That's why she talked to me afterward."

"Oh. Good. Okay. So — jacket?"

"It connects me to you, so I'm attached to it."

"You're wearing it." He smirked.

"Ha ha. You've got your own attachments to it."

"It's my father's."

Did the colors mean anything? "I'm not sure how useful it'll be, but Jural saw the connections to the bombs and the soldiers who put them there."

"So, not very long ranged."

I frowned. She might not have understood it. We'd walked about thirty paces from where she stood talking with Gina and Weston. Preparing myself, I dropped into the awareness of attachments, and easily spotted the green thread from her chest to her pockets where she had the figurines. A variety of colors sprang from her and sprayed out to become filaments threading through the woods. I could follow a single thread deep into the horizon, but had no sense of what it connected to. "Actually, I think it's very long ranged — for whatever good it will do."

Disconnecting from the disturbing awareness, I stood facing the broken bridge, river, and team. Quinn, Weston, and Ben marched toward me.

"Nothing is easy." Dean turned from them and rubbed my shoulder.

"Why are they coming to me? I'm not in charge."

He chuckled and then kissed my cheek.

Quinn scowled, so I pecked Dean on the lips. "Love you," I said.

"I love you, too." He chuckled again.

The sun had tilted toward the west, but not enough for shadows from the surrounding woods to reach the road. Leaning heads together to talk, Roxie and Penny noticed the trio approaching me and Dean.

"We need to change the plan," Quinn announced from six paces away, though still marching closer.

I'm not in charge. "Okay." He'd want some reaction from me, so I gave him none.

"We need to go in friggin' earlier and get them out right after dinner."

I almost laughed. Dean, Roxie, and Penny had fought for that option yesterday, and Quinn argued against it. "Okay."

He stood flustered for a minute, expecting more from me. Weston and Ben smiled at him as if they'd known my response.

It took a few awkward seconds before Quinn jerked around to head back, barking orders as he did. "Len, Andy, Jimmy, get the boats out. We're heading early. I want them inflated and in the water in fifteen friggin' minutes."

Dean sighed. He and Penny had trained on prepping the four inflatable boats. "We probably should at least supervise." Patting my hip, he trailed after the trio.

Our plan had been to travel the six miles downriver at sunset; instead, Roxie propelled the first in a four-boat chain in bright sunlight. Using an oar to keep us from veering into the shore, I sat in the flimsy boat behind hers with Jimmy, Gina, and Isabel.

Compared to our previous boating excursions, it took no time at all before we pulled our boats onto the southwest shore of the Savannah River. Farther down, barriers cut the water like miniature dams, but the Duathua had warned us of this. A rank quarry waited for us somewhere on the other side of the steep, tree-lined incline.

As Quinn climbed to the ridge above, leaving us to deal with the boats, Roxie whirled her fingers in the air. "Anything?" she asked me.

I waved to the west. "Two people on patrol a quarter of a mile away. No one else I can sense." People had abandoned the area this close to another cryptid zone.

Penny and Odie had remained behind with the Duathua to watch our vehicles; we couldn't chance losing our escape route. Len and Roxie were to be stationed here for much of the same reason.

Jimmy's deep voice had a southern drawl to his words. "I'm not very powerful, even with wind, if it comes to a fight." He walked with me, Dean, and Gina as we made up the rear of the Wolf Squad.

We walked on a dirt road with the river and trees to our left and a ridge of earth and brush to the right. "Let's hope there is no fight," I said.

"Isabel knows the camp. She'll be fine, once you get her in." Gina flashed a smile at me. She'd been there when we'd tested my metal-melting skill on a wire fence.

Isabel nodded bravely, but she seemed as nervous as the rest of us.

According to the plan, Isabel would find someone named Lisa, who'd been housed in a downstairs apartment. I'd gotten most of the details from Dean and Roxie. I pointed to Weston and Ben ahead, who had climbed part of the earthen wall to our right. "Checking out the quarry?" I asked.

Dean and Jimmy, the tallest of our group, paused to do the same. "Holy shit," exclaimed Dean.

I scrambled up beside him. "Crap."

Something had carved a massive hole in the ground in spiraling layers wide enough for dirt roads. At the bottom lay a dark lake, perhaps accounting for the stench. Even the tallest building in Columbia would have fit inside the pit. The forest on the far side appeared nothing more than a smudge of green and brown.

The brown dirt had splotches of bleached white, giving it a dirty, stained impression. As we circled around the quarry, we got better views, until it finally ceased to awe me. I'd rather live in the marsh than near this place.

When our road angled to the right, we could see huge, rusted containers on wheels that I sensed the camp ahead. "Ben," I called out.

He and Weston paused, letting us catch up. "What is it?"

I pointed straight ahead. "I'm guessing the military base, though only about twenty people spread out. A couple on a close patrol." Shifting my hand to the right, I continued. "A much larger group, maybe three dozen with guards and patrols. Youth Guard."

"Camp Morea. Can we approach?" Ben asked.

I gestured to the tall pines surrounding us. "Depends. I'll know better when we get closer."

Jimmy's voice rumbled with light irritation. "Maybe they should keep near Caitlyn, instead of racing off ahead." He spoke of Quinn and the bulk of the Wolf Squad, who just now glanced back at us.

Ben nodded. "I'll tell him." He sprinted off with Weston following.

We continued at our easy pace, Jimmy shaking his head. "Most of us would rather you do the thinking."

I knew he meant me, as even Ben would be swayed when I spoke during our planning sessions. I'd avoided the meetings because Quinn just argued about anything I said. Dean, Roxie, and Penny were level-headed enough to keep the Wolf Squad safe. We'd talked half of the people into staying in Columbia, so I only needed to watch over this group.

Quinn didn't wait for us, and we passed freakish blue-green ponds on either side that let off a reeking smell worse than the rest of the quarry. The sand had a sickly, whitish-gray color. The large boxy containers were set on railroad tracks; I kept them between us and the people since the trees had grown sparse.

Quinn left Lorabelle and Weston at a stand of trees where multiple roads split off in different directions from ours. They would direct those we rescued, much like we had at Camp Mystras.

We didn't gather as a full group until the area opened up, threatening to expose us. Quinn scowled at us as and pointed. "That building. Is there anyone on top who can friggin' see us?"

I shook my head. "There's a patrol we'll need to watch for that's circled twice around the military base, but they're not jumping from building to building." Stifling his reply by continuing, I gestured straight ahead. "There's another pair doing a large loop around the camp and what I believe is a school is farthest away. Beyond that, I sense people heading for what should be the front, like they're returning."

"That's not very friggin' helpful." His comment didn't stop him from striding down the road across the open area.

I kept up, pushing down annoyance. I wasn't in charge. Didn't want to be. The sun had pushed far to the west, and a fresh breeze from that direction washed away some of the stench of the quarry.

Ben glanced back as he walked close behind Quinn. "We're still earlier than we need to be. It's only 3:22 p.m."

We left Ben and Gina stationed at the edge of the trees along our escape path.

Gina pointed to the east and spoke to me. "Past that building is the military headquarters."

I nodded; I could sense the couple dozen soldiers clustered in that area. How long before her othersense developed and she could as well? The otherness rumbled faintly from the Youth Guard practicing on the east side of the compound.

Leaving the trio, the remaining seven of us crept south down a road beside the wire fence that cordoned off the camp to the east. Older wooden fences had fallen to rot on the slope, and sparse trees grew on the inside of the compound.

Brush had been cleared around the woods on both sides, leaving us exposed to the closest buildings, but no one hid inside them. We stopped where our woods ended and the road turned to pavement. Our little group settled at the base of the trees, sitting or squatting. The scent of cooking fires wafted past us.

Isabel nodded to a faded cream-colored building. "That's an old hotel that used to house admin before the roof started leaking. It's next to the one we quartered in, that you can't see from here. The shorter ones in front of us are the two warehouses."

Jimmy gestured through the squat metal buildings closest to us. "The barracks are just beyond those. There's a couple roads between them leading to the back of the hotel."

"We friggin' know that," Quinn shifted to the front. "Caitlyn, make our entry there." He indicated the camp fence at the top of the rise.

Swinging his head side to side, Jimmy reminded me of a bear we'd seen on an outer patrol. "No. It's not safe yet. She'd have to risk hanging there when everyone is coming in from practice. We wait like we planned."

Quinn snarled. "Who's in charge?"

I hid a smile as Jimmy leaned his large frame toward stubby Quinn and spoke. "Isabel is. She's taking the risk."

Dean slid off his small pack and settled himself on the leaves, and I sat next to him. Andy and Kira joined us. Jimmy waited until Isabel sat down, leaving Quinn fuming and muttering.

As we waited, the sun dropped behind the woods just to the south of us. We'd brought flatbread, and I chewed through a piece, tracking both looping patrols in my othersense. Youth Guard were returning from practice in the east and the new admin building to the southeast.

"Patrols are switching," I said. Brushing my hands off, I rose, as did Isabel. No one came too close to this section of the fence on their laps. "I count eighteen soldiers total; does that seem right?"

"There were more when we left," answered Jimmy.

Were they drawn away, preparing for the attack on Columbia? I wondered. Studying the closer buildings with a rising dread, even though I couldn't sense anyone in them, I made for the wire fence. Isabel followed close while the others waited.

On the top of the rise, the compound became fully visible, with abandoned trucks and scattered debris of wooden crates and black barrels. Buildings rose in a thick complex of low structures with bay doors and taller hotels farther away. The hearty aroma of cooking drifted in the wind.

I touched the fence at a point just higher than my head and focused my otherness. We knew someone might hear it but hoped it would get lost in the prep for dinner. I could sense the interlinking fence as one vast piece, never ending in my perception, but I focused on the links from my hand to the ground.

The metal bent to my will, as easily as air did, liquefying as if that were its natural state. Gobs of gray dripped to the damp grass to turn solid again. The fence pushed apart in a line when I pressed the toe of my boot to the base.

"Be careful," I whispered to Isabel as she slipped into the compound.

Quinn, Andy, and Kira left Dean and Jimmy to trot toward the woods to the south where they would have another vantage into the camp. At least I knew Quinn didn't plan to sneak in and rummage the admin offices this time.

We waited as the sky marbled with color, flying bugs buzzed our faces, and the Youth Guard settled into a tight cluster at the mess hall. The flatbread did little to compete with the aroma of cooked chicken wafting occasionally from the camp.

When the sky grayed, Isabel brought one of the first Youth Guard to the warehouses ahead.

"The patrols are holding, nowhere near this position," I said. "We're clear." Dean, Jimmy, and I climbed the slope to greet the scared teen at the fence.

The blond boy peered at me as I pulled the wire open. "Caitlyn?" he asked.

I nodded and smiled as he slipped through. "You're safe. Just head down the road, and there will be more of us to point you to our staging area."

He began to cry and wrapped his arms around me, burying his face in my shoulder. "Thank you, thank you."

Swallowing, I patted his shoulder and eventually got him on his way, but his relief at escape from the camp spun my thoughts. Dean and Jimmy joked when the teen ran out of earshot, but I could barely hear them. As much as I hated the risk these rescues presented, they were important.

Eight more Youth Guard followed the first, most one at a time, with a trio in the middle. They were grateful, but not as emotional as the first. I kept my othersense tuned; otherwise, I might have missed a new patrol coming out of the military's buildings and headed right toward Isabel's position.

Chapter Sixteen

"Crap." I pushed through the fence. "A patrol coming right at Isabel." The two soldiers walked briskly, as if hurrying to catch us.

Frantic, I sensed the area again, but it seemed just those two moved toward us. *Not a trap.* I ran through the thin woods toward the corner of the building and hoped the guards didn't see me in the dwindling light under the clouds.

The fence rattled as Dean and Jimmy followed me.

I stumbled over a chunk of concrete hidden in the debris and planted palms down into leaves. Isabel shifted in my othersense, perhaps hearing my blunder. Beyond some calling crickets and frogs, little noise came from the camp.

Dean and Jimmy scooped me up by my armpits. "How many?" asked Dean.

"Two." I resumed my race, knowing that Quinn and his team would see us running. Andy might be the most likely to leap to our aid. We didn't need more of us in the compound.

Isabel had reached the corner of the building and peered out at us, oblivious to the threat approaching from behind her. Three derelict cars parked neatly against the structure in spaces marked with faded white lines. I used the vehicles as cover between us and the soldiers.

"Caitlyn?" Isabel called in a husky attempt at a whisper.

"Get back. Soldiers," I hissed.

It took too long, but she understood, glancing around at the dark shadows and backing up between the buildings. I almost took another tumble on a concrete bumper in front of a door, but kept my balance. In my othersense, one scrambling Youth Guard approached us from the direction of the barracks, but otherwise we appeared undetected.

"What?" Isabel asked in a hushed voice as we raced around the corner of the warehouse.

Dean and Jimmy, despite their sizes, followed without making a noise.

The space between the buildings stretched wide with two cars rusting on the crumbling asphalt. The Youth Guard skittered through a fence and some bushes at the far end, slowing when they spotted our group. "How many more?" I asked Isabel, already leading her away from the corner.

"Just one," Isabel said. A hesitant woman approached, and Isabel pointed. "Dory."

I waved generally to the east. "We've got two soldiers coming down. They'll pass here in a minute. Is there somewhere to hide back there?" We'd reached the end of the alley where I considered a small car as cover. Perfect, as long as the two soldiers didn't come check this way.

"Yeah, there's some brush behind the building." Isabel began to run without my prompting. "Dory." She motioned the teen in the direction of the broken fence she'd climbed over. "Back."

The remnants of wood tilted, with gaps like teeth, and stretched west from the corner of the warehouse, giving us just enough room to line up there. I forced Jimmy and Dean in, taking a position at the corner. I didn't appreciate that I could see a window in the barracks ahead through a small jumble of trees.

The soldiers' voices drifted from the other end of the warehouses to my left. Flickering light from a lantern bobbed at the edges, but the men hadn't come into view yet. Sweeping othersense around the Youth Guard barracks in front of me and to the area surrounding the military building, I relaxed somewhat. The closest Youth Guard were settling into their quarters for the night, ignorant of the rescue.

As the soldiers came into view, barely glancing between the buildings, I heard otherness gathering behind and to my left. They were from Andy's vibrations, then a lighter call, probably from Quinn. I couldn't yell out to stop them, and I wasn't close enough to dampen their attack. Frustration and panic welled inside; I should have known Andy would react.

Flames burst from the two soldiers, and their screams pierced the night. That had to come from Andy, as Quinn had as much skill with fire as I did. The Youth Guard at this end of the building had heard the otherness or the cries, as their rhythms vibrated furiously. The patrol north of us had begun to jog; they would soon close in on Andy's location.

"Follow me," I called out and raced toward the burning men.

Flames engulfed both their bodies. Their searing flesh stunk as they writhed on the asphalt. I trusted my Wolf Squad to follow and bring Dory.

A flare lit the sky over the Youth Squad barracks, casting shadows from the warehouse roof. A few of the Guard had exited the front of the building, appearing unsure about our location.

Andy, Quinn, and Kira had entered the compound to gather at the end of the street by the camp's fence. They wouldn't know about the patrol coming in from their north. Why didn't they just leave?

My group had tightened close behind me, and I raced for Andy. I could see his lanky shape and waved him back. He took a step back, but Quinn stood firm.

"Don't slow down until we get to the exit." I'd need a shield against bullets. The patrol moved too fast and would cut us off. The flare had called the rest of the soldiers, though they bunched up and headed for the Youth Squad barracks rather than us.

Quinn opened his mouth to say something as I reached them. Gathering otherness, I flew past them with my team. I slung up a broad shield for bullets between us and the patrol. Andy and Kira were quick to join us. We were nearly running toward the soldiers.

When the first soldier shot a bullet, I sensed otherness welling from along the fence. Ben. Gina. Andy and Quinn drew in as well, but I soaked it up and strengthened my shield.

One member of the patrol burst into flames along his side and hair from Ben's attack. His weapon sprayed gunfire, but at the ground, not us. Gina lit the second soldier. Her attack didn't burn as brightly as Andy's or Ben's, but she focused on the head, sending the man screaming to the ground. This had turned into a mess.

Both the military and Youth Guard were focused on our exit now. Like a swarm, they shifted toward the sounds of gunshots. I squirmed through the opening in the fence, hoping we'd have enough of a lead to lose them.

"We need to stop them here," Quinn said from behind me.

I shook my head. "We need to run. They don't know where we're going."

Andy and Quinn paused a few feet from the opening, while Isabel and a terrified Dory followed me. I kept moving down the slope toward the road that would lead back to Ben and Gina — and our escape.

The otherness surged as Andy set fire to the roof of the old admin building. It brought me to a stop, along with the others.

"Andy? What are you doing?" It would be less than a minute before he'd be in sight of the mob of Youth Guard rushing toward us. I couldn't let him die over Quinn's foolishness.

I nodded Isabel down the road. "Get Dory to the meeting point." Dean and Jimmy hovered by my side.

Ben had taken the cue from Andy's attack and lit a building inside the compound to the north.

Scrambling back up the incline, I rushed to get to the idiots, Andy and Quinn. Kira lingered at the opening by the fence, unsure.

Andy's second attempt tried to light the closest warehouse on fire, but after a blossom of flame, it died.

Quinn was yelling. "Its friggin' metal! Go for the big building again."

Three Youth Guard turned the far corner of the same warehouse, and they must have spotted Quinn and Andy. The otherness started to gather in three distinct strikes, and I snuffed each of them.

"Andy, c'mon." I slipped on the leaves, and Dean caught my arm.

The flames at the old admin building had taken root, crawling up the roof. The military advanced quickly from the east, spreading around the buildings. Gina and Ben were running to our location.

"There, Andy, see them?" Quinn pointed out the first of the Youth Guard, who slowed when they realized I'd doused their attacks.

We reached them, and I set the wide arc of a shield around us before Andy drew in the otherness and heat seared the first of the Youth Guard. I should have doused his attack. Wincing at the spike of pain the woman vibrated in the othersense, I pleaded with Andy. "Please. Run. We can get away."

Otherness sprang up around us, and I drew it in again. Youth Guard poured out of the alley between the warehouses, where the two soldiers still smoldered. I called the otherness and air.

Sending a gale into the group, I scattered them even as they attacked. I scooped up the otherness growing around our group and kept feeding the storm I threw at them. I hurt them, but at least they wouldn't die. Andy's second attack on the Youth Guard to our right engulfed a teen, and his frantic vibrations pierced my othersense. "Please, Andy. You're killing them."

Ben joined the attack, igniting one of the Youth Guard I had blown back. We didn't need to do this.

The Youth Guard retreated as the first of the military arrived, sending bursts of gunfire into my shields. Drawing in otherness to send a new storm deeper down the road, I swayed as the gale built.

Jimmy took my left forearm, and a moment later I found otherness swelling from him to me. "What?"

He smiled. "I've been thinking about this since you did the group healing. It worked."

My storm raged through the first soldiers, tossing them to the ground. Metal peeled off the side of one of the warehouses. I staggered from the exertion, and Dean rested a hand on my shoulder. He had his gun out.

To my right, fires had started in the dry, rotted wood that had once been a fence. Just beyond, the flames burning the admin building lit the surrounding area. Ben continued to draw otherness and heat where he thought the soldiers might be, and my storm brushed his flames in a streak. Debris around the buildings caught fire.

Using Jimmy's added strength, I cast a new storm to my left, where four soldiers had reached the corner of a building to the north. Ben and Andy followed with bursts of flame, though they couldn't see anything. Discarded boxes and crates exploded in fire as the military were sent rolling away.

"We need to leave," I pleaded with them.

Quinn growled. "Nothing to friggin' do here anyway. We'll torch the forest on the way out, Andy."

Ben ignited one of the soldiers to the left as we retreated. The screams cut into me. Gunshots started up as my storms abated, but the bullets didn't find my shield.

"We didn't need to kill them, Andy."

He didn't meet my eyes as we squeezed out through the fence. "I thought you were in danger."

"The first soldiers, not really, but possible." I stumbled down the slope to the road. "The Youth Guard, though?"

He didn't answer, and when Quinn began lighting up the woods on both sides of the fence, Andy joined in.

Dean nodded at the road ahead. "When the military attack, there will be a lot more deaths."

I swallowed my emotions, and he reached for my hand, comforting me. "I love you," he said.

"I love you, Dean." If only we could live somewhere in peace.

Tired, I jogged with Dean and Jimmy along the road. We'd freed some of the Youth Guard, but these deaths had been needless. Dean's words haunted me on the race back to the boats. There would be times when Tyrell would have my back against a wall, and I might have to kill.

We weren't pursued. Each time I glanced back, the orange glow of the flames grew larger.

When we reached Roxie and the boats, the moon shone full in the east, streaked by sooty haze. She stood on the embankment over the river, watching the horizon. "Rough, huh?"

"Didn't need to be."

"Still sticking with the plan?"

"Andy would have died if I hadn't been there." I couldn't let them go on to Camp Evrotas without me.

Chapter Seventeen

We returned to the vehicles in the middle of the night, and I must have had an awful expression.

Jural eyed me closely, and Penny shook her head. "That effing bad?"

Dean intercepted. "I'll fill you in on the ride. Grub first."

We took off as soon as we packed the newcomers into Len and Kira's van, then drove north along the route the Pahawan had recommended. Clouds played hide-and-seek with the moon as we puttered to a place called Edgefield before turning southeast.

Exhausted, I sat and scanned the area with my othersense. The Pahawan had warned us of random private compounds, all tied to the Savannah Charter.

"Crap." Roxie slowed in an area blackened by fire.

On the road before us was a cluster of burned cars, mostly shifted to one side, but there wasn't much room. This wasn't the first blockage we'd passed. Quinn left a rising cloud of dust from where he'd veered off-road.

Penny leaned in from the back. "You got this."

Jural and the two Pahawan fluttered low overhead, returning from a scouting jaunt ahead of us.

I did sense more pockets of people as we drove farther south. According to Weston, Camp Evrotas didn't sit on the edge of the cryptid zones like the others. He called the training aggressive, and Quinn didn't talk about his time there.

In the dark, we reached the house where we'd planned to rest for the night. It lay five miles away from the university grounds that housed Camp Evrotas. The biggest argument during the planning had been whether to proceed in the dark of the morning or stay out of sight for the day. Spent, I was grateful we wouldn't have to move until after a rest.

We lined the floors of the rotting, molding house. Exhausted, no one cared. Dean held me while I tried to forget the men writhing in flames.

"I don't want to do this," I whispered to him.

"Some nice places on the way here."

More than anything, I craved to be safe and quiet with him with no one around to fight. I wouldn't leave the Alliance. Not just for the security, but they offered stability in our broken world. Hope.

Even in Dean's arms, I couldn't forget the pain and death the Wolf Squad had caused. Sleep proved fitful and elusive before the sun poked through the windows and people began roving about. I finally rose to pee in the surrounding woods, avoiding greetings as much as I could.

Odie escorted me back, and Jural dropped from a perch among the trees to talk with me. "Shall we meditate today? There's plenty of time before you leave."

I opened my mouth to refuse, feeling grumpy, but our sessions often helped ease my frustrations. "That might be good, Jural. Let me grab something to drink and maybe some flatbread."

Jimmy had joined Dean, Penny, and Roxie at our vehicle, and their conversation quieted as I approached. "Jural wants to meditate," I said, reaching for the water Dean offered.

Roxie huffed. "I'd just start snoring."

Penny shrugged. "I'm in. Something to it. Even if I don't see fancy stuff like you lot." She handed me flatbread with a sparse layer of jam. "I'll let Gina and the others know."

I studied big Jimmy as I ate. "That was pretty sharp. I never would have thought that we could share otherness, like in healing."

Roxie had heard the story on the ride back from Camp Morea and turned to Jimmy as well. "Think it would work with water? Who knows when I'll be lugging a caravan of boats again, but any help would be appreciated."

"I don't know, but I don't see why it shouldn't." His southern drawl slowed his speech. "Kira works with water so you could try it with her. Dave or Cindy, but they're back at Columbia."

Isabel and Gina joined us, and I stuffed the last of the flatbread in my mouth and led the group toward Jural. We walked a distance into the woods until the house, cars, and the rest of the Wolf Squad were barely in sight.

We started as before with my simple session. Gina could still hear the hum, but couldn't progress beyond that. When I did my shield example, Jimmy tried along with Jural, though neither managed it.

I felt apprehensive as we followed Jural's toe meditation. My breath tightened as I delved into the intense sight of all the connections between people and objects.

"Caitlyn, do you have keys to one of those vehicles?" Jural asked.

My eyes nearly crossed from the complexity of lines around me, I shook my head.

Jimmy pulled out a jingling pair, and a purple thread banded from him to the keys to the cluster of vehicles by the house. I followed it, swiveling my head, to see if I could identify which one. My focus somehow traveled along the bright line to a dark vehicle rounder and larger than the Jeep.

"Ah, I can see it." My words came slowly, surprised. It appeared as if I could reach out and touch it. Nausea welled in my stomach with all the connections added to the distorted view through the forest and the vision of the vehicle up close.

"Very good. How far can you form your shields?"

I swallowed, not wanting to puke. "Around five to ten yards."

"And that car is farther than that?"

"Oh, yeah."

"Try and use your sight of it to create a shield on it."

"It's too far."

"Try."

She likely knew something I did not. Nodding, I drew in the otherness and focused on the hood that seemed within arm's reach, rather than all the various aspects. Removing the distractions eased my stomach. In only a moment, a robust shield sprang into place against the hood of the vehicle.

My mouth dropped for a second. "How did you know?" I asked.

Jural glanced at our group, as if reluctant to speak in front of them, but answered. "There are descriptions in our stories of those who could heal, or harm, using such methods. Considering your adeptness with the esse, I thought it possible and worth exploring."

"Esse?"

"What you call the otherness."

The intense focus of the surrounding Wolf Squad made me uncomfortable. "Let's go back to the meditation."

Dean and my friends said nothing about it when we returned to the group, and I busied myself meeting the newcomers and dealing with the misdirected symbolism. Andy avoided too much interaction with me, likely sensing my disappointment in his violence at the last camp. We prepared for a late afternoon departure of an eight-mile walk. As before, the Pahawan, Penny, and Odie would stay with the vehicles, along with the newcomers from Camp Morea.

The town of Aiken had not avoided wildfires, and much of the area we traveled had little more than blackened husks of buildings and younger trees. Anxiety nipped at me as I walked, imagining another bloodbath like Camp Morea or Sparta.

As the sun dropped in the west, we walked the last mile along a road that cut through a forest with a variety of trees. The air smelled fresh, and wispy white clouds streaked the sky, but my mood stole the brightness of it.

"Weston and Quinn both swear there is barely any military presence." On my right side, Roxie caught my eye as she spoke.

Unlike the other camps, the army had set up Evrotas at a college, a school of sorts. "Why would they lie?" I asked.

I walked with Dean holding my hand, while Jimmy and Gina took the outer edges of our group. Dean just snorted.

Roxie tilted her head in a shrug. "This whole camp seems odd. You picking up anything?"

Despite having walked through a nearly pristine neighborhood of houses, I'd only picked up half a dozen compounds where people had gathered. "I've got a small group in the direction of the college, but no patrols." So far, it fit what Quinn and Weston had described.

As the forest ended at an intersection across from fields of younger growth, where I could easily sense the Youth Guard barracks, Quinn changed the plan. "Roxie and Lorabelle here," he said.

Dean raised an eyebrow. "Kira?"

"No, she'll remain with Weston, Len, and me."

"Why?" asked Jimmy.

"Cause I friggin' said so." He challenged me with a glare, but his group would be the closest to the barracks, and Kira worked with water best, not fire.

Jimmy checked to see if I'd argue, then frowned. He had a steady nature and seemed to like firm plans.

The wider road we turned onto had clusters of cars pushed to the sides, so we kept to the tall grass, though we could be spotted. I found only three groups of humans. Eight people in what I guessed to be the admin building based on the map, only a couple dozen Youth Guards in their barracks, and another dozen south of that in what I assumed was a school, though I couldn't determine ages.

Quinn's next change came when he had a clear view of the college under the colored clouds of the setting sun. "Andy and Gina, here," he said.

None of us asked why Len hadn't been included as we planned.

"There are people on the upper floor of the barracks," I said. "We'll want to keep out of sight for the next part."

"So, everybody crouch?" Dean asked.

"Probably best," I agreed.

"You should be fine standing, Quinn." He smirked at Quinn's huff.

To the east lay the barracks, a dark, two-story structure with a wide parking lot in front of it. A stand of trees lined the west edge where I, Dean, and Jimmy would wait to send those we rescued across the road to Andy and Gina. I'd been happy with the arrangement, especially after working with Jimmy on air. Anyone attempting to approach I could toss back along open pavement while hidden in the trees.

Tall poles dotted the parking lot, but I didn't find a single car. The lack of patrols seemed unnatural, but we were far from any cryptid zone or people.

Quinn left us with his oversized group and headed for a tree-shrouded building just to the right of the barracks. None of the Youth Guard appeared to react to our presence. He planned on going inside to gather the six that he and Weston believed were potential Wolf Squad recruits.

Dean wrapped me in his arms and pulled me against him. "Let's hope he doesn't muck this up."

I considered arguing that Andy had been the cause last time, but did worry. "Yeah. I've been more worried that Tyrell would be prepared for us. Our raids on the Youth Guard have to be obvious."

During the planning, despite the promised lack of military, Dean and Penny had been sure we'd find a force here. They'd wanted Tika along just for that contingency, but she'd refused. She still hadn't gotten over the damage she'd caused at Camp Sparta.

In the othersense, I followed Quinn inside the barracks, where he met with one of the Youth Guard, and surprisingly left without incident. I tracked him back to his group and checked the area.

"I think we're going to be okay." I exhaled and leaned in against Dean. The growing shadows were cool but not cold.

"Nothing is easy," Dean murmured.

His words kept me uneasy, even when the first escapee trotted out of the barracks and made for the empty building among the trees. I stiffened when I found only one of the five waiting there. "Crap. What is he up to?"

Dean stiffened. "What?"

I found four of our people, Quinn and Ben's rhythm's I could identify among them, running south of their supposed post toward what I assumed was the school. "I think they're going to try and free the kids at the school."

Chapter Eighteen

I imagined Quinn killing the teachers, or rather having Ben torch them. They might have planned the attack on the lab all along. "We have to stop them."

Jimmy put his hand on my shoulder. "You two go. I'll cover this position. The first rescued teen I send out will have a message for Andy to return to help me. We'll be watching for you to come back."

Dean just grunted and kept pace as I ran, stumbling on the uneven ground hidden in the high grass until we got to cracked asphalt. The drive circled to the front of the building, where the first escapee had just left.

A young teen, as blonde as myself, paused when she saw us speeding toward her, but I just pointed back toward Jimmy. "Go, get to Jimmy." My heart raced, mixed with exertion and panic. I couldn't handle another round of murders.

Quinn and the other three had reached the building and slowed, creeping around the far, southern side of the structure. In a hasty sweep of othersense, I found a second rescued Youth Guard running toward the sole member of the Wolf Squad stationed where Quinn was supposed to be.

No one else vibrated with any extraordinary concern, and no hidden troops moved in to intercept us.

We kept to the asphalt, looping in front of the building with the trees and onto another broad, empty parking lot. Across it, a building with a peaked roof had a tree with white blossoms in front. Quinn and his group had stopped, but I heard no otherness called.

"I think they're breaking in," I panted to Dean.

The building became more defined as we drew closer. A lower set of windows hinted at it stretching down a slope, as if built into a hill. The sides were speckled, made of brick.

Otherness rang out from inside. In one window, a white electric light flashed on. I stumbled, flailing to keep my balance.

Other than Vinnie's compound, only one building I knew had electricity: a lab.

Chills shivered down my back as Dean pulled at my arm to help me up. My muscles sagged. "It's a lab, Dean."

"Are we clear?" His calm, no-nonsense tone helped me focus.

I winced, pushing up to my knees as I scanned with the othersense. Five of the Camp Evrotas Youth Guard had crept out to the Wolf Squad, and the only excited vibrations in the rhythms came from inside the building in front of me and those escaping away from it. "Yes, I think."

Memories of electric shocks, needles, and queasy drugs flooded my mind. I didn't want to go inside. Quinn and the others had already killed two of the people in the lab, and a third rippled with pain.

Dean didn't push me but kept pace as I found a step within me, then a second. I had to focus. The road sloped down and around to the front of the building, so I stared there.

A side door opened close to us, and we both froze. A boy, perhaps ten years old, ran out wearing the familiar white gown of the labs. Silver glinted at his neck from a collar. When he saw us, a hint of otherness growled, then faded as he ran.

"Wait," I called, but he just sprinted faster than my shocked brain could think.

"He's free," Dean whispered.

An alarm sounded from inside.

"He's not," I whispered. The claxon had sounded in my childhood, and resurfaced in my nightmares. The braying noise tightened my chest.

In my othersense, I caught the rising vibrations of the Youth Guard in the barracks, as well as others at the admin building. Inside the lab, the last of the active rhythms, outside of Quinn and his cohorts, were snuffed out. My emotions fought between disgust and satisfaction. I hated those who worked at the labs, but couldn't have killed them.

I drew in a long breath. Quinn and his people didn't need my help, and the children had escaped, though collared. The Wolf Squad needed me more.

None of the Youth Guard had left the barracks to race to the rescue; they would have had as much love for the scientists or techs at the labs as I did. In my othersense, three rhythms emerged from the admin at a run, heading for the labs; soldiers, I assumed.

"Let's go back." My tone lacked any emotion as I lumbered into a return jog across the parking lot.

"And Quinn?" Dean asked as he kept an easy pace beside me.

"I'm done trying to protect him."

My dull shock hardened to anger as I ran. The alarm continued to ring from the labs behind us, but only the three from the admin approached Quinn and his team still in the building. Ahead, Jimmy, Andy, and the lone member of Quinn's post, Kira, wide-eyed and abashed, stood with them.

"Did you know what they planned?" I asked her between two breaths.

"No. Are they —"

I shook my head. "They slipped out before the soldiers got there." Waving a tired hand past the woods, I continued. "Let's go."

She gave one glance behind me, then followed Andy and Jimmy plodding through the grass. The moon would rise soon in the east. We picked up Gina on the way to Roxie, and Dean explained in his concise manner.

I didn't pause when we reached Roxie and Lorabelle with the six rescued teens from Camp Evrotas. Waving for them to follow, I turned onto the wooded road that would begin our eight-mile hike back to the vehicles. I'd wait for Quinn and his mob there. We'd leave tonight with the moonlight to guide us.

We might make it to Columbia by morning, and I couldn't find any emotion in me about the return.

Chapter Nineteen

I sensed Quinn and the others approaching as I sat in the Jeep, stewing in my anger.

Their laughing comments as they greeted the others made me close my eyes. They'd murdered the scientists and lab techs. Part of my anger came from my own ambivalent emotions over that.

Waiting for them to settle into the vehicles to leave, I startled when Penny spoke at my window. "You're going to effing want to hear this," she said.

The moon shone bright and full on the back area where Quinn had gathered many of the Wolf Squad around a map spread on the hood of his Jeep. Kira and Gina appeared uneasy as I drew near.

Weston spoke. "I was only there a single night when they were building the camp. They had started by refitting a sawmill with barracks. The military didn't have any presence at all. It'll be easy pickings. Easier than tonight." A number of the group laughed.

Quinn noticed me and ignored me. "Most of the Youth Guard here are considered the rebellious or unteachable, so we might end up with more than we can fit. We've got six seats, eight if they're small."

They were talking about going to Camp Taygetos, which we'd dismissed in the planning as too deep into Savannah Charter territory. Besides, transportation had been a concern. He'd likely get us killed.

I hadn't realized I was shaking with anger until Dean rested his hand on my shoulder. From his other side, Jimmy watched me, concerned.

"No," I said, surprised at the firmness in my tone.

Quinn regarded me from his place at the map. "You're the one who said you weren't in charge."

His statement felt like a punch to the stomach. I'd done this.

Weston smiled in earnest. "We could use your help, Caitlyn. It'd be safer for all of us if you came with."

"She'd probably only feel safer if her crew leads the new people back to friggin' Columbia." Quinn's grin held a malicious twist. "Back to her Duathua friends, while we take care of business."

I searched the faces of the others surrounding the map. Jimmy and Andy would leave with us, maybe Gina. Most of the Wolf Squad would risk themselves. It was my fault for refusing to lead. I'd let Quinn be in charge with Ben and Weston, and the "success" of our past two raids had them ready to take risks at the last camp.

The best I could hope for was to get the new recruits back to Columbia. I wouldn't abandon the others to Quinn's foolishness. "Send the newcomers back to Columbia. I'll go with you."

Dean squeezed my shoulder. "No regrets, love," he whispered.

Yaz was in Camp Taygetos, supposedly.

Thirty minutes later, while Len led the van and a large

truck north, we took the worst route possible, straight up I-20, the one route the Pahawan had warned us the army frequently used. As if an omen, Andy had a tire blow out, and he crashed with Gina into one of the many stalled cars that lined the side of the road.

Isabel worked with me on healing Gina's sprained wrist while Quinn grouched about the delay.

"You think this is a bad idea?" asked Isabel.

"We have no one who knows the camp, it's close to where Tyrell has been massing his army transports for the attack, and the area is populated with people who support the Savannah Charter. Yes. I do." My tone came out sharper than I intended.

"Weston's been there," she offered.

"A single day, weeks ago."

"Their plan sounded good."

"Hardly a plan. Weston wakes up one kid and hopes they know who wants to join the Wolf Squad. What if it's the wrong kid, and they attack him or set off an alarm? Each time, we've had a list of sure people to rescue. This is sloppy."

Isabel remained silent as we finished our healing of Gina.

As we headed back to our Jeep, Dean grabbed my hand. "It'll work out. I love you."

"Even when I'm grumpy?"

"Mostly when you're grumpy."

I forced myself not to smile.

We survived the almost two-hour trip along I-20 with the moon hiding occasionally behind clouds and took an exit at Wire Road east of the Jones Crossing ramp. Wildfires had taken a long section of woods, but I still sensed compounds of people living in scattered areas.

Quinn and Weston pulled our caravan into the yard of

a house caved under a fallen tree. Unlike the low fields around it, scattered woods offered some cover. Camp Taygetos lay southeast of us with over three dozen sleeping there, and no patrols.

Leaving Roxie with Penny and the Duathua, we headed for the camp with only a sketch of a plan where to stage ourselves. The low growth in the field behind the house made it difficult to have clear guideposts for the potentially rescued Youth Guard. Kira, Isabel, and Lorabelle waited beside a taller sapling that we hoped would be visible.

Dean, Jimmy, and I took a spot at the edge of the woods so that Quinn and his group could direct them close enough. I'd pick them up in my othersense if nothing else.

When I sat down to wait, Dean dropped behind me and leaned against my back. "Almost done."

"Until Tyrell attacks."

"There's that."

I followed Quinn's group to their stop where Weston split off, leaving Andy, Ben, and Kira with the squat tyrant. The rhythms at the barracks remained quiet.

"He's inside," I said. "Let's see how this goes."

Surprisingly, Weston woke one of the Youth Guard quickly with seemingly no hesitation. I leaned forward, forcing Dean to straighten.

Two others rose in quick succession and then two more, before three of them joined Weston, heading back to Quinn and the others.

"That was quick." I stood, stretching tired muscles. My othersense still showed no patrols around us.

Dean watched me as I faced the direction of the camp. "All good?"

As he spoke, the otherness rang out from the direction of the camp and I grimaced. "Crap."

"What?" Dean reached for his weapon at his side.

Through the woods, lightning crackled, and the rhythms from both groups flared. The Youth Guard who were with Weston burned. Their pain vibrated from the lightning attack. Weston alone had been unharmed.

I sucked in a breath as one of the Wolf Squad's vibrations, that I recognized, dimmed in death. My hand reached for Dean's shoulder as I swayed. "Gina!"

Chapter Twenty

I ran into the woods, bringing Dean and Jimmy toward the danger.

Camp Taygetos had become a beehive of activity. My heart skipped when four gunshots sounded: a pair followed by two more in a distinct rhythm.

Quinn had turned to flee back to us, Weston followed, and Ben only hesitated a moment before they raced from the erupting camp. Andy remained with Gina.

"Run, Andy," I growled as we continued toward him.

I heard his otherness as he screamed, "Wolf Squad!"

Fire shone through the trees, though I couldn't tell what burned. The Youth Guard exiting the closest building scattered.

When Andy finally turned to leave Gina behind, I slowed. I couldn't save her. I blamed Quinn, but I should have accepted the responsibility for not taking the lead in the first place.

When Dean laid his hand on my shoulder and spoke, I flinched. "What's the situation?"

"Gina's dead. The rest are heading back. The camp is chasing them, mostly." It seemed, once again, that Andy's

rally cry had created some dissension in the ranks, as otherness sounded from the camp and rhythms vibrated in pain.

Weston led the group racing out of the forest toward us.
Quinn and Ben followed, sharp with pain in my othersense.

Dean nudged me gently. "Let's go."

When Quinn saw me, he scowled and said something to
Ben. They turned, drawing in the otherness. Fire erupted in
the forest between Andy and Camp Taygetos. It wouldn't
stop the pursuit, and the damage to the Wolf Squad had
been done.

We had to get to the vehicles and leave. I pinpointed
Isabel, Kira, and Lorabelle and led the way toward them.
Their sharp rhythms vibrated in concern, but they hadn't
left their position. I pushed out my othersense to scan an
alarmed Roxie, Penny, and Odie by the vehicles.

"What happened?" Jimmy asked behind me.

Weston answered shakily. "I — I don't know. They just
attacked."

"You were sure about them?" Jimmy's tone, always a bit
deep, sounded forceful.

"Yes. No. They seemed excited. I made a mistake."

My anger focused on Quinn and me, not Weston. The
plan sucked from the beginning. I circled my othersense to
the camp, where a full riot appeared to be in play between
the Youth Guard inside the barracks. *Yaz. Gina.*

We were almost on Kira's group. "Run! Back!" I yelled.
"Go to the cars!"

I widened my othersense, beyond Camp Taygetos. A
trail of tight clusters moved faster than someone running.

"Dean?"

"Yeah?"

"We're in trouble." I spoke quietly, huffing from the run.
"I think there are soldiers coming."

"On the road?"

"Yeah."

"Will we make the vehicles? Never mind. How many?"

It took me a moment to focus and parse out the rhythms. "Twenty-four." I pushed out my othersense to the max. "More behind that. I can't count at that range."

The vehicles moved faster than we did. The Youth Guard who had recently learned to drive crept along carefully, except for Quinn. We couldn't hope to beat them in a race on the roads. Weeds whipping at my legs, I ran faster.

By the time we dove into the small woods behind the crushed house, the military were driving almost parallel to us. The drone of their engines carried from our right. I hadn't studied the map well. We likely had a little over a minute before they came down the road from which we'd arrived.

"We're trapped," I said to Dean.

Jimmy spoke with ease. "We can link. I've talked with Len. Quinn left."

I spoke single words between pants. "Over two dozen."

The Pahawan and Jural fluttered at the tops of the trees, watching the east. Roxie had the Jeep running, but I continued past, pointing in the direction that I sensed the military.

"Jural, get out of here," I yelled. The Duathua were vulnerable against gunfire. She nodded, fished in her pouch, and tossed me her crystalline fish. I understood; they would find me.

The Wolf Squad slowed, unsure, when I didn't head for the Jeep. I gave Jimmy a frantic nod. We'd have to try to hold them back. Perhaps we'd have a chance. If we drove, they'd follow us with automatic weapons and better drivers.

Andy, ashen faced and grim, jogged up to us, eyes wild. Ben appeared behind him just as pale, but more scared than angry.

"Andy. Ben." A little fire might be needed.

Dean circled to the Jeep, but I knew we had a rifle in the back.

As I reached the asphalt out front, headlights turned onto our road far ahead. Drawing in a shaky breath, I held out my right arm to reach Jimmy and began to pull in a roar of otherness; his power joined mine.

On the left side of the road, the woods continued along the edge, and on the right, low shrubs had overgrown a field or lawn. Visible over the tops of the bushes, the string of headlights leading to the intersection seemed to go on forever. With Jimmy's added power, I reached for the air closest to the intersection, twisting it into a tornado. Malformed, it still blasted one of the vehicles off course to veer out of sight.

I drew a shield in front of us.

"Quinn and Weston are leaving," Andy said, his voice dull.

I could hear the engine and sense them driving away.

Penny dropped to her stomach on the dirt beside the asphalt, her rifle already sighted. Dean slid in beside her.

Mustering another cyclone of white sand from the distant intersection, I flipped a vehicle into the path of another. Not all the cars tried to turn toward us, though. A pair continued forward, ignoring the turn in our direction; perhaps they would circle back around to us.

Worse, three had veered off the road before the intersection and drove across fields on our right side where I couldn't see.

Penny's rifle cracked.

Based on the clusters of the closest rhythms, I'd left two vehicles crashed at the intersection, two had continued northwest, three were driving in fields to my right, and the last two had clipped the corner of the intersection and cut across grass toward our road. I caught one of those with a broad tornado and sent them spilling to the side.

Gunshots were coming in, and Dean and Penny returned them. If we disabled the soldiers' vehicles, we might be able to drive away.

Absently, I searched for the second cluster I'd sensed behind the first. They'd disappeared from my othersense. My heart skipped in panic.

"Where are they?" I whispered. Quinn and Weston had already turned north. I should have sent Roxie to follow with Isabel, Kira, and Lorabelle.

Jimmy cocked his head but said nothing.

I already drew otherness for the pair of headlights that had nearly reached the road. The vehicle kicked up white dust in the moonlight, obliterating visibility behind it. Penny and Dean continued to trade gunfire with our pursuers across the darkness. Of the two dozen soldiers, only three rhythms spiked in pain, and those were in the vehicles I'd crashed.

My energy sagging, I caught another vehicle at an opportune moment when it rose up an incline, and my weak tornado flipped it. While the three vehicles to my right aimed for just behind the crushed house, soldiers spread out to approach on foot. In the darkness I couldn't see them, but I sensed them.

"Fire up the woods on the left side of the road." Bolstering the shield in front of us, which already held a scattering of enemy bullets, I pointed for Andy. Ben, who'd joined him, stood ready despite fresh lightning burns on his ear and neck.

Andy snarled. "Let's do it."

I hated the idea of a wildfire raging out of control, but I had to protect the remaining Wolf Squad.

Thinking of Yaz and Gina, I scanned toward the camp.

As I feared, about ten Youth Guard were running toward our location. I still hadn't found the missing soldiers, either.

Fire bloomed both low at the base of the trunks and high in the canopy about fifty yards down the road.

Weariness heavy on my shoulders, I drew in otherness and began forming a cyclone just ahead of the closest vehicle to my right. They moved slower in the fields, but still veered when I hit. I sagged slightly when they continued on.

The soldiers wouldn't stop, and the Youth Guard would be upon us soon. Sighing, I scanned wide again for the missing military.

"Crap." I found them.

Chapter Twenty-One

"They're coming in behind us!" I yelled, gesturing south down the road.

Jimmy shifted, but Ben and Andy spun around. I took an involuntary step as if I might search with them or escape this trap.

I spoke loudly, over the gunfire. "Dean, Penny." When they glanced over, I gestured toward the crushed house. "Get Roxie and the others north into the woods. Don't stop. We'll be following."

Ben gave me a startled stare, but Jimmy nodded, his firm grip on my arm.

Dean studied me, and I pleaded with my eyes. Penny had already rolled back and jumped into a run, calling to Roxie. We had a couple of minutes before a new force of four vehicles raced down the road to pin us down.

Once Dean headed away with the others and they were crossing the road behind me, I nudged my head toward the house, woods, and our vehicles. "Andy, Ben. Torch it. We're going to retreat into the woods with the shield." Focusing, I created a semicircle around us and backed up one pace.

Andy smiled somewhat darkly, though his response seemed more like him. "Super."

Fire blossomed along the trees and house, then spread inside the Jeep we'd driven.

I looked south along the road. "Something down there, as far as you can muster."

Smoke from the first fire I'd had them set hazed the area to the north, and as I led us off the road, the gunfire stopped. I could sense them trying to pinch us in. "Let's go. Run."

I pulled out of Jimmy's grasp and waited as he followed Andy and Ben. Our Jeep exploded, and in my othersense, the Youth Guard slowed their approach. The three military vehicles still ambling forward only shifted their directions by degrees. I intended to leave them with nothing to follow.

The firelight and bright moon lit the woods well, and some wider trails wound between trees, leaving only small brush and vines to fight through. The sharp stench of burning forests bit at my nose when I inhaled. I let us race deeper for about thirty yards before slowing.

"Can you hit the edge of the woods where we just came in?" I asked Andy.

He grinned and failed to quote Dean in a gruff voice. "Never gets easy." It seemed he was attempting to push aside the grief, but it came out awkwardly.

As he and Ben pointed to signal each other, they created a series of well-spaced fires. Already, the flames consuming the crushed house rose high in the night sky.

I pointed to the northeast. "Same distance there?"

Their expression turned more serious as they lit those fires. I was boxing us in. With soldiers on foot moving in from that direction, I continued to have them light fires in the northeast after another thirty paces. The air was thickening with smoke, darkening the woods.

Keeping the moon on our right, I let Jimmy lead the way

as he cleared some of the worst vines. The military circled behind us, avoiding the fires. Some drove south of us, others returned to the road they'd come in on. The chasing Youth Guard moved away from the growing inferno.

Though not focused ahead, I still felt the spikes of the rhythms in that direction as a gunshot rang out, then a second. I focused on Dean as his rhythm shot up, then began to slow. I gasped, thinking for a moment he might be dying.

Penny's pace hesitated at the front of the group, then turned sharply west. Roxie followed with the other Wolf Squad members, while Dean brought up the rear, moving slower with each step.

Far to the east, two soldiers trotted in pursuit.

Dean wasn't hurt, not badly at least. Pain didn't vibrate in him. However, something was wrong.

I sprang toward him, nearly going down, but pushed past Jimmy. "Hang back," I said.

Penny, Roxie, and the others were gaining distance from Dean as he continued to slow. The soldiers drew closer.

I burst out of the woods into a smoky field of tall grass and low shrubs. A faded metal barn lay in front of us. Beyond, another boxy shape proved to be a trailer as I ran closer.

Dean's rhythms stilled as if unconscious, and he stopped moving about thirty yards ahead of me. The soldiers had reached him. My teeth ground as I sprinted around the trailer.

Dressed in dull black, they appeared as mere silhouettes lifting a limp Dean between them. Fifty feet from them I staggered to a walk and drew in the otherness.

One raised a revolver, and I slammed a shield in front of me, while my pace never faltered. Rage boiled in my chest.

Both men fired dark bullets into the thick shield in front

of me. Shining black specks embedded the air, moving steadily with me. I drew in more otherness with each step. They could not have Dean. I would kill them first.

I chose the man on the right. Wrapping a tight shield about his head, I trapped him inside it. He reacted in a spike of vibrating panic, and I enjoyed it. He dropped his weapon to claw at the hardened air with one hand. Eventually, he released Dean and pried with both.

The other soldier continued firing. He bore Dean's weight but couldn't move.

I wrapped his head as well in a suffocating shield. Speaking with each step, I watched him drop my love and scramble away. "You — can't — have him."

The first writhed on the ground; the second stumbled from me. Their rhythms slowed. They would die.

They deserve to die for attacking Dean.

The two soldiers, adults, were helpless against me. They'd dropped their hand weapons, and their rifles tangled about them as they suffocated.

I gasped, fighting my rage. *I'm not a murderer.*

With a grimace, I released all my shields. One of my victims lay unconscious while the other knelt and raised his hands in surrender, choking.

I staggered the last few steps to kneel at Dean's side, my body trembling with rage and relief battling for my emotions. Laying my hand on his chest, I forced myself to keep from crumbling on top of him. They almost had him again. Would we ever be safe?

Ben stepped up beside me. "Want me to kill them?" he asked.

"No. Get their weapons." I put my hands on Dean's face, checking him with my healing and trying to push the drugs away. Ben had hardened to something dark, and I'd nearly followed him. Eric and I were only supposed to be healers; he'd been killed, and I'd — changed.

Dean didn't wake, not yet. He would. Jimmy leaned down beside me. "We got to go. I'll carry him."

I shook when I tried to stand, and let Jimmy raise me with one hand under my arm.

Andy's pale face studied me. "Where are the others?"

Using othersense, I found the Wolf Squad to the northwest and soldiers to the east hunting for us. I pointed toward Roxie and Penny. "That way." Turning around, I glared in the direction of the approaching enemy. "Can you two set the far edge of this field on fire? We've got more company coming."

We didn't move very quickly with Dean slung over Jimmy's shoulder, but the fire spreading to a glowing horizon behind us kept even those soldiers at a safe distance. At one point, we walked beside the road they'd been using, and then crossed to keep our northerly direction. I couldn't sense a single soldier.

An hour later, with smoke and clouds shading the moon, Dean finally woke. "Let me down, oaf."

When Jimmy complied, Dean folded under his own weight. I knelt beside him. "Groggy?"

"Hear the drums in my head out there?" He smiled toward Jimmy. "I should have stayed on your shoulder."

Jimmy grunted, offering his arms.

"Probably." I leaned my forehead against his. "You had me scared."

"Two darts. How far did I get? What happened?"

Ben sounded proud. "She suffocated both at fifty feet. Something to see."

I closed my eyes and whispered. "I almost murdered them. Why won't they let us be?"

Dean kissed me lightly. "No regrets. Speaking of, help me up."

I didn't like the way he swayed. "Okay?"

"Yeah. Rifle?"

Ben patted the strap on his shoulder.

We moved slower at first, until Dean got his legs, but the forest thickened, binding us with vines. A dirt road leading north helped, and when the moon dropped from our sight, the Duathua found us.

They brought water. With guides for the trip back to Columbia, it only took us half a day's walk to get to near Lake Murray, where a van driven by one of the Alliance picked us up with water and food.

We'd survived a disastrous raid on the last of the camps. I found it hard to believe we'd lost Gina. *Yaz.*

Tyrell's troops would come soon.

Chapter Twenty-Two

After sleeping twelve hours, I stayed in my room mourning Gina until Nur and Jural came to visit. Then I descended into the mayhem that had taken over the Wolf Den. Mattresses lined most areas for the newcomers in both houses. Wolf Squad who I barely recognized greeted and thanked me. Fawn and Tika started to follow me, until Roxie whispered to them.

The air stunk of people needing baths. I was one.

Standing outside the front of the house, the Duathua brought looks through the windows. The sun shone late in the day from a rich blue sky. Roxie and Dean accompanied me, since they'd been the ones to rouse me from my self-pity.

"Good morning, Nur, Jural."

"Seyir," Nur said. "I've come to warn you."

My heart sank, expecting news of Tyrell's army outside the city. "So soon?"

Nur twitched, in a decidedly Duathua expression of confusion, then spoke. "The Elders have agreed to allow petitions to you for those who wish to return, as Wati did. Jural believes it is safe."

If I'd been more energized, I might have glared at them both. "And if I don't want to?"

"That is your decision, of course."

I glanced up and down the quiet street, half expecting to see a crowd of Duathua lined up. "I've had a rough couple of days."

Jural smiled. "Perhaps some meditation?"

I thought of the nauseating complexity of connections and shook my head. "I'd prefer some peanut butter and honey lemonade."

She glanced at Nur. "I'll ask about those."

Chuckling, I believed she might find them. My tone drew somber. "I lost someone I cared about, watched people do horrible things, and nearly murdered people. I just need a day or two to sort out my head. A bath too; I need a bath."

Dean slipped his hand in mine a squeezed. We needed a little time to maybe read or cuddle.

As I hoped that there wouldn't be a line of Duathua anytime soon, two Pahawan crested the trees behind Nur and Jural and dropped toward us.

They landed with grace, glass tridents tucked under their arms. "Seyirs, Grandmother," said one. "We've been sent to collect you. All three of you."

"For what purpose?" Nur asked.

"An ambassador has approached the Alliance." The Pahawan turned to me. "They asked for you specifically, Seyir Caitlyn."

"Me?" I squeaked. The vague memory of the man we'd tied up drifted in my memories of all that had happened over the past week. "Oh." Darker thoughts of them trying to trade me and Dean for peace crossed my mind, but I didn't believe the Alliance would consider that.

"We can take you there now, Seyir." The Pahawan seemed serious.

"You mean fly me there?"

"Yes. We can keep very low, if you'd like."

I can't say I hadn't imagined what it would be like to flit about, but carried didn't sound comfortable. "I really need a bath."

"The ambassador is here *now*, Seyir. Elders of both races are with him."

The part of me that wanted to curl up and hide lost to growing curiosity and even hope. A portion of my mood stemmed from an army targeting Columbia. "Okay. I warned you about the smell."

I wore my original coveralls from Camp Sparta with the sleeves removed and Tika's intricate embroidery patching the holes. Each Pahawan grabbed an armpit with Kudaru gauntlets, and the wind from their wings blew my hair into my face. They lifted me no higher than I might be if riding Bella, but we skimmed the road at a significant speed. On another day, after a bath, I might have enjoyed it.

We cruised right up to the doors of the Alliance meeting hall, and a crowd packed much of the room. Most were humans, but Duathua stood there as well. Nur and Jural landed with us, but motioned me inside first.

The hall buzzed with a quiet murmur, and most ignored me as I entered but moved quickly enough when I shouldered through with apologies. A ripple in the people ahead of me created room before I arrived. Men in long sleeves, women in tank tops or dresses, all seemed to recognize me, though I knew none of their faces.

Half a dozen Duathua and the same number of humans stood on the dais, similar to any Alliance meeting, except for the visitor. None of the people there spoke. Cups and a pitcher waited on the table, but no one sat or drank. I recognized Henweyay and a couple of the others.

I'd hoped for Higgins, the little bald guy, but instead a

tall thin man in a gray jacket and pants stood with an arrogant expression at the table. His pinched face turned to study me as I worked through the crowd. He spoke when I reached the steps of the dais. "Caitlyn, leader of the rebel Youth Guard?"

"My name's Caitlyn, yes." I had no interest in discussing leadership or rebellion.

"I've been waiting. I can begin now that all parties are here." He turned back toward the table.

Henweyay motioned me to step up, which left me awkwardly beside the man.

"Jared Fenrick. I represent the Savannah Charter in these negotiations. Our terms of peace are simple. Our government intends to hold the prior states of Georgia and South Carolina against the cryptid threat. The liberation of Columbia is essential to this. In exchange for your immediate surrender, the Youth Guard, including Caitlyn, will be repatriated into their camps, the Duathua will be given their own camps to live peacefully within, and the humans will surrender their weapons and join the workforce toward the common good." The nasty man regarded me like a cockroach that had come too close. "Dean Valdina will surrender himself to the military for transportation to the labs."

I hoped I stunk worse than I thought I did as I stepped up to Jared Fenrick. "Dean's not going to a lab. You can't have him."

"You would have thousands of your people die for one werewolf?" The man sneered.

My heart skipped, suddenly unsure if everyone else on the dais would support me. We'd run if we had to. Surely the Duathua wouldn't agree. We could leave with them.

One of the Alliance humans, a tall woman with squared

shoulders and short blonde hair, tilted her head and stared at Jared. "We would die for freedom. For everyone."

He spun toward her. "These creatures have affected — controlled — your minds. They aren't human."

She chuckled. "We noticed; the wings were a hint. See, Henweyay there saved me and my boy from the Oni long before we reached Columbia. What you call control, we call friendship. It is what people do; help each other."

A heavy man with a gray beard down his chest nodded his head. "We don't lock up our children and kill those who don't want to be a part of the Alliance. We will fight you." He looked out to the hall of attendees, and they responded with a murmur of agreement.

I wanted to cry at the big man's words. It grew hard some days not to blame my time at the labs on my parents.

Jared straightened. "You'll die."

Another of the humans, a woman with a pitch black braid, raised a hand and scanned the other Alliance members. "Please bring back to your government a counteroffer. Leave Columbia to the Alliance, a one-hundred-mile radius from this location, and we can establish trade between our two peoples. Our ability to forge simple metal items will be a useful commodity. Your military can be better spent protecting your borders from the Oni and werewolves."

With a snort, Jared shook his head. "In time, these Duathua will turn on you. They've already enslaved you. We know you outnumber them. Rejoin humanity. When our army arrives, all you need do is not resist. Our new arsenal will decimate the Duathua and free you all."

"Why did you come here?" I asked.

He seemed surprised at my question. "To offer peace."

"No. This is the same liberation they taught us at

school. Higgins seemed to have a different viewpoint. He could actually conceive of cooperation."

"That fool has been silenced." Jared's chin lifted, as if he hadn't intended to say what he had. His lips twitched.

I remembered Higgins's comments about Tyrell's power. "So not everyone in the Savannah Charter agrees with Tyrell, and you were sent to ease the situation back home, not negotiate. You can go back and say the Alliance refused, so that war is justified."

His glare told me I'd hit close to the truth, so I pushed. "When you're not parading as an ambassador, what is your position?"

"I'm not answering a girl."

The big man with the beard coughed. "I'd be interested to know who they sent as well. Unless it's too embarrassing."

Jared's pinched nostrils flared. "I'm the chief accountant at the quartermaster's office, not some farmer."

The blonde woman laughed. "I'm a farmer. Biggest coop of chickens, too. I didn't think they still had use for a pencil pusher. But it reads about right, now that you admit it."

I wasn't sure why someone would push pencils, but I appreciated the way her comment blustered Jared.

Staring above them, he spoke in a clipped tone. "These negotiations are done. There will be no peace. Escort me back now."

Two Pahawan at the bottom of the dais stepped forward, their Kudaru boots clicking on the floor. Jared glared at them but stepped down.

The hall opened a path, but angry murmurs grumbled as the ambassador for the Savannah Charter passed by. I trembled, unsettled by the entire conversation.

The big man studied me. "Who's Higgins?"

I grimaced. "At Camp Mystras, we got caught by a man, not military. A minister of some department. We tied him up before we left. He said the military never let any of the Duathua ambassadors through. Tyrell holds some sort of power over the government. It sounded like not everyone agreed with the war. They certainly don't understand the Alliance."

The blonde woman scoffed. "So the military sent us someone who might appear like a non-combatant as an ambassador, but he's still in Tyrell's pocket. Doesn't seem to help us."

Henweyay spoke after being notably quiet during the entire proceeding. "I understand the Wolf Squad has grown to over thirty Seyir. Jural speaks most highly of your success. How is training proceeding?"

I sagged. "The last day has been a little rough."

Henweyay glanced at some of the others. "Our time appears limited. We caught one of their scouts on the bridge. I-20. We believe they'll attack there."

"I'll get back to it, then." I forced a smile, pausing only long enough to nod to the other members. No one stopped me before I turned to leave.

I'd have to organize those I could into training. Jimmy's new linking would have to be tested. A few, Ben and Weston at least, I believed would stick close to Quinn, but I wouldn't fight over control of the Wolf Squad.

Chapter Twenty-Three

As the Alliance members began discussing logistics for the war, I reached the back, where Nur and Jural listened beside the two Pahawan who'd flown me there.

Jural tilted her head. "Very well-spoken, Caitlyn."

"He was a dick."

She paused. "I might be misinterpreting that. Perhaps slang?"

"Yeah, slang." I shifted for the door, as it seemed Jural and Nur were intent on listening to the Alliance.

"It seems we have problems in the east as well. The Oni have set their human slaves to building bridges. The Pahawan have been busy these past couple of days as well."

I blinked, unsure how to consider the statement. *Slaves?* With a shiver, I waved off the two Pahawan. "I'll walk." I needed a moment alone.

The blue sky with white puffy clouds felt too cheery as I stepped outside. Some of the Alliance had moved to the open air to talk in groups, but no one gave me a second glance. I watched my footsteps as I kicked the dim shadow I cast from the overhead sun. The warmth baked the earth, teasing rich scents of growth and life from the grass and brush.

Candy?

I lifted my nose to trace the aroma and nearly tripped when I caught Moonjir walking a step behind my left shoulder.

"What are you doing?"

Exaggerating, he extended a large furry foot as he stepped. "Managing not to fall, it seems."

I relaxed, almost surprised to see him after what seemed so long, though it had only been days. "Should have expected you."

"Horrors. What have I done to become predictable?" His eyebrows, pale against blue, pink-tipped fur, rose high and questioning.

I chuckled. "What sage words have you brought me?"

"You've got all the words you need." He shrugged. "Learned a few tricks while I was off, despite some rather unusual bad luck."

Stiffening, I thought of Gina and the Youth Guard who had killed her. We were trying to rescue them. "That wasn't luck. We were betrayed."

"Indeed. Have you decided?"

"Decided what?" I snapped.

"Popcorn or gummy bears? What goes best with a movie?" He snorted at his gibberish as if it made some humorous sense. "Who's in charge of the Wolf Squad?"

"I'll lead them; for the battle."

"All of them?"

"Some might choose otherwise. Their call."

"A powerful move. True and faithful arising to the trumpet's call. A symbol of hope among the smoke and ruins of the battlefield."

I hated being a symbol. "There's no rebellion."

"Just because you have words doesn't mean they are true in a sentence."

"I'm tired of talking." As always, Moonjir frustrated me. If he'd had something insightful to say, then I'd missed it. "Is there something important in all this?"

"All of it. Trust yourself, Caitlyn." He rose into the air, angling forward like a flying Duathua. "Enjoy the ride." Moonjir zipped ahead, fading as he did so.

I continued walking, grumbling about "gummy bears" and "symbols," when I spotted Penny riding Bella toward me at an easy walk. We'd talked plenty on the trip back from Camp Taygetos. Odie grew excited when he spotted me.

She stopped a few paces away, turning Bella. "Ride?"

"Nah. The walk isn't bad."

"I'm going to have to bring my effing boots to Donny for some new leather." She lifted her foot to show me the worn sole. There wasn't a hole in it yet.

Bella clopping alongside, I told her about the meeting at the Alliance hall. "We had an ambassador from the military."

"Roxie told me. You got to fly. Enjoy it?"

"I guess. Anyway, a real jerk. Might as well have been one of my instructors from the camp spouting all the nonsense about the Duathua and the holiness of humanity."

"Bet they wanted you and Dean."

My lips tightened. "Yeah. The humans in the Alliance stuck up for us, and for the Duathua. That was nice."

"So effing war?"

"Yeah."

"You going to suck it up and start effing leading?"

I nodded. "Took me long enough, didn't it?"

"Well, count me in as your effing honor guard, general."

"Honor guard, where'd you get that?"

"Dean has me reading fool books."

I smiled. We had a library going in our room of mostly fantasy, but Dean had gathered some science fiction, history, and philosophy as well. Someday, maybe we could grow food and read instead of sweat and fight.

When we returned to the Wolf Den, I poked my head inside until I found Roxie talking with Tika in the main room. "Gather everyone out back. We've got news."

She smiled and nodded. "Sounds good."

The more recent members, resting in the stale air of the main room, sat up or stood expectantly.

Dean and Ben prepped some wrinkled onions in the kitchen while a pot simmered over burning logs in the fireplace. We cooked there as much there as we did by calling heat from the otherness. The aromas had me hungry.

I grabbed some water to drink, still wanting a bath. "Met with Tyrell's guy. That didn't go well."

Still peeling down to the usable onion, Dean cocked his head. "Anything new?"

"Supposedly some arsenal, whatever that means. We didn't agree to his terms." I drank, finishing the cup. "Have you ever heard of gummy bears?"

Dean chuckled. "They're going to throw candy at us?"

"Two different conversations. I'm calling a meeting outside."

He nodded. "Aye, Captain." Brushing his hands off, he eyed Ben. "Coming?"

Ben smiled weakly. "Of course."

The backyard, mostly pines, had plenty of shade beyond the small screened-in patio. Fresh grass sprouted in bursts between beds of dried pine needles. A warm breeze promised a hot summer to come and at least didn't blow from the direction of the latrine. The Wolf Squad trickled in, with Andy being the only one who sprinted around the corner of the house.

I stood leaning against the trunk of a pine and grew calmer when Dean sat at my side and rested his back against the bark. Roxie dropped to the grass beside Tika. My smile grew when I saw how close they were. *Not just love, but lovers*. I glanced at Dean, aching inside.

His expression harder than ever, Andy forced a ready nod to me. "Let's do this, Wolf Squad," he offered. The loss of Gina had devastated him, but he kept it hidden behind energetic comments. Those who didn't know him might not think he cared.

Quinn, whom I hadn't seen since he'd scurried into his Jeep and driven off from Camp Taygetos, came around the corner with Weston at his side. They both stopped at the patio, while most of the Wolf Squad began taking seats around and behind Roxie and Tika.

Unsure if everyone had arrived, I started. "We just had a meeting with a representative of the Savannah Charter. I won't call him an ambassador because there was no negotiation. He just stated that the humans had to surrender while we and the Duathua go to camps."

I let them murmur and didn't let on when Tika grabbed Roxie's hand. "No one surrendered or even discussed it. The belief is that Tyrell's army will hit the southern I-20 bridge. We'll be expected to help, but I'll only ask if you're willing."

Quinn's face darkened at my last comment, and he took two steps from the patio, jamming his hands in his pockets. "And are you willing, or afraid of the fight?"

I smiled, wondering how far I needed to go. "Let's just say I won't be hopping in a Jeep and leaving everyone else with the mess."

He grumbled low enough that I didn't need to respond. When he stalked away, Weston remained.

"Jimmy has taught us something new, with a type of linking that can amplify the distance and power of an attack. A number of you healers have already experienced similar when helping me. I've worked with him on air a couple of times and prefer him to demonstrate, and hopefully teach you, this method after the meeting. Maintaining our distance from the soldiers might be very helpful in keeping us safe."

Focusing first on Penny, then Roxie, I moved to the part that would determine who would be willing to risk themselves for an Alliance they hardly knew or understood. "This afternoon, I'll ask Penny to lead us down to the bridge, where we can see what we might do. With Jimmy's new linking, I'd like to consider groups based on our best skills. I can pair up with those adept at air. Roxie with water. Ben and Andy for heat and fire. Tika for electricity and lightning." I pointed out those I mentioned. Test the efficiency for linking in large and small groups, then come up with what works best for each of you. Healers can get with Fawn and Isabel, as they've healed in a circle with me."

I drew a long inhale. Many of the newer faces had grown more interested as I elaborated on the training. There were a couple more timid holdouts and a pair of stony expressions. "We can talk tonight about what we learned and see how that might help in the defense. The most important aspects are communication and safety. No charging knights." I tilted my head toward Andy, but smiled warmly. "Jimmy?" As I motioned the big teen up to my spot, Dean stood to escort me to the back.

He leaned in. "Damn. Where'd that come from?"

"What?" I frowned.

"All leader-like. I'm ready to sign up." He chuckled. "Just teasing. I love you. It was good. Proud of you."

I found his hand and squeezed it. "I love you too. Let's hope we survive this."

"There's that. No regrets. We might lose some. Can you handle that?"

"No," I said honestly. "Do I have a choice?"

"Still gas in Quinn's Jeep, I bet."

We moved over to the patio as Jimmy explained in his slow drawl. He quickly pulled Len from the group to demonstrate; many of the newcomers knew the long-faced teen from the ride back to the overfull Wolf Den.

A bath would have to wait. Getting the Wolf Squad organized might save some of them, and I couldn't think of anything more important.

Chapter Twenty-Four

My bath came that evening in the Saluda River under the bridge as we scouted the area based on Dean and Penny's recommendation. They suggested we should learn the terrain the enemy would have to deal with. The river ran swiftly in spots, but it could be crossed. Tyrell's soldiers would not just attack over the blockaded bridge, but through the dense forests lining each side of the water. Fire could become an enemy to the Alliance as well if it got out of control.

Henweyay and a wiry gray-haired man who wore hunting camos tracked down Dean, Penny and me on the south shore. A rotting white house promised some cover for the attackers, and Penny wanted to booby trap it with explosives.

Henweyay gestured to her companion. "Samuel Pence. Marshall of the human troops. Caitlyn, leader of the Wolf Squad, Dean, Penny and Odie."

The freshly shaved man wore his hair bristled short like Len's. His weathered face had lines, but few seemed from smiling. He thrust out his hand to me. "Call me Sam." He gripped my hand with solid firmness, but didn't squeeze like he had something to prove. "I'd like to agree on a time to coordinate plans. I can set up a command tent at the junction of Bush River Road and I-20 where we can schedule meeting times."

"That would be good. I'll bring Roxie, Dean, and Penny."

He studied me. "You *are* young." Continuing with a shake of his head, he spoke quickly. "No disrespect. Just the opposite. Henweyay has often spoken of your missions."

The otherness roared, and fire the size of a house blossomed over the river, hissing and throwing up steam before it disappeared. Sam whistled.

Dean spoke in the silence that followed. "Have we considered some controlled burns? Both sides could start some devastating fires. If it catches on the Alliance side of the river, we might lose on that account."

Sam responded with a slow nod. "There's an old railroad track about a thousand feet back from the shore just behind the lagoon and wetlands on both sides of I-20."

"Saw the water. A couple of ponds." Dean shrugged. "Fire will sweep right around them."

"Man-made, in the days before the Sorrow. You're right. Lot of dry forest still. The tracks are just on the north side."

I smiled. Dean and Sam seemed to get along, without a lot of wasted words.

Henweyay pointed to the sagging house. "Are you thinking of setting up on this side?"

Penny grinned. "Just a tripwire. Always trap where the rabbit might hide."

The Pahawan's nod seemed distant, as if her thoughts had already moved on.

"Where are you thinking of putting your people?" I asked.

She glanced aside. "The last couple of battles have

shown us our — limitations — when placed against human weapons and powers. With our diminished number, we will remain scouts, perhaps messengers during the upcoming battle. Jural had hoped to learn your soft Kudaru, but there might not be time for that."

I remembered proud Halimay, who died in the attack at Sumter. It had to be difficult for a warrior to be rendered obsolete. "I've always relied on Pahawan information. If we'd been more careful at Camp Taygetos and took the time to use the scouts, we might have avoided such a deadly trap." I gestured toward her armor. "Is there any process to make the Kudaru less shiny? It has to make scouting that much more difficult."

She spread open her gauntleted hand and lifted it to catch the sun low in the west. "It is a consideration."

We spent a short while together with Dean, Penny, and Sam clustered around us. I agreed to meet at the command tent at sunrise before Henweyay took flight to meet with a group of Pahawan.

Sam left with us to return to the blocked bridge. "I think more rests on your group than most would like to admit," he said.

We marched uphill in front of Penny, Dean, and Odie. Roxie and her water team sent a roar of otherness to raise a ten-foot wave racing along the river. "I wish that wasn't the case," I replied.

He frowned quizzically. "Why?"

"Most of us don't want to kill. We're willing to defend, but would rather not kill anyone."

He turned forward, watching the brush and terrain. "I guess that's a good thing. People still have a bit of apprehension when it comes to all of you. When things calm down, I think you'll find some parents approaching you."

My eyebrows rose. "With kids like us?" Dean had asked Nur once, but her response had been vague.

Sam nodded.

The vehicles blocking the bridge formed a mass you had to climb over at first. Metal groaned under our soggy boots and scraped under Odie's nails. Deeper into the blockade, a thin opening the width of one person led down the middle. At the far end, I could make out the Wolf Squad gathering in the shadows of the thick forest. My stomach growled as I thought of the walk back.

All except Quinn and Weston had shown up, and even the fresh faces appeared engaged. They spotted us crossing with Sam, and furtive glances peeked over the rusted cars at their end.

Roxie hopped up and sat on a faded blue rooftop to watch us, so I introduced her to Sam. He greeted her, then said his goodbyes and wove through the mass of teens waiting for us.

Andy jogged up, smiling as if his usual relaxed self, but his eyes still showed grief. "Everyone's here. Back to the Wolf Den?"

"Please. You lead. It's straightforward, but most haven't been out this far from the Wolf Den yet."

He barked out for the Wolf Squad to get moving, his imitation of the military back at Camp Sparta.

During the forty-minute walk back, I tried to relate Moonjir's conversation to Dean, Roxie, and Penny.

"He's right," said Penny.

"About being a symbol?"

"Yeah. I see the way Wolf Squad watches you. But you live up to it, too."

I frowned. "How?"

"You care about them. It's not just a show."

"We're all about to be at risk." We'd just been at a

bridge, planning to risk our lives to help defend the Alliance. Most of the newcomers couldn't help but freeze at the sight of a Duathua, but they'd quickly grown willing to help.

"How does he know about movies?" Dean asked.

"The theater things?" I truly didn't understand myself.

Dean shrugged. "I guess there are plenty of older people, like my family, who talk about them. Does he just sit around invisible and listen to conversations? Creepy."

We were all a little damp from our improvised bath in the river, but I felt better than I had in the morning. Gina's death still rose in my thoughts.

Jimmy dropped back to me when we were closer, sounding pleased about the success the different groups had achieved. "I think some people work better together than others. What I mean is that Andy had a large gathering of fire people, but when Ben matched up with two of the newer recruits, they were more powerful than everyone combined."

Roxie nodded. "Same here. Kira and Dave alone created an eight-foot wide waterspout. We should have everyone pair up, then add in members to get the best teams."

I waited for Jimmy to continue, but he simply glanced back at me.

"What do you suggest?" I asked him.

"Not only what Roxie does, but see if some of the healers can join in with other skills."

My strongest ability was healing, but air came a close second. At the camps, we trained on everything. "Good idea. And consider Tika, whose main ability is electricity; she's also decent in water."

The edge of Roxie's lips twitched, as if she might smile. "Fawn," she began as she pointed at the shaved head just a few yards in front of us, "can work with air, but barely."

Jimmy strode faster to catch up with Fawn and draw her back to us. She smiled as she asked, "What's going on?"

"Would you be willing to try something with us? Linking to work with air?"

Her reaction seemed almost reluctant. "Okay."

"Draw on my power. Blow the tops of those trees." Jimmy offered his arm as we walked.

Fawn paused, then grasped his forearm. "I'm not very strong. I doubt you'll see anything. How do I do this?"

Jimmy's voice held a calm quality that made it easy to work with him. "Just feel my otherness, then pull on it." His call rumbled like rolling thunder.

She shrugged thin shoulders, then gasped. "Wow. I can feel that."

"Go ahead. Use it," he urged her.

The treetops to our left bent, blustered, and a couple branches snapped. Fawn stopped to stare, and we joined her.

"I never could do that." Her voice sounded incredulous.

Jimmy rumbled a chuckle. "Yet, you just did."

Fawn, Jimmy, and I took turns linking and working with wind as we walked. The best combo came when I led and drew from their power. Roxie moved from our group to walk with Tika, and that made me smile. Another part of me fought with envy as I thought about Dean. We had our love, but the physical closeness we both craved eluded us. *Love, not lover.* I winced at the thought.

Despite being housed in two buildings, with a third in the midst of repair, the Wolf Squad jammed into mine with Ben's promise of a warm meal. The living and dining areas exploded into a gaggle of conversation, while half a dozen of us worked to get a meal together. The camaraderie seemed to have deepened with our training and excursion to the bridge, despite the impending threat it implied. I kept breaking into a smile.

Dean leaned into me as he brought roasted and chopped chicken for the stew pot. "I'm going to need to scavenge up books. When we get through this."

"Did you lend out some more?"

"Fawn is voracious — and Timothy. I ran up for three books while cooking."

"Nothing's easy." I quoted him.

He chuckled and patted my hip.

When everyone had eaten and I'd finally removed myself and Dean from the conversations, we crept upstairs, where the voices were a dull murmur. Cooler air flowed through our windows, and only a couple of bugs had made it through the patched screens.

We stripped and dropped to the mattress, and arousal swept me quickly into Dean's arms. His chest burned warm against mine, and our kisses grew from temptation to satiation. The caresses started innocently enough before developing into more targeted exploration.

My heart dropped when Dean released a throaty growl and sprung up and away. Using othersense, I could feel his heightened vibrations, close to shifting.

Rising to my knees, I kept to the mattress. "Fight it," I pleaded.

He moved to the window, silhouetted by stars, and spoke in a husky whisper. "I am."

His form remained human, though he vibrated sharply. In a quieter, more human voice, he continued. "I'm sorry. I love you."

I rolled to my back, confident he wasn't turning into his werewolf form. My envious thoughts imagined Roxie and Tika together. "I love you, Dean." Tears filled my eyes.

Chapter Twenty-Five

I had three days of the light mayhem of training and getting to know the Wolf Squad before Sam and Henweyay showed up at the Wolf Den. We were in the middle of our prep for a communal dinner when Jimmy came to me in the kitchen.

"Company," he rumbled quietly at my shoulder.

Considering our numbers and the focus on Tyrell's army, word spread faster than I could get from the kitchen to the street out front.

Dean and Roxie were behind me as I exited the front door. They, along with Penny, had accompanied me each morning to the command tent. The planning and preparations benefited more from their presence than mine.

Sam's tense, wiry frame shifted as he waited, while Henweyay's head scales might have been bristling.

"Tyrell?" I asked.

Henweyay spoke in a muted voice with her eyes flicking to the building behind me and the faces likely peering from its windows. "Troops are flooding into the staging area at Leesville. We believe they're going to move tonight. I've got every Pahawan scouting the roads." Her long fingers twitched. "Are they ready?"

To kill or die? "Some. Most." They were kids like me.

She studied me for a long moment. I hadn't been very reassuring. "It is going to get very rough. Very messy."

"We know."

Sam exhaled with a murmur. "Kids. Too young." He raised his chin, inhaled, and spoke louder. "I've always hated conflicts, but this is worse. Still, our regular militia can't stand long against their weapons without your people. Most of our job will be to make sure they don't get to you or past you."

He gave Henweyay a nod before asking their question. "Can you have them all at the command tent in the morning? If we send word, they're moving tonight. Say, two hours before sunrise?"

I agreed, checking with Roxie and Dean after the fact. We watched Henweyay and Sam walk away in silence before Dean rested a hand on my shoulder and spoke. "It had to come."

The tension of waiting had melted with the training and planning, but now it hit me like snow in the face. "What if we lose? What if they get through and kill us — the Duathua?"

He squeezed my tense muscles. "Retreat. We've discussed it. Pahawan flares, and we move north."

My stomach churned, turning any plans for supper into nausea.

Roxie cleared her throat. "Everyone's going to be curious. We should put on a good face."

I didn't turn, but practiced a confident smile. Sam's forces would protect us until they couldn't. The Wolf Squad would need to devastate Tyrell's forces. We'd done it at Camp Sparta. "Happy face. I got it." I turned and marched us back to the Wolf Den. If I didn't smile, at least I wasn't grimacing.

Jimmy opened the door. "This it?" His even temperament helped me, much like Dean's did.

"Yeah." My mouth twitched. "We should plan on getting an early night's sleep. We might be heading to our positions at the bridge before daylight."

I spoke to the crowd clustered in the entry as much as I did to him. Fawn rubbed her shaved scalp and turned back to the kitchen, where Ben watched from the deeper shadows. We'd need to prepare supplies to bring as well, and he was in charge of that. Word would spread to everyone, and I doubted many would get much rest.

Jural had not given up on meditations, and she arrived with Nur around dinner time. They appeared on the back patio while we were cleaning up and soon had a couple of the Wolf Squad chatting with them.

Because I wanted to cancel and focus my stressful thoughts on the impending attack, I forced myself to attend. "I probably need this," I told Jural.

She touched the back of my hand. "I'm glad you see that. We can skip attempting to make soft Kudaru as the time for its use has passed. Tika will probably learn before I do."

My presentation lacked energy, and we had fewer attendees than usual. Weston arrived late. He'd been holed up with Quinn in the other building.

My ability with Jural's connections came with no effort. She always brought me a new object to touch, sometimes more than one, and I'd learned to filter the mayhem into a single set of links. Today, she brought a worn leather glove that could only have come from a human.

"Let the esse guide you to the source, then out from

there." Jural spoke better than most of the Duathua, with inflections that mirrored humans.

I nodded. She'd been pushing me to this since we'd returned from the last disaster. Green and purple lines blended and twisted about each other, heading behind me. Somehow, I knew generally where they led, not that I saw the location, but I knew the owner of the glove's direction and guessed them to be just over a mile away. That part came easily.

"Touch them with the esse. Coat them — like spice on a chicken."

Grimacing at the analogy, I found my fingers splaying out as I washed the otherness over the source. Without any physical imagery, I knew a web of colorful lines in varying strength emanated from them. One, orange and red, appeared attached to the small pouch at Jural's side. With a smile, I pointed.

"Very good. You are adept at this, Caitlyn." She withdrew a coin and showed it to me. "This belongs to the owner of the glove. It was her father's for many years, and she carries it to remind her of him."

Dean whistled. Later, after Jural and Nur had left and we'd slipped into our room, he mentioned the session. "Still not sure how useful it is. Cool, but what can you do with it?"

I considered when I'd moved the shield down the road to a car using the connection from the keys. "I'm not sure." Describing the shield, car, and keys, I flushed, as it sounded rather useless.

"We just need to collect their keys." Dean smiled and kissed me. He pulled me close, walling away thoughts of the impending attack.

Before we were asleep, a Pahawan scout brought the alert that Tyrell's forces had begun their march. Two hours after setting the Wolf Den into a buzz, we cuddled on our mattress again. The clouds drizzled with a brisk wind. None of us would sleep well.

Our timekeeper, Ben, woke us in the dark, and the houses stirred into action. Everyone had a small pack or satchel of water and food.

Penny waited outside in scattered showers with Belle and Odie. "Effing lovely day for a war."

Clouds hid any stars, leaving us in nearly pitch black. "I think I prefer this."

While I wore his jacket, Dean opted to head out into the rain shirtless. Penny wore her long coat while Roxie just had on her coveralls. Most of the Wolf Squad wore theirs with jackets or ponchos.

My job would be to sense the area and direct the attacks through a Pahawan messenger. Dean and Sam had worked on multiple sets of maps to create grids and pinch points where fire or water would be most effective. I'd have Jimmy, Fawn, and Len with me to create air attacks. Linked, I could drop tornadoes nearly anywhere my othersense reached. In this kind of darkness, I'd be one of the few who could see. When the sun came up, it wouldn't last.

The Wolf Squad stretched in a wet line, slogging the forty minutes to the bridge. As we neared the command tent, scattered groups of humans joined us with rifles and smaller weapons.

A dark form flew above us and landed beside the white tent that glowed from lamplight inside. "That's a Pahawan," I said to Dean.

"Yeah."

"Their armor, it's dark." Henweyay had somehow incorporated my suggestion. The Kudaru didn't reflect the light.

"Hmm."

I peered back at the line of Wolf Squad trailing behind

us. "Jimmy, can you send the different groups to their positions? I need to check inside."

"Yep." Rain had flattened his hair to his forehead, but he still loomed.

Roxie gave me a pat on the shoulder before heading to gather her group. Penny and Dean followed me into the tent. Len and Fawn waited at the flaps.

The large tent had a makeshift table in the center with a map and a lantern hanging from supports above it. Chairs, cots, and crates rested near the cloth walls with a couple more lanterns lit.

Sam's aide, Lauren, a thin woman who wore glasses and wet camos, noticed us first as we reached the edge of the table. Like many other humans in the Alliance who had been in the command tent, her reaction to Sam's integration of the Wolf Squad into the battle plans had been reluctant. "They've stopped in Lexington," she said.

I didn't recognize the location. "Why?"

Henweyay pointed to a place on the map. "Don't know. Maybe just a quick formation before they move the last eight miles to the bridge."

"Or," Sam's tone sounded tired, as if he hadn't slept, "they're going to head north to the dam. In which case, we have a lot of people to move quickly."

Dean stepped around to Sam's side. "You said the road is nearly impassable to the dam."

"It is; for vehicles. Potholes the size of Jeeps and a washout. We've counted three dozers accompanying them, so we assumed it's to attempt to clear the bridge for the rest. I just don't like them pausing at the junction that could lead them north."

Lauren pinched her nose. "Maybe trying to get us to split our forces."

Sam grumbled. "Might just work."

After half an hour of theorizing and continuous reports from scouts, I grabbed one of the chairs, then leaned back and closed my eyes. That lasted a short while before I began pacing, heading out to speak with Jimmy, Fawn, and Len.

"We're concerned they might aim for the dam." I offered a weak smile. "They've stopped south of there."

Jimmy straightened. "What's the plan?"

I shook my head. "*Which* path is the question. Just be ready to alert the others and make a run for it."

Another Pahawan, masked in the new darkened armor, fluttered down from the rain and headed into the tent. I followed in case they had word of movement.

Instead, there had been one Pahawan scout injured with sniper fire and continued reports of the army sitting in Lexington. Waiting wasn't my best skill.

About sunrise, Weston and Quinn strolled into the tent. Neither of the teens approached the table, but Henweyay knew who they were. Since we'd returned to Columbia, Quinn had ignored most conversations and meetings. Weston had come to the command tent a few times. There had never been a restriction against anyone attending.

Sam and Henweyay worked with Dean to plan potential positions around the dam area, but no one except the Pahawan scouts were redeployed. Weston paid more attention than Quinn, who seemed more focused on scowling than being present.

I missed a comment, but the others around the table had gone silent, their eyes on me. An ominous growl of thunder outside set the tone.

"What?" I asked.

Lauren pulled off her glasses and rubbed her eyes. "We have a motorcycle and driver. Can we run you up to the dam just so you can 'sense' the surrounding area to make sure we aren't being infiltrated?"

Dean's lips tightened, and I guessed he didn't like the idea. Sam and Henweyay studied me.

"Yeah," I said. The waiting had my skin itching. I doubted any of the Wolf Squad were happy sitting in the rain for hours, not knowing what was going on. We'd hurried to ready ourselves for a battle none of us wanted, and now I almost wished for it to start and be done with.

Lauren nodded to herself and headed for the tent flap. She stopped when a Pahawan burst in and circled the table to Henweyay.

"Helicopter." The scout spoke the word awkwardly.

A chill rolled across my shoulders.

Chapter Twenty-Six

I imagined a fire throwing helicopter bearing down on us inside the tent. My feet shifted, but I remained in place.

"Where?" asked Sam.

"It landed with their army. I was sent immediately."

Sam relaxed. "We'll get a report if it moves." His eyes went to me. "You brought down the one at Sumter; can you do it again?"

I'd nearly killed Dean. "It's not my most — *precise* ability, but yes, if I'm close enough."

He nodded with his usual solemn expression. "We'll have to switch around our plans. An Apache or anything like that can decimate our defenses if it's left running loose. We don't have anything that can bring it down besides a lucky shot. That'll have to be your primary concern."

The Wolf Squad was first, but they'd be targets, so I nodded in agreement. My pulse throbbed in my ears. Perhaps I could bring it down with something more under my control, like a tornado.

"Lauren, get the driver ready to take Caitlyn wherever this helicopter targets." Sam's expression darkened, and a hint of guilt lit his eyes when he looked at me. "This really tears a hole in our plans. If I were them, I'd lead with the 'copter. Bring in the troops once defenses are softened."

A second scout returned, letting gray light inside and bringing a report of no movement beyond the army's scouts, who had spread out in no particular formation. Henweyay and Sam marked the helicopter's location on the map, along with troops, and discussed reasons why Tyrell might have hesitated.

To torture me, I thought. Restless, I paced the tent, avoiding the edge where Quinn and Weston whispered to each other. Lauren entered with a muscled man in his thirties who stood at the flap opposite the teens.

Sam and Henweyay included me and Dean, planning a layout of Wolf Squad if we needed to defend the dam instead of the bridge. They focused on a section close to the Saluda River.

"Early on, we built a defense platform in the old electrical towers here. It's a climb up, but the view of the area across the river is good." Sam swept his fingers along the dam and the road there, then down the river. "I'd have troops protecting access from below."

"A platform?" Dean asked. "How many can it hold?"

"Dozen. It's made for snipers, with an overhang and rails. We've got three such stands, but this one in the middle is best for Caitlyn to use her abilities. If we need to defend the dam."

Despite the storm, the clouds let in gray light each time a scout came in to report. I didn't need Ben's watch to know we were hours past the expected attack. Still, when Quinn stepped up to the table, it surprised me.

"We should attack the helicopter while it's on the friggin' ground. I can get a group together to do it." Quinn addressed Sam, as he still had difficulty with Duathua.

Henweyay responded. "They've set out a lot of scouts. The helicopter is deep in their troops."

"Not friggin' afraid," Quinn said.

Weston stepped up beside him, eyeing me. "We only need to get close enough to get eyes on it. Ben and Andy can set it on fire. Tika could help."

My chest tightened at the mention of the Wolf Squad members. "They've got scouts who'll be watching for us to try something."

Quinn's lips twitched as he turned to me. "Not friggin' afraid," he repeated.

I shifted to face Sam to argue, and found him watching me. "They'll get themselves killed," I said.

He nodded. "They'd never get close enough without getting caught."

But I could. Even Henweyay's eyes focused on me. Maybe I *was* the one afraid. "Do you think this is a viable idea?" I asked Sam. "For me to go?" I knew what Dean and Penny would say, but destroying that helicopter without losing members of the Wolf Squad might save lives.

He closed his eyes as he wiped a wrinkled hand down his face. "Assuming they don't move it before we get there. Yes. If I had a seasoned squad trained to infiltrate, I'd risk them." Taking a deep breath, he reopened his eyes and gestured at Quinn. "Sending them is suicide; without you. You're all too young."

I bristled, but Weston spoke. "We are. We've also managed to get out of a few scrapes, with Caitlyn's help."

Quinn nearly growled. "Don't need her friggin' help."

Weston shook his head. "To get around the scouts, we do."

My stomach churned. Dean and Penny would want to go. Jimmy and the others would as well. "I'll do it. I can get us through, locate it, then back up and take it out with air."

If Tyrell didn't move it. *If* he didn't attack before I reached it. *If* this wasn't bait.

"I'm going," said Quinn. "With or without her."

Weston just nodded.

Dean sighed, and Penny shifted the rifle on her back. "Watch Odie for me?" she asked Lauren.

I stepped closer to the map where Lauren had marked the helicopter. "We'll need a route. Dean? Penny?"

Dean cocked his head but approached. "Three or four-hour walk from here."

Henweyay's face formed a stiff, light smile. "On foot, perhaps. I can get you closer by wing. About an hour out in most directions." She drew two fingers in a circle up to the area marked by pins where Tyrell's scouts had been spotted.

Quinn choked at her comment, and I hoped he'd refuse, but he didn't.

Ten minutes later, we had a plan. Henweyay sent a scout to retrieve Roxie. I didn't want to involve her, but a couple water areas might need to be bridged, and no one else had mastered her trick. Weston promised he and Quinn would follow the plan, though I didn't completely trust them.

In less than an hour, we were deposited in a rain-drenched forest with a map, compass, and an enemy ahead of us in my othersense. According to maps, we had a mile and a half to navigate.

"Shame you don't have the keys to the helicopter," Dean chided.

I sniffed, amused. Perhaps Jural's training could prove useful, just not in this case.

Chapter Twenty-Seven

As a dozen Pahawan began pairing up with the Wolf Squad, I had to explain to Jimmy why he wasn't coming. "With us gone, I need you to keep the Wolf Squad calm and in order. The waiting is going to wear on everyone."

He wiped wet hair off his forehead, visibly distressed. "It's not safe. If you need to link, only Quinn is any good at air."

I patted his large forearm. "Once I mark the location of the helicopter in my othersense, then I can back off and flip it with a tornado. I won't need to link."

"You've got to get close to do that. What if they spot you?"

"We'll be very careful."

He stared, almost a glare, for a long moment, then wrapped me in a hug. "You'd better be."

The rain eased down my back under Dean's jacket as Jimmy squeezed, but I didn't stop him. He'd made himself my protector, along with Penny and Dean.

The two Pahawan scouts who carried me wore the darkened armor and didn't carry their tridents. Gray light from the clouds showed a tinting to their Kudaru, like some of the old car windows we found. Through the armor, the details of the Duathua's faces and skin disappeared at a short distance.

Skimming over the cars on the bridge, I could see the river below better than the trees lining the shores through the rain. My chest tightened, but the scouts had a firm grip. Penny carried the simple map wrapped in a plastic sleeve. Her long black coat whipped behind her between the two Pahawan who carried her.

They warned us, but the first time they rose from a creek bed to lift over the tall pines, my heart froze. We traveled over some dark woods, dropped to backstreets or muddy dirt roads, then climbed again. I focused on Penny and Dean ahead of me.

I let my othersense range around us, but mostly ahead. The Duathua had distinctly different vibrations, and as we drew closer, the number of hidden Pahawan we passed surprised me. The last part of the trip wove us above Twelvemile Creek, where we barely squeezed between overhanging trees at some points, and Tyrell's scouts began popping up in my othersense.

A pair of his men occupied a building ahead of us, and I mentioned it to the two Pahawan carrying me. One nodded. We were near the end of our trip, and the rain had soaked me through to my underwear.

When they dropped me beside Dean, his expression appeared grim. "You okay?" I asked.

"Not a fan," he said.

Penny chuckled. "I'd rather it wasn't effing raining, but otherwise, I loved it."

I tucked Dean's jacket tight around my soggy coveralls. "There are two scouts in that direction."

As they released her, Roxie sunk into the moist ground. With a shiver, she scowled. "I'd dry off, if I could." We'd agreed to use as little otherness as possible and only when absolutely needed. There might be Youth Guard among the patrols.

Behind us, Quinn grumbled to Weston. They both had opted for weapons, and I hadn't forgotten his stupid gunfire at the Santee bridge.

As we left, I waved to the Pahawan scouts, who hid themselves in the branches of the surrounding trees. They'd be waiting for our return, and Henweyay promised to relay any important messages there, like if Tyrell started moving the army.

Penny, with a compass, led the way ahead of us, back toward the river. Dean walked on my right and Roxie on my left.

"That river — creek isn't deep," I said.

"No need for a bridge," Roxie agreed.

Dean glanced back and grumbled, "Holster those weapons."

I turned, gesturing around us. "There are scouts within earshot, but not close enough to see us. Let's not alert them."

"Not going to friggin' fire it."

Roxie didn't turn. "Like last time."

Weston put his weapon away, and Quinn followed suit after a glare. We reached the shore of the creek a couple minutes later, though I focused on my othersense. From Henweyay's description, we were well over a mile away from the bulk of Tyrell's force and the helicopter.

Penny stepped into the flowing water and sunk knee-deep, nearly toppling headfirst. "Ef me."

I caught the back of her long coat and Dean sloshed in to grab her arm. "Short people problems," he said.

"Ef you." Penny dug her boot out of the mud and shook off Dean's grasp.

The four of us went through as a group, grabbing support as we could. I almost wanted to watch Quinn and Weston struggle but restrained myself. The opposite shore proved slippery, but we had trees and brush to grab for support as we climbed.

After a few trees, silhouettes of buildings loomed ahead of us, and Penny checked with me.

"To our left, and deep behind us to our right."

She reached the wood's edge, peering in that direction. "I can make out a building there." We kept to the trees, then darted for a passage between the pale structures.

We wound down the apartment complex, as large as any in Columbia, littered with abandoned cars. She stopped at an overhang so she could check the map. "We good?" she asked me.

I gestured to the left of our path. "I've got a pair we're getting closer to, but they're not patrolling. Stationary."

"Main road ahead we have to cross. I'll veer us away from them just in case they have a good view."

"We're wasting friggin' time," grumbled Quinn as he tried to get out of the rain. "They'll move the damned thing before we get to it."

Penny got us across the wide road, between two long buildings, through backyards, and into copses of trees. We traveled a while before I sensed a growing number of troops. They thickened into a dense line of people, as if they clustered on a road.

"What's a mile ahead of us?" I asked. We had reached an area lined with industrial buildings. One leaned precariously from past weather, but she made for an intact awning to get out her map.

"I-20," she said, checking the map. "Ramps for an exit. The helicopter."

"If it's still friggin' there." With no room under the shelter, Quinn hunched in the rain.

He grumbled even louder when I diverted us around another pair of Tyrell's scouts. They surrounded us, but the only patrolling groups were much closer to the thick mass that I guessed waited on the highway.

"We're going to have trouble," I finally said. We'd just exited the edge of some woods onto asphalt pockmarked with brimming potholes.

Penny stopped, and Dean cocked his head at me. "Why?" she asked.

I gestured left of due south. "The army ends there, lined up on what I guess is I-20. They continue west. They've got moving patrols between us and the bulk of the people. Stationary scouts straight along your path and to the right where this road leads."

Dean peered across the street to the south. "There's a church steeple. Not high enough for you to get sight of the helicopter. The terrain rises. Are we clear in that direction?"

I grimaced and shrugged. "Aiming us directly toward the troops."

"No regrets. If we get you up on a building there, maybe you can get sight of it."

The rain blocked us from seeing very far, but it seemed like our best choice. Unless I wanted to run between patrols.

We continued down the exposed asphalt and Penny pointed to a pair of tall electric poles.. "Climb that? Should be able to see for a distance."

Towers. "We'd need rope and a hook to get to the first rung," I answered. Towers were all over Columbia and around the river, but they'd been designed to avoid climbing.

Dean pointed past them. "Those buildings. I think there's a gas station sign below them. Maybe built on a rise."

I couldn't see as well as his watchful eyes, but there were angled shapes to our left. In my othersense, the patrols ahead roved past one of the stationary pairs. "Let's give it a shot."

Gates with barbed wire protected a number of warehouses with rusting trailers parked beside them. The trailing end of the army seemed close to the last of the buildings in my othersense. Penny used the butt of her rifle to twist the wire into snapping, and we climbed over.

Weston pointed to the buildings on the adjoining property. "I think I saw movement." His alarm had Quinn reaching for his holster.

"There's nothing." My voice snapped sharp. I had dozens of rhythms to track, but none where he pointed. Farther east, yes, but not close enough to see.

He studied me, then Dean, before he nodded. "Shadows, then."

"We need a way up." Roxie craned to see past the trailers close to the buildings. The roof arched high, as if to two stories, but the tops of the containers didn't come close to even the lowest slope.

Walking the drive, I cringed at how close we were getting to the tip of the army. I could make out trees between us, but we were nearly on top of them in my othersense. Beyond the dull sound of rain, it felt oddly silent for the number of soldiers piled there. At least they weren't moving and heading to Columbia. *Why* did *Tyrell wait?*

"There." Dean jogged ahead, pointing to a truck and trailer parked on a ramp leading to the building. He didn't wait for us as he scrambled up rungs on the side of the cab to get to the roof. "We can make it," he called back to us. His chest glistened in the rain and his jeans clung to him.

Dropping to lie down, he patted the side with the rungs and smiled at me. "No regrets."

The truck seemed to grow taller as I approached. The sun-faded paint appeared slick in the rain as I grabbed the door handle and climbed up. My feet slid on the rungs, but Roxie smiled below, as if she'd catch me.

Dean grabbed my arm when I reached the top, and I found the footing to be no better on the roof. He steadied me, then jumped the gap between truck and trailer as if it were nothing. When I tried, he caught me before I plummeted into the tubing and wires between the sections. Against the relative silence, the sounds of creaking metal forced me to wince.

The trailer roof sagged under our weight, and water pooled around our boots. The rear was backed under the edge of the roof with only three feet to spare. I could climb that. Penny had followed us but remained crouched on the trailer.

"Easy, now." Dean climbed first, and lay down to offer his arm. Water sheeted off the metal.

"I'm going to kick you if this doesn't work."

"Fair enough."

"I'd fall off the roof trying." I navigated the roof well enough, and we moved up.

"Likely." Dean had a firm grip on my arm as he knelt by the peak of the roof. "Bingo."

I peered over the top. The bent overhang of a gas station stretched in front of us. Beyond that was a road, and farther lay the curving asphalt of a ramp visible through the rain. In the grass inside the looping road, waited the helicopter. I matched my othersense to what I saw, noting the troops in a line to the south and the scattered rhythms waiting in makeshift tarps near the craft. Two people were inside.

"Got it," I said. We could retreat off these barren streets,

and then I could unleash a tornado. The Alliance wouldn't
have to worry about the helicopter.

A gunshot rang out in the storm. It took a frantic second
before I knew it came from below, where Roxie, Quinn, and
Weston waited.

Chapter Twenty-Eight

"Quinn," I growled.

Dean and I scuttled down the roof before he jumped to the container. Nothing close threatened us in my othersense, but the rhythms of the nearby troops had spiked. The wandering patrol on the main road made a beeline for us.

"There's nothing there. Caitlyn would have warned us." Penny's sharp, berating tone sounded low against the beating rain.

The trailer roof groaned under our feet, where streams of water pooled under our weight. My pulse raced, and I pushed away a rising resentment of Quinn. *I don't know what happened.*

"She's not friggin' here. Weston saw it too." Quinn motioned with his gun.

Dean hit the roof of the truck cab loud enough that all of them turned to us. "Time to leave," he said.

Penny and Roxie nodded, splashing toward the gate. Gauging the approaching patrol, I thought we could make it without using the otherness. Dean scrambled halfway down the rungs before helping me.

"I'm not even going to ask," I muttered under my breath. If I had to, I'd send a tornado at the closest pair of soldiers, but hoped I wouldn't have to cause more of a commotion than we already had. I trembled, partly from being startled, but mostly in anger.

Quinn and Weston studied us. "The helicopter?" asked Weston.

"It's there." On the wet rungs, I didn't dare look at him.

"Well?" Quinn asked. "Are you going to do anything about it?"

Hitting the ramp with a splash, I ignored him and ran. Troops were moving around us, angling in toward our location but twisting around obstacles. Quinn and Weston would follow.

I tensed when a roar of otherness grew between the warehouses and the gas station, but it gathered too far away for any genuine concern. Lightning crackled down, striking with brilliant arcs on the far side of the building.

Roxie and Penny had almost reached the gate, glancing over their shoulders toward me and Dean. We were too slow; the faster patrol would arrive in time to prove troublesome. Running as fast as I could, I drew in the otherness, knowing that whoever had thrown the lightning would hear me.

My tornado struck the two soldiers, scattering them both into the air. Even through the rain, I could hear it rumble.

I'd already announced our presence, so I called the otherness again for the helicopter. The net of soldiers around us had grown tighter, with pairs of scouts approaching from the north while trails of soldiers streamed from the troops to the west and south.

"All good?" asked Dean as he kept pace beside me.

"It will be."

My tornado hit where I believed the helicopter waited. The rhythms of those around it spiked higher. Pain vibrated from those inside, and I cringed; it couldn't be helped.

I spread my othersense wide to determine what kind of trouble we might have as we escaped. A single pair worked their way in from the east, but I could handle them. My shoulders tensed as I imagined Tyrell's entire force chasing us on our retreat to Columbia, but his vehicles needed roads, and we'd be cutting through woods.

"Finally. Idiots." Dean turned from where he'd been looking toward Weston and Quinn.

They were running to follow. If Quinn hadn't fired his weapon, we'd be slipping away without being chased. Instead, soldiers bled from the dense group at the highway toward our warehouses. They weren't our closest problem. Another patrol from the west moved too fast. They had to be driving. *Damn it Quinn.*

Roxie and Penny had cleared the gate and lingered on the outside. I yelled and waved them on. "Go!" Their reluctant trot to the northeast frustrated me as much as Quinn and Weston's delayed retreat.

We spread out in a long line, and Tyrell's forces were closing in. I pulled in the otherness and focused on the fast-moving patrol. They'd turned onto the road we were heading for and picked up speed.

I slipped as I focused a broad, rough tornado into their path. They skidded north, their tires screeching above the rush of wind and droning rain.

Dean glanced. "How close?"

"We'll be fine. I'll have to watch out for Weston and Quinn, though." Quinn had caused the problem, and now he slowed us down.

One patrol lingered near the corner of our street,

perhaps having witnessed the previous windstorms I'd created. The stream of soldiers pouring from the highway toward the intersection of our street worried me the most. I couldn't stop that many.

Hitting the gate and rolling gracefully, Dean landed on the other side and waited to help me. Boots sliding on wet metal and arms flailing, I crawled over like a dying beetle.

Quinn and Weston weren't that far behind. The gray rain hid the soldiers that I could sense entering the south end of the warehouse area.

Dean and I cut to the right of the drive where trees and brush offered cover. Across the grass led to the road and woods we'd entered through, so I felt comfortable pausing there to wait.

"I've got dozens coming up a road to the intersection with ours," I explained to Dean, gesturing along the west. "A pair hiding at the intersection. Four that I scattered earlier; two of those are injured."

"Will Weston get here on time?" Dean asked.

I nodded. "Should. I can scatter the lead soldiers if I need to." My chest tightened as someone called a roar of otherness over the warehouses. "Youth Guard."

Lightning, a massive array, lit the storm as it stabbed across the metal roofs and onto trucks and containers. Weston and Quinn were clear but illuminated as if it were a sunny day. Quinn had about ten paces until he reached the gate and Weston fewer than that.

"Damn." Dean tugged me back farther, toward a broken rail fence and the road we'd be escaping down. "Where are Roxie and Penny?"

I searched. "Walking toward the woods. They're clear."

Another vehicle cut out from the main tide of soldiers and squealed tires as it turned at the intersection. My strength ebbing, I called the otherness and focused a tornado into their path.

Lightning cracked behind the warehouses as if in response, striking the asphalt we'd been running down.

The speeding truck swerved around my storm, headlights lighting nearby trees. I caught it with my next tornado; its passengers flipped out as it toppled backward.

Weston hit the gate much like Dean had, stopping to lend Quinn a hand. *Hurry you jerk*, I thought. I blamed them both for this mess, but I needed them to survive. The front group of the troops were at the intersection, running down the road toward us.

As Quinn reached the top of the gate, gripping Weston's hand, lightning cracked down behind them in brilliant white. The strike wasn't close enough to injure them, but they stood out, poised on the fence.

Quinn paused, and my mind registered the gunshot after he started to fall backward. His rhythms already dulling in death, he slapped onto the asphalt.

"Shit." Dean tugged at me, though I resisted.

Shock wrestled with my sudden guilt over my anger at Quinn. He'd been a jerk, and screwed up, but I didn't want him dead.

Three more gunshots cracked through the droning rain.

Weston went down beside the gate. He wasn't dying. His rhythms were pitched, but steady.

The otherness formed, nearly close enough for me to grab. Lightning struck the road ahead of me and Dean. Water sizzled and steamed to curl in a mist against the rain. Hair on the back of my neck prickled. My nose flared at the almost pleasant scent.

Dean jerked me away. My feet slid in the muddy grass. "Weston."

"Can you stop all of them?" Dean asked. He didn't slow.

I sensed the army running toward us. "No."

"No regrets." He nearly dragged me until I was running with him, leaving Weston to Tyrell's soldiers and the lightning crashing down behind us.

Belatedly, I drew in the otherness and formed a shield behind us. The electric attacks were closer to Weston than us. His rhythms spiked in pain before we were too far away. "We're abandoning him." My voice croaked, pleading past the lump in my throat.

"Yes."

Dean led us off the road toward the woods, where Roxie and Penny waited. I shook from exertion and swirling emotions.

Roxie glanced behind us. "Quinn?"

"Dead," Dean answered without explanation. "Weston's likely captured."

Or worse.

"The soldiers?" he asked me, forcing me to focus.

They were spreading out, some to Weston and the warehouses, more racing down the road behind us. In short, clipped words, I told Dean this.

I hadn't liked Quinn — at all. That made his death awkward and difficult, churning shame into the shambles of my emotions. Weston I'd liked, and leaving him tore me open.

Dean studied me as we ran down the crumbling asphalt of the drive behind rain-shadowed buildings. "There will be more," he said.

"More?"

"More will die. I'm sorry. You did what you needed to do. The helicopter was our mission. Quinn shouldn't have fired his gun. He was — a liability. Always was."

His words didn't help, but I knew them for the truth. I didn't want this, any of it. The destruction of the helicopter would save lives, just not Quinn's. *What would they do to Weston?*

"More." I repeated the word with a wince.

Chapter Twenty-Nine

I jogged with sluggish strides, and we slowed to a brisk march. My mind replayed the gunshot that seemed to be delayed, as Quinn had already dropped. The rain poured off buildings, pooling into streams along the road. Water-soaked branches swung in the breeze.

"Are we clear?" Penny asked, dripping water from her chin.

With an effort, I scanned the surrounding area with othersense. My focus returned, afraid I'd let someone sneak up on us.

Tyrell's soldiers swarmed about Quinn's body like flies. "At the gate, dozens." I couldn't separate Weston from the other rhythms.

Roxie jumped beside me. "What happened with the helicopter?"

"I took care of it."

"Then we did it." She spoke in a reassuring tone, not excited, but encouraging.

"Yes."

Penny, behind Dean, spoke loudly over the wind.

"What was Quinn doing firing that effing weapon? Did he want us to get caught?"

Roxie answered, as if she knew I wouldn't want to speak about it yet. "He and Weston kept saying they saw someone moving. They had each other riled up."

Someone far back by the gate used the othersense, and lightning crackled behind us, too far away to be our concern. At best, it hit the area of the road where we had turned off.

"They'll torture Weston," I said, nearly under my breath.

Shivering, Roxie marched faster.

I cast another wide circle with my othersense. No one threatened us ahead, but we had a long way before we reached the Duathua scouts. The soldiers' initial confusion near Quinn's corpse resolved into a distinct squad following our trail, while most of the soldiers returned west down the road.

"That was quick," I said.

"What?" Roxie asked at the same time as Dean.

"They're following us. One group is. The rest are heading away."

"Weston talked. Maybe." Dean tugged at my sleeve, getting me to hurry. "We're going to have to move faster." He broke into a jog ahead of us, winding around trees and difficult brush.

Tired, I often slipped and stumbled, but we threaded through the woods onto backstreets. My energy sagged, and I fought my muscles to keep pace with Dean. Penny remained behind us, and more than once I caught her peering back as if the soldiers might be close.

To the north and south, patrols waited. I'd sensed them when we arrived. They didn't move. However, others sprang up from the army behind us, fast enough to be in vehicles. Uncomfortable with my thoughts, I finally called through the rain. "What if Weston told them about the Duathua?"

"Assume he did," Dean said.

"Then they'll be waiting for us." I almost slowed.

"Not a lot of choices. That's why we're in a hurry." He jogged a couple silent paces, before continuing. "Quinn. Weston. Those were sniper shots. High caliber."

"Okay..." I pitched my tone, so he'd explain.

"If you sense someone at a location that might have a roof or who could have eyes on us, we need to be more careful."

Those who had followed us from the gate trekked into the forest for a while, then returned the way they'd come.

His new concern set me to obsession as I tried to peer through driving rain toward the closest scouts. They weren't moving, but I couldn't tell at this distance if they were perched up high or sitting in mud. It grew frustrating.

We reached familiar warehouses, and Dean nudged his chin in the direction we'd be heading. "How's it look?"

I sensed wide around our location. "As clear as when we went through."

"Any unusual activity?" Dean stretched bare shoulders as he jogged. "Can you sense as far as the Duathua yet?"

Identifying the lone pair we'd passed before, I found no one else waiting. The area between them and the cluster of Duathua remained empty, as quiet as it had been when we arrived. I described it all to him.

"Strange." Dean scowled.

"You expected them to be waiting here?"

"I did. They are. They know about your ability, though. Weston would have told them."

"Maybe not." My chest tightened, remembering Selina's

torture. "He might have said enough to get them to stop." Weston might have even lied, sent them somewhere else.

"Search for little clusters behind the Duathua and far to the sides. Up and down that main road."

Surprised, I found them. "Yeah. There's a group of eight just north of the Duathua. A group of four and a separate pair northwest of us." I gestured as I spoke. "Almost ten to the east, maybe down that main road. They're all just waiting."

Dean slowed, motioning our group toward a small canopy. "Let's think this through."

I was too tired to think and happy to just slide down against the wall and breathe. Penny pulled out the map, and they kept questioning me about positions. We used the distance from us to the Duathua as a measurement so they could guess the location of Tyrell's soldiers.

The wind had died down, and the thunder had moved south. The storm was passing, leaving us in the wake of Quinn's gunshot and Weston's capture. *I'm tired of running.* "What if we just attack them?" I asked.

Dean frowned at me, but Penny raised her eyebrows and spoke. "Yeah. We've got two badass effing Seyir with us. Sneak in behind that group of four to the north along with the other two and trash 'em. It'll put us close to the Duathua, then we just wing it out of here."

He turned to scowl at her. "It's dangerous."

"And they won't expect it." She grinned, mocking his voice. "No regrets." Holding up the map, she pointed to the locations where we believed the four were waiting close to the pair. "It's about half a mile. Straight north, close to this effing pond or whatever, work our way around them, then hit them from behind. Six of them total. I'm good for two."

As she said the words, I knew she meant to kill them, and my resolve wavered. I rose, pointing on the map. "I can scatter them, then we run down this road, and meet up with the Duathua. Nobody needs to die."

"Nobody else?" Penny asked. She drew in a breath and waved an apology. "Sorry. I'm good with that. Air power it is."

Roxie studied me, and as she opened her mouth to say something, Penny interrupted her. "People are going to effing die today. Might have to accept that."

Quinn first. My stomach roiled, but I nodded. "We agree. Wind." With over a dozen other soldiers waiting nearby, we'd have to move quietly, then attack and run for the Duathua.

Dean and Roxie mumbled their agreement, but they weren't enthusiastic.

As we cut near flooded streets and through backyards, the wind shifted to a milder breeze from the east, and the rain lightened. A few minutes later, I had a clear sense of the pair directly ahead of us and the four to the right, closer to the Duathua.

"I think the pair are up higher. A building." Trees blocked our view, even with the rain letting up. "One of the four is a Youth Guard. Maybe."

Penny pulled us into an overhang of a well-preserved building, one of many in the complex we'd wound through, to pull out the map. "If we can come in the rear, behind the two on the roof, effing snipers, you can take them out, I'd bet. From there, can you reach the four hiding here?" She poked the one spot and swept her finger east. "About a thousand feet."

I nodded and used the river line to mark where I sensed the cluster of Duathua, then north to a few smaller roads. "This is where the eight are waiting."

"Can you hit them as well?" asked Dean.

"Perhaps. It might be better to wait until we're on our way to the Duathua."

"Unless they split up," he said.

I sagged. "Roxie. Okay to tap you?"

She shrugged. "Of course. It could get crazy though."

Penny folded the map and grinned, almost eager.

With Twelvemile Creek just ahead of us, we skirted an old pool filled with green growth and slimy water to enter dark woods. A moss-covered floodgate offered us easy passage over the water and continued in a levy straight north. To our left, a murky pond rippled from the rain, and dots of white hinted at flowers.

Across a low field rose a high, brick building that appeared to have been built over time, with random sections tacked in place. Twice the height of the building was a brick smokestack coming out of a small extension.

Crossing the field would leave us exposed. Letting my othersense overlap my vision, I gestured to the roof. "Up there on the far edge by the road."

Dean smiled, pointing to the pond. "Let's go wading."

I wrinkled my nose at the option, but we had little choice.

We slogged through muck that reminded me of the marsh where we'd lived. After a minute, we climbed out at the back of the building. Around the structure, a path led between walls and a raised parking lot with rusted cars. Rain had formed a river that still drained down the worn concrete. The walkway led to a front corner that I peeked around while sensing the scouts. To the south, they were side by side and nowhere near the edge of the roof I could see.

"Roxie?"

She offered me her arm, and we pulled in the othersense. Her surprise flowed through the connection when I started walking into the parking area where a trio of rusted pickup trucks were parked.

I wanted to be ready to run for the Duathua as soon as I hit the three targets with varying intensity.

The first tornado, a small gray tube, whirled above us and whisked the snipers over the side of the roof.

With a grimace, I sent a larger cyclone that roared as it hit the four between us and the Duathua. The Youth Guard there had called the otherness as soon as the first of ours sounded, but they were too late. Metal shrieked and glass shattered as their rhythms spiked in pain.

Holding steady against Roxie's arm, I threw two at the far group and felt some satisfaction as they scattered. "Let's go."

Penny dashed ahead of us, rifle in her hands. Dean followed her, pacing to keep a couple of steps between them. Roxie and I jogged behind.

The snipers were unconscious, both crumpled on the road. I focused on the four tossed inside their vehicle. Two were unconscious, the Youth Guard vibrated in pain, and a fourth struggled to exit the vehicle.

Penny cut across the main road, leaping over a rivulet at the gutter and running to a driveway beside a house with a crumbling porch. We planned to cut through the woods to another street that we'd take toward the Duathua.

The soldiers far to the south might have heard the tornado, but they hadn't moved yet.

I'd made it to the drive when three distinct gunshots sounded. In a panic, I tossed another tornado at the four wedged in the vehicle and sent it skidding with a crash. The gunfire had come from one of them.

Neither Dean nor Penny, visible in the woods ahead, vibrated with pain.

"That was a signal," I shouted to Roxie, and we sped to catch up with the others.

The vibrations of those far to the south spiked, and a reply of three shots echoed from that direction. They knew where we were and where we were going. I needed to get us safe. *But how?*

Chapter Thirty

Roxie and I reached Dean and Penny as they doubled back to check on us.

"Are you okay?" Dean's intense eyes studied me as I ran.

I waved him forward. "Just a signal. Hurry."

My concern spiked as I tracked the soldiers closest to us. Two of the eight north of the Duathua were speeding toward our friends. Most of the group had been disrupted, but another pair moved eastward with purpose.

Far to the south, the bulk raced toward us in fast vehicles, but others circled east as well. If Weston had told them about Twelvemile Creek, they'd try to intercept.

"Dean."

He slowed as we broke through the woods onto a street that would lead most of the way toward the Duathua. "What is it?"

"I think they're going to try to cut us off along the river." We'd passed a couple bridges on the way.

"Then we don't use the river."

As we raced down the road with Penny in the lead, I scanned north toward Columbia. There were a few stationary scouts dotted about and a pair patrolling in a vehicle, but we might be able to weave through them. We might have to.

The woods were soggy where we left the road, but it seemed to cause difficulty for the two who had broken away from the eight as well. They'd moved swiftly at first, then slowed to a near walk.

"There's two soldiers close to the Duathua," I said between breaths.

Penny kept a distance ahead of me, but heard my comment and dashed faster.

My skin prickled as the threat loomed closer to the Duathua. Not only were they our quick escape, but I cared about them. Tired, I drew in the othersense and dropped two small tornadoes on the stalking soldiers. It worked in two ways. First, it blew them off course, but more importantly, it warned the Duathua.

Splitting into two groups, they moved out of position and slipped to the sides. They wound through the woods, and I felt some pride in their stealth as the two soldiers continued straight to the area where we were supposed to meet.

As we drew close, Penny caused a slight glitch as she snapped a branch underfoot. I couldn't see her through the trees and rain, but the closest soldier paused at the sharp sound.

One of the Duathua darted up behind him, I guessed on wings, and the man's vibrations spiked. His gunshot made me wince, then his dying rhythms chilled my emotions.

Dean had said it earlier. *There will be more. Ours and theirs.*

The second soldier went down when he turned toward the gunfire. I shivered as his rhythms died.

Penny's vibrations were tight and fast, so I yelled to her, "It's all clear. They're safe."

The first Pahawan, cloaked in their new dark armor, we came upon appeared to form from the grays and shadows. They stood beside the soldier's body, where Penny scavenged his weapons and belongings.

She tossed something to Dean. "Grenades. I kept two."

I continued walking toward the meeting area where the Duathua had loosely regrouped. In two minutes, I stood with my hands on my knees, dripping water off my nose and explaining the situation to the Pahawan scouts.

Dean shoved a water bottle at me. "Drink."

Roxie had dropped onto the soggy ground and leaned her back against a pine. Penny had grabbed water and disappeared to search for the second soldier.

When I finished talking and the Duathua discussed our proposal to abandon the creek, Dean hovered to make sure I drank nearly a full bottle. "How does it look out there?"

Despite a heavy weariness, I scanned with my othersense. "Tyrell seems focused on getting ahead of us. Not coming for us. The four we left in the car have spread out but not moved after us too far." One of those was immobile and unconscious. The others were injured.

Penny returned, offering Dean another hand grenade. "We're going to have to remind Sam they have these."

The Pahawan agreed to have me lead our escape by relaying enemy positions to the two Duathua holding me, so that they could avoid any danger. The others would follow. Once we were clear, the extra scouts who had carried Quinn and Weston on the way in would race ahead and report our situation.

I was too far away from the mass of the army to know if Tyrell had moved on Columbia after I'd destroyed his helicopter. In this whole mess, we had one solid success.

The deaths that had rattled me earlier faded as we escaped past the army's scouts. We soon rose above the trees, and they blurred if I peered below. Eyes on the gray horizon, I focused on the return to Columbia and whatever news awaited us there. In the woods around the bridge, the Wolf Squad waited with limited supplies. Jimmy would have taken care of them.

Tired, exhausted, I'd have to put up a confident front for the Wolf Squad, even as we explained about Quinn and Weston. Dean's words echoed between my thoughts. Tyrell's soldiers intended to destroy the Alliance. *The worst is yet to come.*

Chapter Thirty-One

I stumbled when the two Pahawan eased me down in front of the command tent. Water pooled downslope, and a pair of open-topped Jeeps collected rain.

Jimmy, drenched and squishing as he jogged over to meet me. "They said Quinn was dead. Weston captured. Are you okay?"

"Tired." I checked on Dean being lowered before I moved for the tent flaps, drawing Jimmy with me. "How is everyone?"

"Some bored. Some scared. Too much time just sitting there." As he stepped under cover, Jimmy pressed his temples and squeezed along his scalp to ease water out of his hair.

Sam eyed us, standing in the same place I'd left him hours ago. "Food over there. Eat something. I can tell you what I know in one sentence. He's not moving."

Tyrell. Why would he wait? My stomach growled as I headed for the crate with the flatbread sandwiches. Grilled chicken wafted as I picked it up. "They told you about Quinn and Weston."

"Yep. Sorry to hear." His condolences lacked any real depth. Like Dean, he probably guessed it would get worse.

The sandwich of cold roasted chicken tasted better than it should have. Chewing, I mumbled. "What do we do now?"

"We wait. I've sent some troops to the dam and wired surprises there in case they pick that route. I've got every transport we have ready to relocate us. It'll still take half a dozen trips. Your Wolf Squad will be in the first."

Lauren cleared her throat and took off her glasses. "How much will Weston tell them about our plans?" she asked delicately.

Dean stepped beside me, resting a warm hand on my shoulder. "Assume everything he knows." From his pocket, he pulled one of the grenades. "Expect these. We collected a couple."

Weapons clattered at the front of the tent as Penny placed them on the ground. "I got one automatic, too."

"Like Sumter." Sam sighed and wiped his face. "It's going to get nasty, if they get close." The latter part of the comment he added after studying me. He thumbed toward one of the folding chairs. "Need to rest?"

I'd inhaled the sandwich, and weariness clung to me like a blanket. "Yeah."

As Dean asked about the plans for transport, if the need to move came, I slid into the chair. Water dripped from my coveralls. Jimmy joined the conversation, and their voices droned.

When I woke, Dean held a mug of something steaming in front of me. Sluggish, I didn't reach for it at first. "What's that?" I asked.

"Black bean soup. You've been out for hours." He lowered the mug with a metal spoon sticking out so that I might see the contents. "It's hot."

Straightening, I didn't trust myself not to spill it, instead, I wiped my eyes and face. Stifling a yawn, I asked, "Anything?"

"Nope. Would have woken you. Jimmy's taking care of the Wolf Squad. Rain's letting up. Rest is good. So is food." Dean winked. Raising his eyebrows, he gestured with the mug. "Want me to feed you?"

I waved him back and stood, stretched, and felt like my moisture-wrinkled skin stuck to the coveralls. "How long can Tyrell just sit there?"

Sam glanced over his shoulder at me. "We're guessing they're hitting at nightfall. All of it is a good strategy. Waiting and making us potentially divide our forces. We're not a regular army, trained to stay at our post. I've had a few people moving out of position, and plenty threatening to. Your man's done an excellent job keeping the Wolf Squad in place, considering—" He stopped, eyes darting away.

"—considering how young we are," finished Dean. "He's right. Jimmy's done well. We should tell them. Nightfall."

I took the soup.

Sam gestured to Dean. "Good. It'll help hold them in place. Just three or four more hours."

The beans with onion and garlic were good. I hoped Jimmy had been able to get the Wolf Squad warm food. Spread along the bank of the Saluda River in clusters, they waited in the rain.

Tyrell might still be torturing Weston. I had to do something. Shoveling in the soup, I made my way past the table. Penny sat on a crate with Odie beside her.

"Where's Roxie?" I asked.

Penny winked. "Visiting the Wolf Squad, she said. Finding Tika's group, I bet."

"Want to come with?" I asked.

I handed Dean my empty mug. "I'm going to go check

on the Wolf Squad. Hold down the tent?" He'd want to be here, in case news came in.

He frowned, but nodded. "Be careful."

"Love you."

Dean leaned in and kissed me. "I love you too."

The rain had lessened to a dreary drizzle, though the ground had given up trying to soak it up. Little rivers ran off the asphalt, waterfalls splashing as they sought the river. The current would be stronger and better for defending.

Penny checked on Bella. "She doesn't mind the rain too much. I don't like leaving her geared up all day, though."

Jimmy jogged toward us from the bridge, swinging a large orange container. I'd seen the military at Sparta use a similar cylinder for carrying water. His expression curious, he called out to us. "Something happen?"

I shook my head and offered a comforting smile. "Just wanted to check in on everyone. Come with us."

He relaxed and hefted the container; it appeared empty. "Let me drop this off. I can catch up."

"We'll wait." My coveralls were hardly dry from the morning's excursion. I smoothed back my hair and tilted my head to smirk at Penny. "Tika's group first?"

After Jimmy joined us and we started toward the bridge, I commented on an obvious tear in the leg of his coveralls. He shrugged it off. "Tore it on one of the old trucks."

I frowned. "On the bridge?"

"No, the big trucks around Andy's post at the silos east of the bridge. I was hurrying and not paying attention." Jimmy's southern accent made light of the incident, but he'd been working nonstop throughout the day.

"How are they doing out there?"

"They're dry, but bored. They were all a little upset about Quinn and Weston."

He led us down the empty section of the highway ramp that led to the bridge, keeping us to the right side. Tika's lightning group had a post at the railroad tracks just behind the burned area that Sam and Dean had prepared. With all the rain, was little worry about fire spreading. As the ground sloped down, we walked beside asphalt to a muddy hill. Jimmy kept me from sliding on my ass more than once before we reached the bottom and headed east.

The area stunk of burned wood on the south side of the tracks. I could sense Tika and her small group hidden in the trees ahead. From her familiar rhythms, Roxie was with them.

Sam had his people armed and scattered about where they had a view of the river. I could find them easily in my othersense, but rarely physically saw them. They blended into the brush as well as Dean or Penny could.

We heard Nadia's voice from a few yards away. The boy who eventually responded with an acknowledging grunt was Patrick, who Tika had picked for her team.

"It would make sense. They might have planned on the threat being enough for the Alliance, but now that we've taken down their helicopter, they have to come up with a new plan. You know it was Quinn who had to have pushed for the assault. He was never one to sit around and wait."

I scuffed my foot on the oversized gravel near the rusting tracks loud enough that at least Roxie and Tika turned toward us. When Isabel stood, Nadia trailed off. The young Patrick paled when he looked over.

"How is everyone holding out?" I climbed up the muddy incline to their position under a large live oak. Odie checked in with everyone before settling with Isabel.

Nadia smiled. "The rain's nearly stopped. I feel like it rains more up here. Is that possible? We're close to the mountains, right?"

I let Nadia chatter for a bit. She kept the group lively, when we might delve into darker thoughts.

I waited a while before coaxing Tika into speaking. "I actually miss the little berets." As a sly smile slid on my face, she returned it.

"I forgot about the hats. I don't miss those patrols," she said.

"Didn't mind them. I wasn't good at training."

Tika appeared surprised. "I would have thought — at least air."

"I would have focused on healing, if I could have." Eric rose in my memories, and I fought a wince. "I could control air better than heat or water. Some things changed when I really had to use them."

Tika frowned when she noticed Jimmy's coveralls. "I should have brought my supplies."

He chuckled. "Like we thought we'd have nothing better to do."

Nadia jumped in about the berets, and how they'd be too wet by now. In most conversations, she didn't like being left out of doing most of the talking.

When I prepared to leave, Roxie said shy goodbyes to Tika before joining us. My lips twitched in a near smirk, and she rolled her eyes. "Don't."

"Why not? You're squirming. I'm happy for you — both."

Jimmy seemed awkward by my teasing, but Penny just beamed.

"Tika's sweet," admitted Roxie.

"So are you," I countered.

She snorted and laughed. "Rough and gruff."

"So? At least you're not preaching all the rules to me anymore."

Roxie rolled her eyes. "What rules?"

We checked on her small group just to the west and let Jimmy loop us through all the positions. The rain eased to occasional whimpers of wind and drops that might have come from cloud or tree; I couldn't tell.

When we reached the sandpit labyrinth of machinery and equipment where Andy had holed up half a mile east of the bridge, Jimmy pounded on a silo wall to get the Wolf Squad's attention.

His red hair dry, Andy peered over the edge a couple stories up. "We moving?"

My neck pinched, trying to look up. "No. Came to check in on you."

He scrambled over the edge onto the ladder and climbed down. "You okay? I mean, after Quinn and Weston and all that?"

"As good as it gets." My feelings changed every few minutes, and Dean's words haunted me. *More would die.*

Fawn's shaved head peered over, and she began climbing down more delicately. Len came after. Those two were part of my team with Jimmy, and I'd grab them to take up my position at the north end of the bridge.

"I'm ready to get this going. Just waiting on the word." Andy jumped the last few feet to land in the sand.

A ring of heads peered down from the top of the silo, most from Morea and Evrotas.

"I'd rather it not happen at all," I said. "I don't believe I'll have that choice."

He leaned down in a conspiratorial whisper. "Too much longer and I'll have a mutiny on hand." His head cocked, and his eyes squinted, staring behind me. "Pahawan."

As the Duathua swooped down toward us, the darkened Kudaru armor stood out against the light gray sky. Their voices loud, they circled as they called, "The dam. They're moving for the dam."

Penny swore and led the run back toward the tracks. As I followed, Andy whistled and shouted to his silo crew. "Move out. Careful with that ladder."

My chest tightened and felt hollow. I didn't have a great understanding of the positioning at the dam. Most of the conversation in the command tent today had been planning for it, but I'd missed a lot. Dean and Penny would be with me when we set up my position, and they had the details.

I just needed to get there in time.

Chapter Thirty-Two

Running beside the tracks, I chastised myself. "Should have been at the command tent."

Ahead, Penny's dark coat whipped, making her appear a vengeful spirit. Roxie kept pace beside me. Jimmy and Andy were behind, only because they didn't use the full length of their legs.

Would Dean wait or head west with Sam and the others in command? *He'll wait.*

Dampened, burned brush and trees to my left stunk as the rain barely sprinkled. My footing threatened to topple me a number of times as random chunks of rock dislodged from their places between rusting tracks.

I ran past trees where the gray sky appeared to scrape their green tops. The sun had sunk but left little hint of its position against the clouds. A pair of dark silhouettes formed at the crest of the canopy ahead before they dropped to the opening along the tracks.

Nur and Jural sped toward me, and my steps slowed, unsure of the message they'd bring. Penny stopped and turned as they flew over her head.

"Caitlyn, with us." Nur's voice carried a tense tone, one I'd rarely heard from her.

I glanced at Roxie without hesitating as I stopped and spread my arms for the Duathua to grab. "Good luck. Stay safe. You too, Andy. Jimmy, see you there."

As they grabbed firmly under my arms and lifted, air from their wings beat my wet hair into my face. The clouds proved higher than I'd imagined as we rose above the trees, cutting northwest over the forest. "Dean?" I asked.

Jural answered. "Sam and Lauren are dropping him off to meet you at the Nest."

"Nest?" I asked.

"His name for the platform they've set up for you."

That likely had some meaning in his quirky humor. "How much time do we have?"

She remained silent for a bit. "None, really, from what Henweyay explained. The first vehicles will arrive at the east edge of the lake by the time we get you there. The troops on foot, maybe an hour after that."

Trees, structures, and roads flashed under us in a nauseating blur, so I focused on the horizon where dull gray met with dark forest. *There will be more.* I almost wretched. How many more could I lose to Tyrell? *Eric.* Thinking of my friend tightened my jaw. *Where will you be, Selina?*

In my othersense, I found many of Sam's people already dotting the forest as they moved into position. Pahawan patrolled from nearby to the south. I found Tyrell's vehicles at the edge of my senses to the southwest, speeding in our direction in a wide line.

Ahead, electric poles spiked an open area, with some of the wires dangling and others taut. It wasn't the Nest, but similar from the description and perhaps where Roxie would be posted. I turned, trying to peer past Nur on my left, but couldn't see the Saluda River for the trees. Dean and Sam had all but one of the water teams along the river, the last at the end of the dam near Lake Murray.

I sensed Dean ahead and made out the spiked poles of the Nest. The gray sky only remained light in the west.

The Nest had been built at the top of a forest of electric poles, where wires stretched outward in some configuration from the past. The towers grew in rows from cracked concrete that stretched as far and wide as a parking lot. On the highest spires facing the dam, newly added wooden bridges stretched from rough platforms affixed to the metal structures. Some had walls and two had ceilings, forming little shacks. The river flowed to the south, escaping Lake Murray through the dam to the west. Three of Sam's snipers held positions there, while a couple dozen patrolled the base almost to the shore.

Navigating the thick metal lines, Nur and Jural brought me down on one of the bridges, and I yelped when it swayed underneath my feet. The cables that stretched along like railings gave me something to grab.

The pair of Duathua released me, then rose. "We'll be back after we check in with Henweyay. One of us at least." Jural nodded, diving north through the tangle of wires and poles.

Unsteady, I slid my hands on the lines as I shuffled toward Dean, who waited on the platform ahead. It had two walls and a roof, but only railings where they joined the flimsy bridge as I crossed, another cutting in from my right, and the one beyond.

"Don't fall," Dean said in a teasing tone.

"Shut up, Dean." His taunt had the intended effect. I glared at him and crossed the last few steps with false confidence.

He offered a hand that I ignored as I stepped onto the steady planks of the platform. "Jerk."

"Glad you didn't fall." His gentle smile faded, and he rested a hand on my back. His skin had dried from the earlier rains. Even his hair appeared its normal messy wave.

I pulled my eyes off him, studying the crates and water bottles stored in the shack. The metal pole in the center dominated the space.

"What's going on out there?" He nodded toward a thin slit in the wall facing the dam. Someone had tacked a map on the wood beside it.

I could see the blockade of cars silhouetted against the lighter gray of the sky. As high up as we were, the horizon of the dam rose above us. Peering down, I could make out the dark, rolling waters of the Saluda River and the shadows of the tree-lined shore across the way.

Beyond the shore, I sensed the Pahawan gliding on their patrol and the first of Tyrell's vehicles moving sporadically toward us. "A few are coming." Glancing from the window slit to the map, I drew a finger along the road that led over the dam. I pointed to a spot far from the Saluda River. "Here, I think."

He sighed. "We've got time. Sam's setting up camp a few hundred feet north of us. Henweyay will take a position in that platform back there." His gesture toward the wall behind us didn't tell me much.

"I thought she planned to be with Sam?" Perhaps I should have paid more attention.

"Changed. Weston might have given up the Nest. Sam bolstered the troops along the shore as well."

I frowned, then nodded. "Henweyay's Pahawan can get us out of here quickly, if needed."

"Yep. I approved." He squeezed my shoulders with both hands. "You ready?"

"No regrets," I lied as I leaned back into his hold.

"Nothing is easy."

Penny and Jimmy were the first to join us. Below, I could sense our positions filling up with Wolf Squad: Roxie's and another water group to the east. The vibrations to the northwest should include Tika, though I couldn't identify her at this distance like I could Roxie. My nerves still seemed on edge, but my pulse had eased since the flight here.

Tyrell's people had slowed their initial incursion, and the first vehicles had spread out and stopped. Four-man teams milled about, but none had come closer. Dean pegged pins into the map at my best approximation of the positions.

"Effing odd," Penny commented. "Why not just bring it on?"

Dean nudged his chin toward me. "They know she's able to find them. They've got a plan. Need to wait for their foot to arrive, anyway."

Nur and Jural landed on the bridge, setting it to sway in a sickening manner. They walked to us without noticing.

"Henweyay hopes you have a report," Nur said.

Dean pointed to the map. "Not much of one. I think they're waiting for their troops on foot to arrive."

Jural waved long fingers at the cluster of vehicles about a half mile away. "And these?"

I shrugged. "Raced up here, then stopped." Glancing at Jimmy, I continued, "We can disrupt them, but I expect we'll have a lot more soon."

Penny nodded.

Nur studied the map before stepping onto the bridge and flying off, leaving Jural behind. Below us, two Wolf Squad were climbing up, and I assumed Fawn and Len.

When I turned to the south, Dean frowned. "What?"

"They're moving. A lot of them." Weston must have told them how far I could sense. All across the southern edge, rhythms flared in a mass. Vehicles sped along the road, but a wide wave came for us, aiming toward the river.

As I drew my hand in an arc across the map, a distant thud sounded. A second came behind, a third, then too many to split them up. "What's that?" I asked.

Dean peered through the slit, and I leaned over to look. The murky gray of the southern sky gave no hint of the army approaching, nor what the sounds had been. I turned just as a flash blossomed to the west of us. The blast trailed behind it as a second explosion hit the shore below us.

"What is that?" I crouched at the sounds. The hits came all around us, lighting the metal towers with orange flashes.

Dean's lips flattened. "Cannon. No, mortar. Maybe artillery. Sam would know."

A chill raced up my neck. In my othersense, rhythms spiked with pain. Two were below, near the river, but more to the northwest. "Tika. I think her group got hit. It could be Andy."

I scoured the troops moving toward us. "How would I find them, Dean?"

Jural put her hand on my shoulder. "We should get you down from here. I think they are targeting this place."

Jimmy moved closer to me, as if he agreed.

"They missed." My tone came out sharper than I intended. I wasn't running. "Dean?"

"They'd be small squads. Clustered. With activity."

I smiled, knowing my target. "Jimmy?" I reached out my hand, and he offered his forearm.

He called the otherness, and I drew it in to focus on those first vehicles that had come over. Others passed on their way to the dam. The soldiers on foot hadn't reached them.

A distant thud sounded, and I snarled. A second fired before my first tornado touched down. My next was sloppy, but effectively scattered the crew. A third mortar sounded before the first blast exploded to my left.

In a frenzy and hoping I wasn't wrong, I slammed a third down on a hapless team, almost satisfied at the spikes of pain I brought.

Around me, flames blossomed in the darkness. The Alliance suffered and vibrated in pain and death as I sent one tornado after the next until those first little clusters were torn apart.

I shivered at the continuous calls for the otherness as I waited for another dreaded thud from somewhere I hadn't hit. It didn't come. "Dean?"

"I'm here. We're okay." He and Penny had been placing pins on the map where I'd pointed earlier.

"There will be more," I whispered. Among the Alliance hit by the weapons, some had died, and others were dying. They might be my friends. I found Roxie's pitched vibrations, but she didn't seem hurt.

In the otherness waiting in Jimmy, I felt Len join our circle. They'd made it up here, and I hadn't even noticed. I'd been too focused on destroying those weapons. Acrid smoke wafted in the breeze.

Jural touched my shoulder, and I jumped. Her voice remained calm. "Henweyay's Pahawan is here for a report."

"They're coming." My distracted voice cracked.

Dean spoke from his place at the map. "Caitlyn, do we have this right?"

I glanced at the arc of pins and nodded. We'd rehearsed for a different location, but I adapted. "Tell Roxie to start a wave for the opposite shore in thirty minutes. The first of the soldiers should be there. Have Tika — have them strike the middle of the dam road as soon as they can. Tyrell's vehicles are working through. Andy's fire teams too." I rattled out the directions, but the voice sounded like someone else's.

Jabbing a finger on the map along the road over the dam, Dean barked a light question to me. "Here, Caitlyn?"

"Up and down from that area."

"Targets DR7 through DR9," he said quietly behind me.

I heard a Duathua flutter away, but Jural kept her hand on my shoulder. "You are doing well, Caitlyn."

How could anyone do well in this mayhem? Fires burned below in sodden trees, and the people who were dead and dying around me could be Wolf Squad.

"How will I know what's happening to the Wolf Squad?" *How will I know who died because they followed me?* I thought.

Penny answered from her place at the maps beside Dean. "Henweyay will keep us updated if we — lose a team. Time to get to work, Caitlyn."

She meant it was time for me to send in my wind. Time to kill.

Jimmy's calm accent made it easier. "We're ready, Caitlyn."

The Alliance counted on the Wolf Squad; counted on me.

Chapter Thirty-Three

I sought out the closest vehicles that wound their way through the Alliance blockade of abandoned cars. The first tornadoes I sent were small and targeted, roaring in the distance. Through the small slit in the side of our Nest, I stared at the dim clouds and shadowed trees, while I targeted with my othersense. Some missed, and I had to hunt down my prey. In a few cases, soldiers died in my attacks. I'd begun skipping away from those pained vibrations, searching out any who continued forward. Those behind showed no fear of my wind and barreled past.

"Updates?" Penny asked. She'd hung a small lantern beside their map. A square contraption, it had tiny shutters on all sides, and she only had one open enough that they could see.

Those aiming for the river seemed to come as one, though they spread out and made for sparse targets. Roxie, the other water team, and I would have to deal with them soon enough.

"Yeah, sorry." We'd practiced this in the command tent. I scanned the map, tapped on the forward position of the vehicles, and stroked a general curve for the bulk of the soldiers on foot. Turning my othersense below the Nest, I found active patrols of Sam's people along with the wounded. Two knots of Wolf Squad, one Roxie's, marked the shore to the east, while the rest dotted areas in a northwest line from my location. There were wounded among them, and possibly dead.

"It's going to get bad when they reach the river," I said.

"Sam knows." Dean's tone distracted, he still flicked a smile to his face, knowing I was watching. "We'll be ready. Tika's group will move down here if the bridge is clear. Andy and Ben's fire teams can handle the road."

Lightning lit up the west. Huge bolts crackling onto broken cars set one to explode in a blossom of red. Glimpses of the dam blinked into view in the bright light of the strikes. The attack crawled south, driving into Tyrell's troops. I smiled, not for the destruction and mayhem caused, but because I knew Tika had survived. Would Roxie have blamed me? I would have.

Still drawing otherness from my circle, I scanned the area of the lightning storm. Soldiers died there, and I'd become numb to it. I would love it if they gave up but they wouldn't.

Just to be sure, I sent a pair of tornadoes into the area where the mortars had been. I didn't want those to be set up again. The smoldering fires they'd left were dwindling, but the sharp scent of smoke caught my nose.

One at a time, I attacked the fast-moving soldiers in vehicles, hitting clusters where I could. The line of soldiers on foot marched on the road as well; I'd get to them in time. No matter the havoc I laid upon them, they weren't stopping. Destruction an endless task, my glazed eyes stared at the southern horizon. A wall of dark night seemed to approach as if to smother us.

I blinked, fatigue catching up as I swayed.

Jimmy's voice was firm and reassuring. "Fawn?"

Lorabelle had come up with the suggestion to have a healer on hand to keep our energy levels higher. Drawing through a circle of people still taxed the Wolf Squad. As Fawn pressed her hands on my free arm, I paused my attacks and let her healing refresh me. All the healers had been assigned to teams. There weren't enough.

A Pahawan scout from Henweyay arrived to report to Jural and Dean. "Two dead in F2. One wounded in L1 has been pulled back. Sam wants a time of arrival to the river shore."

Ben's team was F2, the fire group farthest north. "Who died?" I asked.

"I do not know their names, Seyir."

They wouldn't know the name of the wounded, either. Perhaps it would be best not to know. I scanned Tyrell's soldiers on foot. "The first should hit the river in about fifteen minutes. Tell them I'm guessing."

I retrieved my arm from Fawn and with my finger drew two new lines for Penny on the map. It bulged in both spots as if they were blocked in the middle. What blocked them didn't matter; they'd be here too soon. Selina would be among them with the Youth Guard.

"How's the road?" Dean asked.

Returning my attention to the vehicles, I prepared a tornado as I spoke and tapped the map. "I've got them under control at the moment. When the soldiers on foot arrive is when we'll need everybody to pile it on."

According to the map, the widest part of the river lay in front of the Nest. Where it thinned, they'd have to cross in front of Roxie or farther to the east.

Dean pointed to the dam and road where the water flowed out. "Fifteen minutes?"

I nodded. "Twenty at most."

He turned to the scout. "All northern teams on DR6 through DR4 in fifteen. Two-minute breaks between attacks."

A day ago, these rehearsed directions sounded awkward and odd, as if part of a game. Now they meant death and survival.

Doing my part, I dropped another tornado, clipping a vehicle and sending its three occupants tumbling eastward. As they approached, the soldiers on foot were swept up in my attacks. Compared to the mass marching toward the rivers, they were the rarity.

Dean sent Jural off with an update when I had several fast-moving vehicles slip through those on foot to try to reach the river. I caught some but had to shift focus back and forth between the road on top of the dam and those approaching Roxie. *Too many.* My chest tightened as I flitted between targets like a moth.

"They are getting through. I can't keep up." My tone petulant, I straightened. "How soon before Tika's team begins firing?"

"Six minutes."

Soldiers in vehicles could reach Tika's position before that. The Alliance had people around her, but I doubted they were soldiers. "Farmers with weapons," Dean had called them.

I focused on the bridge road, hoping Sam's people would find those who had reached the shore before they could threaten Roxie. When she unleashed her water, they'd have no chance.

A single soldier, perhaps on a motorcycle, evaded my first tornado even though I stood a thousand feet from where he wound through the blockade.

From my left, a gunshot echoed, then two more.

I focused on the elusive soldier and caught him

perfectly. His rhythms spiked with pain and terror; he shifted violently north before his vibrations calmed, perhaps into unconsciousness.

Gunfire spattered up and down the river. Pain took one of Sam's people on our shore, but the shots continued.

A pair of Tyrell's soldiers sped in a vehicle along the road over the dam, and I caught them as they slowed. The soldiers on foot spread across the first part of the dam, some keeping to the road, others heading for the shore. Dean had been concerned that snipers could hit us easily from that distance.

Before drawing in the otherness for my next target on the dam, I scanned the river by Roxie. The enemy had entered the water east of her. "C'mon Roxie. Hit them."

The regular gunfire set the tempo of my pulse. I unleashed my next attack, sending three soldiers tumbling down the east slope of the dam to their deaths.

At some unspoken signal, Fawn returned to my arm, pushing away the fatigue. I paused as she did so, tracking my next two targets who moved through the soldiers on foot. They were so close.

Roxie's team and the second group drew in the otherness, and over that roar came the river rising and clawing at the southern banks. The closest soldiers were swept away; others ran.

"Roxie's group. W1 and W2 just cleared the shore."

Otherness roared from the northwest as those teams prepared to attack. They were early. Fawn worked to restore some of my strength. My mouth was dry, but a drink could come later.

At the far edge of my othersense, a pair of rhythms moved impossibly fast from the south. "Dean." *Nothing could move like that.*

I peered through our little slit.

Below us, a small spray of fire darted toward the ground under me. The sight made no sense to my weary eyes.

Flames sprouted from the back of a long, pointed cylinder. The image seared into my memory as it moved faster than any vehicle I'd witnessed. The fire at the rear illuminated the dull metal cylinder and the nose that curved gracefully to a dull shaded tip.

In the space of time it took me to catch that glimpse, the pair of absurdly fast-moving rhythms passed overhead.

Dean didn't get a chance to respond.

A moment after the strange object disappeared below us, the explosion behind us lit our little room like daytime and slammed me against the thin wall.

Chapter Thirty-Four

I panicked as the world shifted. My ears rang from the explosion. The sturdy metal pole of the Nest groaned and began to tilt forward and to the side in a slow but determined movement.

Jimmy grabbed my arm. I'd lost them all in the shock of the blast.

Where's Dean?

Slipping sideways, only Jimmy kept me from toppling through the opening at the side of the Nest. Someone, maybe Fawn, pressed along my right leg as I stared at the open air and the sagging bridge.

Penny glided on her side to the rails, silent against the roar in my ears. Her hands stretched toward the metal pole in the center, too short to reach.

Jimmy braced a thick arm to the roof with his left hand, keeping me and Fawn from falling.

"Dean!" I couldn't hear my voice beyond the dull hum of the word in my jaw.

Outside, a cable snapped, and the Nest lurched forward, abandoning its sideways tilt. Our little building swung so that the wall, map, and slit were at an equal pitch to the floor.

Dean and Len slammed atop us in a pile while Penny crawled and grabbed onto Jimmy's boot. The Nest came to a lurching stop. A tangle of panicked bodies pitched into Jimmy and whatever wood we scraped against.

I imagined us dangling toward the Saluda River below, but the towers weren't that high. It would crash into the ground before that.

I shifted, searching for Dean. Fires burned behind us in the direction of Henweyay's platform. The light reflected on the cables of the bridge and adjacent towers. I sensed our little group first, finding Dean close behind. Everyone's vibrations spiked in fear, but beyond bruises, no pain.

Below us, my othersense detected Pahawan on the ground. Sam's people lay among them. Many were dead, some injured and perhaps dying. Farther out, people raced toward us. Two Duathua flew toward the Nest; the one in pain I recognized as Jural. Nur helped her. They couldn't fly us all down.

Dean's hand rested on my shoulder, and I grabbed it. "I'm okay," I said, but doubted he could hear me.

That hadn't been a helicopter. *A plane?* We'd read about them, but I'd always found it hard to believe in flying. *Where was it?*

Our little lantern had either extinguished or toppled out of the Nest. Only the glow of fires lit Jural and Nur fluttering at the edge of the opening, as if they feared adding their weight to our precarious roost.

Jural held onto a shard of metal wedged into her side. Her thick skin bled around the wound, but not as much as I would have expected.

My heart raced selfishly as Nur lowered Jural's mass into our sagging structure. Had she come to be healed? A little more weight might send us all to the ground. With Tyrell's weapon flying overhead, though, it might not matter.

Leaning against the floor, Jural sidled toward me, reaching past Jimmy for my hand.

I had a fair understanding of Duathua bodies and wasn't sure that we could save her. Teeth clenched, I crouched and shifted around Jimmy's legs. I could at least melt the metal out of her. I glanced back for Fawn to help, though she'd been wedged under Dean and Len.

Jural spoke, though I couldn't understand her over the ringing in my ears. She held my hand back from the metal protruding from her.

I frowned until she pulled free her Kudaru fish and showed it to me. Pointing it toward the metal in her, she waved her hand toward the sky.

"The metal is from the plane?" The tube had been a bomb of some sort. She wanted me to sense it with her strange method. "And do what?" *Whatever I could.* I nodded.

I started dropping into that overwhelming perception before I even touched the metal. Nausea roiled in my stomach at all the connections of us stranded in this death-trap, pitched to smash to the ground.

Focusing, I found the threads belonging to the metal. Two were the strongest.

One led to the south, and at the end of the bright line, I found Tyrell. Somewhere far from the limits of my othersense, he stood on the flat top of a building. His crew had binoculars trained in our direction, though I doubted they could see this far. Perhaps they waited for signals or just enjoyed seeing the fires from mortars and bombs. Tyrell had a host of tense scouts or assistants waiting for his commands. Maps had been mounted to boards and propped beside him. He wore a cruel grin, and I hated him more than ever.

Eyes closed, I flipped to the other connection and sucked in a sharp breath. A massive triangle of metal, the plane flew sideways in a slow arc with flames roaring out of engines. The tops of the helmets of the pilots faced me through glass that covered their cabin.

"What could I do against something like this?" My voice hummed in my bones. I opened my eyes and searched the faces of those around me.

Jimmy smiled confidently, and I nearly cried. Dean gave me a grim nod, obviously seeing the panic in my face.

I closed my eyes, panting against a tight chest, and followed the thread back to the turning plane. The bomb had been meant for me — for us. Weston must have given up our Nest. I didn't blame him.

Would they attack again? *Of course they will.* Tyrell would make sure I died. The Alliance would not survive once the troops crossed the river with us in disarray.

With a jerk, our Nest dropped.

I screamed, flailing into Jimmy and Dean. Finally, I could hear my voice.

Jural toppled onto us. The wall had become our floor. The wood groaned.

Metal scraped and shrieked as we jolted to a stop. I froze, waiting for us to continue falling, but we'd hit something.

Fumbling for my hand, Jural forced me back to the metal shard slick with her blood.

Jimmy found my other hand and placed it on his forearm before reaching for Len. The otherness of the circle grew. We were Wolf Squad, teetering on the precipice of our deaths, but fighting with everything we had.

Closing my eyes, I followed the strange connection back

to the plane. It was leveling out, and I saw the pilots' visors. As I studied the craft, my view shifted. Bright flames fired out the back.

Three bombs, like the one I'd seen, hung from the bottom.

I formed a shield, but it wavered. The pilots glanced about their cabin as if alarmed.

The next well of otherness I called from the circle roared in my ears, and my body lightened in that odd effect I had on gravity. Vaguely, I sensed the others piled against me, shifting in surprise. I might topple us all. No matter what, I had to stop the plane.

The next shield I built started on the sharp tip at the front, before coating the metal inch by inch as it worked toward the bombs hanging from the bottom. The soft Kudaru held, though I fought for every bit. Air moved by too quickly, making it difficult to gather.

The otherness screamed from the circle, and hands held me in place from drifting away. I couldn't ease up.

Every bit of progress took too long as I crawled the shield toward the bombs. If the first shield had worked, it would have been done by now.

Voices, dull and distant, sounded around me. Dean tapped my shoulder, but I couldn't stop. The next bomb might hit us directly. My almost weightless body felt correct rather than disconcerting.

"Almost." I spoke to myself as well as Dean.

Shield thick and reaching to the pointed noses of the weapons, the soft Kudaru shuddered with the plane. *A little farther.* My panting sucked in breaths, but my lungs felt empty.

At the tips of all three, my shield wavered, searching for air.

A clamp at the top of one bomb released, and I shoved

what I could in front of it. Flame blossomed at the tube's rear, and it wiggled free of my shield, slapping into the other bombs like a frantic fish as it fought its way free.

If it hit, I might die — we all might die — but I intended to hold on as long as I could. There were still two bombs attached underneath.

I packed more air into my growing shield.

The plane vibrated stronger, as if firing the weapon against my shield had been too much for it. Forming another layer became impossible as the shudders nearly wrenched it from my view.

In one quick second, the plane flipped, the flaming engines at the rear over the nose.

The torrent of flames from the engines snuffed out. My vision, so close, had me flinching as the massive craft toppled toward me. In shock, my view backed away. Terrified men struggled in their seats as the craft toppled out of control.

"I killed it," I said in awe.

The plane flashed dizzily as it pitched to its side, wing flipping to wing against the dark, cloudy sky.

When the bomb exploded to the northwest, echoing through my ringing ears and shaking our unsteady perch, I released the shield still glued to the plane.

My eyes sprung open to find dark armored Pahawan evacuating Penny and Fawn. Len's body dropped from where it had drifted, tethered only by Jimmy's firm grip.

Dean pressed against me with renewed gravity. Jimmy slapped to the wall turned floor.

Jural's eyes locked on mine as she said something, but I couldn't hear her.

I'd killed the plane, and we were being rescued from the deathtrap.

Dean tugged at my arm, but I focused on Jural. *She*

can't die. Using what little strength I had left, I melted the hateful metal and poured the warm liquid into my palm. Before any of them could force me out of the Nest, I drew more otherness from Jimmy and healed what I could of her wound.

Chapter Thirty-Five

I waited as a Pahawan and Nur flew Jural into the night. "I think she'll live," I told Dean.

He nodded, perhaps because he heard my words, or because he wanted to placate and get me outside to the waiting Pahawan who were swarming about in the air.

Before I let them take me from the ruined Nest, I tested the metal glob with Jural's strange perception. It led to the shattered ruins of the plane on the shore of Lake Murray to the west — and to Tyrell, who waited bewildered in the south. His attendants were reporting on something, but I could only see, not hear.

For a fleeting moment, I wanted to cloak his head and mouth with a shield and suffocate him. The image caused my pulse to surge.

"Dean, if Tyrell died right now, would it end all this?"

"Doubt it. Someone would take charge."

If I could be sure that his death would end the attack, I would have killed Tyrell and lived with my conscience.

Dean nudged me with more insistence toward the opening, and I complied. Strong Kudaru-armored hands grabbed and lowered me to the ground.

Our Nest wasn't as high up as I'd imagined; it leaned upon a lower tower. Three others behind were toppled to the concrete. One of those had been Henweyay's. Bitter-scented smoke rose from a crater. I spotted two bodies in the darkness.

Gunfire rattled at the shore. I could sense Tyrell's army still pressing toward Roxie.

Penny rubbed an elbow that Fawn worked on, but Jimmy and Len appeared uninjured.

Last to leave the Nest, Dean strode toward me after the Pahawan brought him to the ground.

To the northwest, a dying fire still had orange flames licking at the night clouds. I reached out with my othersense, and my breath hitched. Ben's fire team had been located in that area, but I found no one nearby. "Ben?" I yelled at Dean.

"I don't know." Concern hung in his tone.

I wanted to check on Ben, but we needed to regroup. From my othersense, Tyrell's army hadn't retreated because they'd lost the plane; just the opposite.

Tika's team sprayed the dam's top with lightning, causing me to flinch. Andy blossomed a line of fire down the road to follow her attack.

"Let's get back from the river." Dean gestured north beyond the crater.

Jimmy hovered close to me, as if I might fall. Penny spoke with one of the remaining Pahawan. Len knelt on one knee, taking deep breaths. One of Sam's people limped beside the shore. More of the Alliance moved toward us from the north, probably drawn by the disaster.

I turned southeast, worn from my effort with the plane, and focused on Tyrell's front encroaching even into the water to the east. "The foot soldiers are still making for Roxie's location. Shouldn't we head there?"

Both Dean and Jimmy put their hands on my shoulders and guided me north.

Penny jogged up. "The Pahawan are regrouping and checking in with Sam. They'll be back in five minutes."

Dean pointed past the crater. "They can find us on the other side of that."

"Sounds effing right." Her voice dropped as she placed a hand on my arm. "Ben. He's dead. One of the team survived."

"I did that. When I tried to stop the bomb."

She cocked her head and shook it, lips pursed. "Not your fault. You can't take that."

I had killed Ben — and more. My victory turned sour. I wanted to climb into a hole somewhere. They wouldn't let me, friends or enemies.

When the otherness welled around us, I took precious seconds to glance in surprise from Jimmy to Len, who was still kneeling a few feet away.

The night exploded into white light.

A brilliant stab of lightning struck Jimmy. He froze mid-breath, locked in a tremor of death. Crawling lines of red had etched his gentle face.

The jolt from his hand on my shoulder slammed me into the air. I flew back until his tortured body disappeared from my view. Limp, I hit the ground and rolled helplessly across gritty concrete until I stopped, facing him. *Jimmy.* My breath hitched as I choked a sob. He'd been the kindest and gentlest of all the Wolf Squad.

His rhythms dead, Jimmy stared sightlessly at the cold stars. He had no reassuring smile, just a final expression of surprise.

This can't be happening.

Tears blurred my vision. Short, snotty sobs spattered

out. He had saved me and been at my side during the worst. We'd survived until now. *Jimmy.*

My muscles wouldn't work. I tried to reach for him. Even if I had stretched far enough, he couldn't be healed.

I flashed back to Eric's death at Camp Sparta, and rage ignited inside.

The strange scent of electricity and Jimmy's burned hair and flesh reached my nose. Somehow that awakened me in time as the otherness gathered close, and I drew it in and snuffed it out.

"Selina," I croaked. My muscles jerked as I tried to stand, or at least sit.

She'd killed Jimmy, as she had Eric. Tears poured down, blurring my eyes, but I saw with my othersense.

Her strike had knocked us all down. The others were alive, though dazed and hurt.

Selina stood to the east, closer than the river. I should have sensed her coming near.

The rhythms of another familiar Youth Guard accompanied her. It took me until his first gunshot to recognize him. Weston, his vibrations spiked with nervousness, was with her.

The otherness came again, and I took it from her.

Weston drew in the otherness, but instead of attacking, he worked with air near him and Selina.

Three yards away, Penny fired back. Fawn lay beside her, unmoving but alive.

My leg trembled uncontrollably when I rolled to my knees. Jimmy's body was a blurry shape in the darkness, a silhouette against the paler concrete. The surprise of finding Selina crumbled against my renewed, burning rage.

Dean fired his weapon in two quick shots, then called out from behind me. "He's got a shield."

I blinked against tears, trying to stand. Weston had

betrayed us all along. He'd even learned what he could from me and used it against us.

Selina called the otherness to a spot in the north, and lightning pierced into a Pahawan flying there. The dark armor glowed before the Duathua dropped to the ground, their vibrations dying.

Snarling, I called a roar of the otherness and dropped a tornado onto Selina and Weston. Only a dozen yards away, the wind whistled past me, tugging at my coveralls.

Weston's shield held somehow. They crouched low and didn't budge. When my wind guttered out, they began moving toward us. He continued firing, and a bullet ricocheted off the concrete two feet to my right.

Selina called the otherness over Len, and I barely reached it. Using it to form a shield in front of myself, I realized I couldn't protect the others. We were spread too far apart.

Dean shifted to his werewolf form. I could feel it in the connection we had and through the otherness, yet his vibrations had not spiked to the level of emotion that usually caused it.

"Dean," I called out.

Otherness surged, and a spray of Selina's lightning took down two of Sam's people as they ran toward us from the north. More would die if they tried to come help us.

I stood straight and wiped my eyes clear. Selina struck behind Dean, far enough that I couldn't grab the otherness. In that light, I could see the Wolf Squad coveralls she wore. Weston still had his. Tika had embroidered our emblem on it for him. He'd betrayed us and brought Selina. She'd taken too many from me. *No more.*

Racing north, Dean moved out of my range where I could protect him.

I couldn't bring them down with a tornado, so I called

the otherness to her and drew in air. I formed a shield around her, something like the coating I'd created around the soldiers who had drugged Dean, but different.

My feet shifted as gravity failed, but I ignored it, pressing the usual soft Kudaru into a creation even beyond the regular Kudaru that the Duathua formed. The thickness of my knuckle and dense, it covered every inch of her body and clothes, from her hair to the soles of her boots. It locked her like a statue as it snapped into place. *For Eric. For Jimmy. No more.*

Weston jumped back from her, forming a new shield and retreating as he fired at me. Two of his bullets hung in the soft Kudaru between us.

Selina's expression had been locked in determination, but I could sense the immediate panic she vibrated.

I jolted as my feet landed on the concrete. Gravity had returned.

Selina had once been my closest ally. She'd become my hated enemy, but I still felt dread at what I'd done. Her body encased, she couldn't breathe. The rage over Jimmy's death drained away in an icy chill. "I'm sorry," I whispered to her.

She tilted slowly, then clattered to the concrete. For a moment, I expected it to shatter, but it was far sturdier than regular Kudaru.

Even as Weston and Penny blasted gunfire, I stood frozen as Selina passed into unconsciousness, heading for death. Eric and I had only wanted to heal, not lead, and certainly not to kill.

Behind me, Len cried out, and his vibrations spiked in pain. One of Weston's bullets had found its mark. It broke me from my morbid focus on Selina's death throes.

My head snapped to train on the traitor and the shield he'd stolen from me. Reaching into my own, I touched one of his bullets and used Jural's strange perception to draw my focus up the connection.

My view became as if I stood a yard from him, so I reached out and absorbed the otherness he used for his shield. I would not kill him as I had Selina; I couldn't. His eyes widened, and I prepared wind, but Dean moved quicker. A blur of silver fur darted out of the darkness behind Weston.

Chapter Thirty-Six

I released the connection in horror as Dean ripped open Weston's throat. Staggering backward, I swayed on weak legs.

Jimmy lay where he'd died, his face mottled from the lightning and eyes staring at something beyond this horror. His burned flesh clung to the air. My heart broke again at the sight of the gentle teen.

Gunshots fired to the southeast, where Roxie's othersense roared. Tika still assaulted the top of the dam with sequential strikes. The road smoked with burned cars, and the gray plumes glowed from hidden fires.

Fawn had risen at some point, and she crawled toward Len, who stanched a wound on his leg with both hands. As she saw me moving with shaky steps, Penny straightened with her weapon ready, but only Sam's people moved through the towers toward us.

I stretched out my othersense, dismayed at the size of Tyrell's army at the shore and crossing east of Roxie's position. They'd move toward her eventually, clashing with Sam's defenders.

Deep to the south, a familiar dull thud sounded. I knelt

by Len as the mortar blasted on our side of the shore, just a hundred yards west of me. They'd recovered their weapons.

"That was Weston," Len said.

"Effing playing us all along." Penny stood guard over me.

I drew out the metal of the bullet from where it rested against Len's cracked shin. The tibia, according to Dean. I found him jogging toward us, in human form, and sighed. Together, Fawn and I began healing Len.

The mortar let out another thud, and I ignored it while I healed Len. Sam's people surrounded us in a wide arc facing the river. We might not win. Jimmy had died for nothing.

"Dude, pants." Penny's tone carried more humor than annoyance.

Len lay back, relaxing as we helped the body repair, the flesh pressed against nerves. Movement from the night sky and my othersense told me a Pahawan approached.

Dean collected his pants and spoke as he climbed into them. "Caitlyn, how do we look?"

Remaining kneeling, I released my otherness healing Len and rocked back to my heels. "It's not good. They've made it over the river to the east. Here, they are right across from us on the other shore."

He frowned. "We need to relocate you. Somewhere safer."

I didn't disagree. The mortar explosion lit the area with orange; it had ranged deeper north, but still west of us. We'd have to move Tika's team. *Where is safe?*

The Pahawan approached. "Sam wants you to retreat to his location and station there. I'm to bring back a report."

We needed to pull Roxie back, maybe just make a run for it. *Evacuate Columbia.* "They've crossed the river maybe three-quarters of a mile up. I can work on slowing their approach. They are all along the shore. The mortar — I can't stop it."

"Effing Tyrell's probably firing it himself." Penny eyed the shore, as if hoping to find a target to shoot at.

I reached into the pocket of my coveralls, pulled out the metal, and let the strange perception bring my odd vision to him. He remained on his flat rooftop, binoculars to his eyes. An attendant with a lantern held a map ready. "No, he's far away, beyond my othersense." Through the unusual connection, I *could* drop a tornado on them where they stood.

Dean crouched down and spoke. "Can you reach him? Kill him?"

The casing I'd created around Selina would work through this connection, like the shield on the distant plane. It wouldn't stop his soldiers. "No, I couldn't just assassinate him." It differed from a soldier firing a mortar when the threat was imminent.

"Why not?" Penny's tone came sharp and angry.

Because I wasn't a murderer or a soldier. *Tell that to Selina.* I hated that I'd done it, but didn't fully regret it. Tyrell had created the labs, if I could believe Higgins. "Could I live with myself if I did that to Tyrell?"

The question wasn't meant for them, but Penny swore in response. "Ef, I could."

"Send him a message then." Dean nodded at his own suggestion. "A threat to his life might work better."

The mortar thudded as I thought about Dean's words.

Tyrell brought down his binoculars and barked a command I couldn't hear. What message?

Reaching deeper north toward Tika, the mortar explosion lit my closed eyelids.

Weary, I drew in the otherness and collected the air around Tyrell to replicate what I'd done with Selina. What

I created was intricate, driven without anger, and took everything I had.

In my perception, he dropped his binoculars. Both of his hands went to his neck where I'd formed the wide collar. His usually cold, controlled eyes were wide, and for the first time I saw panic in them. I waited as his attendant raised the lantern, likely reading aloud the words I had inscribed there, "Retreat. I can find you anywhere."

Tyrell spoke, swallowing against the constraint, but I couldn't be sure he'd taken me seriously. I formed a ribbon of soft Kudaru and enclosed it tight above the collar long enough to see him react.

True fear lit Tyrell's eyes as he dug at it futilely with his fingers. I watched, not experiencing the pleasure I thought I might, before I dispersed it.

Dean supported me as I swayed where I knelt beside Len. "Did you kill him?"

"Worse than that. I collared him. Sent him a message."

Through the connection, I watched as Tyrell gave orders, tugging at the collar I'd given him.

Some of his people stared in disbelief while others rushed to complete some command. Red flares fired near Tyrell, shading his face with light; I hoped they were the order to retreat.

Opening my eyes, I let the dark southern horizon overlap the perception of my strange connection. Through smoke and the veil of night, I saw no flares, and my hope sagged.

The mortars thudded once more.

Then, a pair of red streaks rose from far to the south to burst, lighting distant treetops. Two more sets, much closer, launched from due south and the southeast. The light seemed to carry across a wider range of the forests.

"Ef me. Did you do that?" asked Penny.

The last two sets were nearly at the shore. "Are those signals to retreat?" I asked. They lit the sky so bright that I pulled up a shield between us and the shore. We sat on the ruined ground of the Nest with little cover and light illuminating our position.

"Let's hope so," Penny answered.

I searched the southern shore of the Saluda River with my othersense. The rhythms milled in no discernible direction. We waited, and I watched the rhythms.

It took seconds before I could confirm. "They *are* retreating."

Chapter Thirty-Seven

Two weeks after Tyrell abandoned his attack on Columbia, I stood behind the Wolf Den waiting for everyone to gather. Seven engraved Kudaru gravestones stood under the pines where we'd laid our fallen Wolf Squad. Jimmy had been given the center with Ben and his team, Heather and Keith, to the right. Jodie, Drew, and Michael lay on Jimmy's left.

"We'll do our best today, in your memory, Jimmy." I murmured.

"He'd like the pines," Moonjir said from beside me.

I flinched at his sudden appearance, but tried not to show it. "How would you know?"

"He really liked those big blue Morning Glories. They'd do well under here."

Sighing, I played along. "I'll consider that. Thank you."

"Big day," he said without turning from Jimmy's grave.

"We'll see. I don't trust them."

"They might surprise you. Checked in on Tyrell lately?"

As usual, my frustration rose when talking with Moonjir. "No. Not since — no."

"Not since you collared him. Quite poetic of you. Still keep it in your pocket, I see. How's Dean? Meditations going well with Jural? Speaking of surprises."

I turned facing him. "What are you trying to say?"

Moonjir cocked his head toward me and waggled a whitish eyebrow among his blue and pink fur.

"What?" I demanded again.

"No spoilers. I believe I'm going to have to wander off to find some excitement somewhere now."

"Don't let me stop you."

"You'll miss me."

I frowned. "You're leaving? Permanently?" If I were honest, yes, I'd miss not seeing him on occasion.

"Nothing is permanent." As he spoke, Moonjir faded.

Footsteps scuffed behind me. "Talking to yourself?" Roxie asked.

Turning, I found her holding Tika's hand as they approached. "Moonjir."

She faltered, glancing around. "Where?"

I pointed beside me. "Gone now."

Tika squinted at me and scratched at her nose. "We couldn't see him."

"He does that." I shrugged.

"Anything interesting to say?" Roxie asked.

"Expect surprises. No spoilers."

"Useless, as usual." She glanced around and shouted. "I hope you heard that!"

"You ready?" I asked them.

Tika cringed, but Roxie nodded and spoke. "We'll do our parts."

"Wolf Squad!" Andy yelled from the back porch as he came out. Others exiting with him and those heading from the other two houses answered his call.

Including Penny, we had twenty-seven in three buildings, with a fourth that some members of the Alliance helped us restore. Five Wolf Squad were still under Udal's care from their wounds during the fight. Over twenty Wolf Squad would meet with the Savannah Charter's new ambassadors.

While the Wolf Squad gathered, I found my fingers touching the glob of metal in my pocket. Moonjir had been right that I kept it with me, but I hadn't checked on Tyrell since the day after the battle.

Dean stepped out of the house behind Andy's group and flashed a quick smile. He wiggled a water bottle. The days were getting warm, and even this close to sunrise, it threatened to be a hot walk.

As the teens congregated, I drew in a deep breath.

The strange connection came easily from the metal of the bomb. I found my view of a gray room where Tyrell lay on a simple bunk. At first, I thought it some type of plain barracks, then I found bars painted black. Turning my perception in a circle, I guessed him to be in a jail. *This is a surprise.*

A smile curled my lips. I felt no remorse for the collar I'd left him with. They hadn't found a way to remove it, and that pleased me as well. The Alliance had buried Selina in her casing by the banks of the Saluda River, alongside what remained of Weston. I'd hardened some at that battle, and though I had lost any regrets for what I'd done to her, I hoped I'd never be put in that situation again. Today, we'd see what the future held.

As I released the connection to Tyrell and his cell, Dean studied my face as he walked toward me. Stopping, he took my hand, leaned in for a kiss, then whispered in my ear. "What was that smile for?" he asked.

"They put Tyrell in a prison cell."

His grin widened. "That is pleasing news."

Led by Penny on Bella, the Wolf Squad marched to the meeting. Odie bounced about, checking in with everyone. Fawn, her head freshly shaved, walked with Len, who still limped. Andy had become fast friends with Keith. Lorabelle and Jerome had become an item since the battle, or at least that's when Roxie and I noticed it.

The Wolf Squad had grown closer over the fighting. We'd lost people we'd cared about and grown to rely on those we'd barely known. They treated me less like some character from one of Dean's books and more like the clumsy person I could be.

On the broken asphalt of the highway, people joined us on the trek to the hall. Many still greeted us shyly, as if we were different, but more had smiles and comments about the crisp sun in the sky or the healthy crops the spring had gifted us with.

Crowds milled about the parking lot of the hall, and Penny trotted off to find a place to tether Bella. Duathua and humans packed the inside. They made way for us. Sam and Lauren had promised us the space at the foot of the dais we'd requested. I'd been explicitly invited, but they'd made the accommodation when I requested it.

The room quieted at our procession. Bald Harris sitting at the table alongside a tall gray-haired man in a suit surprised me. Three Duathua I didn't know had joined them, along with the tall woman, the bearded man, and the woman with pitch black braids. They all studied us as the crowd parted for our clustered group.

The heavy man with the beard smiled. "Ah, Caitlyn of the Wolf Squad."

A twitch, almost a smile, touched the lips of Harris as he

recognized me and Dean. The tall man in the suit beside him glanced at us and swallowed.

The woman with the black braids gestured for me to join them at a seat beside the table. I waved off the offer. "We'll stay here." Standing in the middle, I had Roxie and Tika on one side, with Dean and Andy on the other.

Tanya Roberts, the black-haired woman, introduced herself and the other members of the Alliance, then Harris, and the nervous man as Kip Atwood. She seemed to take the lead for the Alliance as she reiterated what she'd offered the prick, Jared, who'd come seeking our surrender. "We're hoping we can secure a peace with the Savannah Charter that includes trade opportunities for our mutual peoples."

Kip appeared to be the spokesperson for the Savannah Charter. "As we've stated in our overture, our goals are peace. We would like some assurances that the Wolf Squad will no longer be raiding our territory, though."

I stiffened; this had been a sticking point in the Wolf Squad discussions. Roxie prepared to answer, but Jarvis hadn't noticed and spoke. "How about Tyrell? Why isn't he here to assure us he won't be attacking?"

"They've put him in jail," I said.

Kip, already pale, blanched, and his hand touched the collar of his shirt. His lips quivered, though he didn't speak.

Jarvis glanced from me to Kip. "In jail?"

As Kip appeared unable to pull himself together, Harris patted his partner's arm and replied. "After his push to attack your Alliance and his retreat, there were some changes in our government. Some of those he opposed, along with others, arranged for his removal from leadership. His attempted coup failed. Calmer heads have prevailed, shall we say. Yes. We've arrested Tyrell." The slight smile that had grown faded. "We are willing to set borders and negotiate for trade; however, we need certain assurances from Caitlyn."

I nudged Roxie, as she had the opening part. She cleared her throat to get their attention off of me. "There are some of us who will leave the Alliance, if needed, to pursue our goals. The first is no more labs."

Andy spoke eagerly. "No more forced Youth Guard."

Tika's voice squeaked with nervousness as she spoke her bit. "Instead, Seyir, those with abilities — and their families will be welcomed in Columbia, or wherever we are located."

I drew a long breath. "If the Alliance and the Savannah Charter agree to this, then there are volunteers within the Wolf Squad who will help maintain the borders against the werewolves, Oni, and the other cryptids." Dean had suggested I speak the part I didn't want to. The majority of the others had insisted, so I continued, "Otherwise, the Wolf Squad will move from Columbia and continue to free those who wish to be freed."

I desperately wanted to be safe and quiet with Dean somewhere, but we'd voted as the Wolf Squad.

Jarvis laughed, not derisively. "Damn. These kids keep surprising us."

Kip finally found his voice. "We can't make those agreements. There would be witch riots all over again."

"After your losses at Columbia and this failed coup, how will you protect your borders? What happens when the Oni build their bridges?" Dean asked.

"Bridges?" Kip squeaked.

One of the Pahawan spoke. "They have their human captives building them now. We have destroyed two."

I knew from Nur that the Duathua agreed with the Wolf Squad's stance. The idea of the labs and the Youth Guard had never been accepted.

"We are assuming," I said, "that the Alliance would have no concerns about accepting Seyir and their families if they wished to immigrate to Columbia."

Tanya glanced among the Alliance members before answering. "We would not refuse anyone from joining the Alliance."

Dean gestured to Kip. "Then there is no need for riots, if those who wish to leave are allowed."

"I can't make that agreement." Kip shook his head, obviously flustered.

Again, Harris laid his hand on the other man's arm. "I am confident the Savannah Charter will accept those terms. Dismantling Tyrell's labs was already discussed, and the camps were a source of concern. We can bring these as solutions to an already difficult debate."

Jural's calm voice caused me to turn. "He speaks with more authority than the other."

Aided by Nur, Jural walked into the group of Wolf Squad. Jerome moved to her free side, offering to help.

Kip sagged, his eyes drifting to Harris, who studied me and Jural equally.

"And," Jural continued, "I believe Harris is especially interested in our offer of forging."

How she knew this, I couldn't guess, but his mouth parted at her comment. "I do have a strong interest in rebuilding, and that will take reforging components we cannot replace presently." His tone carried an incredulous note to it.

She chuckled. "Then you might want to get your people more comfortable with the Seyir who can accomplish that for you. You will start with this treaty and grow smarter from there." She stopped behind me and rested long fingers on my shoulder.

Harris wet his lips. "A tentative agreement. I will need a written treaty with defined proposals that include trade parameters for our new Congress to ratify. I need only a promise that the Wolf Squad will not interfere during that time."

"How much time?" I asked. Dean had said there'd be a delay.

"A month."

I shook my head. The Wolf Squad had agreed to halve whatever they proposed. "Two weeks."

Harris took a deep breath and nodded. "Two weeks. I'll make it happen."

"What is your position now?" asked Dean.

A long moment passed before Harris replied. "Speaker of the House. It is an old position from before the Sorrow."

"And your title when we met you?" Dean asked.

"Minister of Reclamation, before they stripped it from me and tossed me in jail after talking with you two." Harris smiled.

As it seemed we were near the end, I tapped Tika. "One last request," I said.

Tika produced the Kudaru sheets she'd lovingly inscribed. With the teachers Nur had provided, Tika's ability with the hardened air had blossomed. "There are eight letters here for our families. I would appreciate it if you'd deliver these." She climbed onto the dais and offered them to Harris.

He searched the Wolf Squad. "Just these? Not more?"

I hadn't seen the point and had been more focused on getting Dean to agree, which he had. He'd been dear to his family.

"For now," I called out.

When we returned to the Wolf Den, I worked in the kitchen with Dean to help prepare a celebratory dinner. We'd cut up a sack of potatoes, and Jerome had us working on onions. He'd taken over some of Ben's culinary duties and done well enough to get nicknamed "Chef" by most of us.

"Where did we get that much honey?" I asked Roxie.

"Lauren keeps bees. Who knew?" She and Tika chopped pecans and folded flatbread for a kind of dessert.

"She's got one, you know." Tika rubbed her eyes with the back of her hand. "One of us. I think she's thinking of letting him work with Fawn's group."

The scents of cooking chicken and onions blended with fresh and dried herbs. Hunger nibbled at my stomach.

Jerome inspected Dean's and my work. "Yeah, she's come out a few times to watch us at Pat's blueberry fields."

I winced at the mention. Fawn had gathered all the healers of the Wolf Squad to learn a growing ability from a pair of Seyirs adept at the skill. She'd been trying to get me to go, but I hadn't taken the time. I would, soon. Using the otherness to stimulate crops came naturally to those who'd lived on Denya all their lives.

"Going to need more buildings for the Wolf Den." Dean chuckled. "Momma Caitlyn."

I laughed, then brooded without replying. We'd been so busy since the battle that we'd crashed every night when we hit our bed. Anything more romantic hadn't seemed like an option. Dean had even mentioned being concerned that he'd turn and scare off the new Wolf Squad recruits. *What kind of future did we have?*

"Hey, where'd you go?" he asked quietly. Leaning toward me, he brushed his bare shoulder against my coveralls, but we had knives dicing.

I forced a smile and shook my head. "Nothing. Blueberries will be nice this summer."

"Yeah." His tone told me I hadn't fooled him.

We were slicing carrots, the thin rounds Jerome preferred, when Dean stopped and leaned in conspiratorially. "Hey. Negotiations are over. The new building is going well; everyone's pitching in. We never did get that picnic out by the lake."

"I'm not sure I want to go anywhere near the dam. Besides," I pointed my knife at the carrots, "I've kinda got to be at this big cookout this afternoon. Did you forget?"

"North side of Lake Murray, far from the dam. I've got a line on a little boat and my eye on some of those islands. We sneak away, after dessert. 'Cause, honey and pecans." He lowered his head to catch my eyes. "Date?"

I agreed, and excitement built as we sat about eating while Keith and Patrick played their guitar and harmonica. "So, what's the plan?" I asked Dean. "Are you talking overnight?"

He winked. "Weather looks good."

"Bugs. Nothing but bugs."

"Nothing is easy."

I leaned into him, ignoring his warmth despite the hot afternoon. The new Wolf Guard had found their places among us. New friendships — and relationships — had blossomed. Their enjoyment sometimes chafed when I imagined Dean shifting and running away in his silver fur because of our passions. I had never found a cure. *It's not fair*.

We celebrated our survival. Others of us had not made it through the battle; our joint Wolf Squad demands, accepted by the Alliance and sent off for deliberation by the Savannah Charter; and hope for our future. Some of our group wanted to continue fighting, but against the Oni and werewolves, while the rest of us wanted peace. I'd be happy to learn how to help plants grow with Fawn, make true Kudaru like Tika, or see how my knack with metal might help with forging.

When our little celebration died out and the kitchen was full of Wolf Squad cleaning up, Roxie caught us carrying bedrolls down the stairs. "Running away from home?" she asked.

I fought a foolish grin. "Just for the night."

She raised her eyebrows, eyeing Dean. "Good luck."

"Thanks." I gave her a hug. "Take care of the kids." I doubted luck would help, but even just being alone with Dean felt romantic.

As we slipped out of the house, hoping to avoid too many conversations, Odie raced up to us. Penny followed him and appraised our loads with a grin.

"Are we camping?" Her lips twisted impishly. "Want company? We could get a group together. Let me call the others."

Dean patted her head. "Think they'd hear you from down there?"

Penny jabbed him in his side. "Get out of here. I'm hitting your library, by the way." She gave me a smile, but a hint of sadness clung to it, as if she knew the disappointment I'd have. "Have fun."

As we walked westward, the sun dropped into our eyes. We talked about the Wolf Squad, the plans for the Wolf Den and the Alliance, and the promise of peace with the Savannah Charter. What we didn't discuss was *our* direct future. Those conversations had ended in the swamp before the battle at Sumter.

The fisherman and his family lived far north of the dam,

so we never revisited the damage from a couple of weeks ago. The man gladly set us up with a dingy that reminded me of Dean's.

I sat watching the sun threatening to set on the lake as Dean rowed. Familiar marshy smells threaded in the wind. "You going to start fishing again?" I asked him.

"I'd like that. I've heard there's boats to salvage. Things are settling in Columbia."

"I'm not really a fan of fish, you know."

He shrugged as he rowed. "I can trade."

On the lake, the worries and stress of soldiers and the Wolf Squad floated away. "This was a good idea. It's hard to have my own thoughts at the Wolf Den."

"That's the truth." He turned to check his bearings and dug into rowing again. His muscles tightened with each pull, and he smiled roguishly when he caught me looking.

"Is that your island?" I asked, nudging a chin toward a small bit of pines jutting from the surface.

"Like it?"

"Is it dry?"

"White pine, soft as feathers. Yes, dry."

When we arrived, the ground proved a little higher than it had seemed. Enough that he could drag the wooden boat up onto the cushion formed of delicate needles. It *was* soft. Nothing grew but the pines, except at the outer edges, leaving it feeling open yet cozy.

Dean made a show of setting out blankets and our supplies, including an extra dessert he'd smuggled out of the celebration. "When Andy figures out his still, we'll bring peach liquor."

I lowered myself to the blanket, watching the reds and oranges color the few clouds in the sky. Dean's scent and firm body had me twisting inside as I both wanted and feared intimacy. When he slid down beside me and wrapped me in his arms, I asked, "Are we here for when you turn? Someplace isolated? Safe?"

"Hmm." He nuzzled against my neck. "Don't worry. I'll be talking to my toe."

I pulled around to frown at him. "What?"

He kissed me, long enough to ignite my desires. When I pressed us apart out of fear of his rising emotions, he just smiled. "Jural's meditations have helped. She's odd, what she seems to know."

"The toe meditation?" It had led me to her strange perception of connections, but I couldn't see how it could help Dean. "I doubt that can cure you."

His hands found my sides, stroking already awake nerves. "It's not about a cure." Gently, he rolled me into his arms, then laid us down together. "You can't save me, Caitlyn."

I nearly cried. "Don't you think I know that?" We'd tried everything to the point of nearly killing him.

Dean leaned down, breath hot against my neck as he spoke. "It's always been up to me. She's been teaching me how to control my body." Kissing the side of my face, he turned my lips to his.

We kissed, and he didn't turn. In our connection and the othersense, I knew his passion grew. His hand stroked me, pulling me closer, firing my own desires. Pulling from him one last time, I whispered, "What if it doesn't work? What if you turn?"

"Then we try again another night." He chuckled in a deep, throaty tone. "Nothing is easy. I love you, Caitlyn."

We didn't have to wait for another night.

Long after the stars came out, I fell asleep on my lover's chest under the whispering pines.

We'd love a review - anywhere! Goodreads, Amazon, your blog, or TikTok

Acknowledgments

We want to thank everyone who have supported us along this path. Our friends and family have been there for us, offering love and encouragement. We can't thank you all enough.

About the Authors

April Davis owns a bookstore in rural Florida, runs bookclubs, edits novels, cosplays, and reads a wide variety of genres.

Kevin A Davis travels nearly every month to convention and events as a speaker, vendor, and even staff.

Find us at
Sorrowborn.com

Also by April Davis & Kevin A Davis

The Sorrowborn Trilogy

Path of Sorrow and Wind

Alliance of Bonds and Storm

Home of Fire and Tempest

Sorrowborn.com

Grab some free short stories from Dean, Caitlyn, and Roxie set just before the trilogy begins.

Join the newsletter with the download of Dean's short story *Never Give Up*

https://dl.bookfunnel.com/d8rkbkphxt

or get Dean's story without a newsletter signup

https://dl.bookfunnel.com/v7szegjy27

Follow the links at the end of the story to download Caitlyn's story, then Roxie's

Also by Inkd Pub

The DRC Files A fantasy series by Kevin A Davis

The Khimmer Chronicles A fantasy series by Kevin A Davis

Spooky, horror, fantasy, science fiction, LGBTQ+, mystery, and explicit romance anthologies. Find them at InkdPub.com